I0735242

THE DOGS BITE

Mariano Morillo B. Ph. D

WORKBOOK PRESS LLC
187 E Warm Springs Rd,
Suite B285, Las Vegas, NV 89119, USA
Website: https://workbookpress.com/
Hotline: 1-888-818-4856
Email: admin@workbookpress.com

Ordering Information:

Quantity sales. Special discounts are available on quantity purchases by corporations, associations, and others.

For details, contact the publisher at the address above.

Library of Congress Control Number:

ISBN-13:   978-1-958176-28-3 (Paperback Version)
                978-1-958176-29-0 (Digital Version)

REV. DATE: 16/05/2022

THE
DOGS BITE

MARIANO MORILLO B. PhD.

CONTENTS

DEDICATION

To the unwavering fighters, who have not wavered in spreading the truth, in order to liberate society.

To those who have understood that to denounce is to liberate, and have made a utopia of their existence, putting their actions in justice, and justice, above the perks.

"Like a soldier with his rifle, I hoisted my pen like my sword, to write heroics in battles."

PREFACE

The Dogs Bite is the novel where the possessions and the possessors dance and shake their hands, while one and the other depend on a superior force that induces them to show the possibilities of being for the self-delight of the spirit.

A kind of social outcasts apparently, lacking a logical reasoning, is welcomed in front of Bulley's facilities, a food supplying corporation that allows them to rehearse the daily survival game, where they work on their own creating their own jobs becoming micro-businessman entrepreneurs of transport, managing to get out of misery, and although they have reached an apparent maturity, they return to the condition of their childhood, wanting to justify the content of their reckless actions, involving themselves in actions of conspiratorial bribes, which lead from odebresch to the corona virus, so that the evils and kindnesses that irritate one and delight others, lead them to behave like a pack that terrorizes with its barking.

All this is generated according to an arranged script for the exercise of existential validity on the planet.

That is why the power of God teaches that there is no other greatness than His breath, because only the spirit defines the value of things.

Without the rehearsal of life, and its assignments, the possessors would not be able to show the influences of their possessions.

In the science of the spirit, and even to achieve results in the industry of religions, it has been necessary the elevation of the levels of consciousness that have been defined in the existential rehearsal, because the influences of the possessions merit the levels of consciousness, for the comprehension and valuation, because each one, shows the selection or assignment at their level of consciousness, that is why, when the pandemic diseases attack humanity, man in its survival, looks for a way to preserve itself above the possessions, because without the interaction of both versions of matter, everything remains in emptiness, however we can't forget that "everything that is seen, was made from what was not seen".

Like Terence, "nothing human
is foreign to me" and today I
give you these fragments of
everyday life, fiction, and reality.

ALLEGATION

The mechanics of the planet earth had generated questions without answers, and this condition had induced a questioning of the global society, the reason for the irrational actions of the human being, which induced them to act as an insensitive machine.

Mariano Morillo B. PhD. It is the social interpreter of cultural historicity, who seeks to awaken the reason for being in action, in order to find the inner response to social change in the universal context.

Humanity in a curve of ascent has reached the climax of its arrival to find itself in front of a decline from an indescribable height where the mystery of the unknown, posed a series of risks that would induce it to reflect on being, or not being.

Knowledge saves, man is terrified of the unknown, but now man has become mute and the machine is absorbing his thoughts, and not being able to express his free action, he will have to distance himself from the machine to become him again, and to think again, because it has always been better to "think before speaking, not to speak and then thinking".

And the machine kept all the thoughts, and man had become addicted to the machine and did things, reckless things that generated a radical social condition, which induced him to want the control, without the capacity of his self-control.

In this novel, the author leads us to interact in a world of fiction and reality, where we will escape the social tension of the conceptual aberrations, even without being foreign to what has been presented.

The events generated by the author imply that not all dogs bite as they bark, and such a condition leads us to awaken in a reality of comprehension, for self-salvation.

CHAPTER 1

THE DEBATE

In the beginning, when the Gods and their descendants ruled, all was love, passion, and distinction, and they were not concerned with the phenomenon of expansion that would later come to preoccupy mortals.

The sovereignty of the power they exercised, strengthened and defined justice, wisdom would fl ow from every decision, and "harmony would reign every day, and life would be born like a melody."

Misunderstandings were solved as actions of experiences of solidarity and mercy.

Everything was a party, because reason was based on love, because love was the reason for being, but it happened that ignorance wanted to overcome wisdom, and in the fight for hegemony, what seemed to be, was obstructed to see if it was not, but in any circumstance, it had already been conceived to be, and as it already was, it continued to be.

Everything was framed in the path of an awakening, regarding each existential step, since life would trace the path that before birth we had chosen, and then we would ignore on the path to the destination, and for that reason many times, we found ourselves self-conscious, surprised and startled by what surprised and startled by what we lived" Gibon explained with confidence, to Professor Saez, and his students, with whom he had an open debate. Gibon was a guest of the professor, and served as his assistant in the chair of history philosophy.

Gibon was always a man of love, but the circumstances of destiny marked his path and suddenly, life presented him with a song that if he couldn't sing, he would have to listen to it.

The fact was that Gibon was a being who loved to please his fellow man even if he harmed himself, and many wanted to take advantage of him.

The stories of radicalism against humanity disappointed him to the extent that when he was told that life must go on regardless of what happened, he was assaulted by torrential tears, especially when he was told about the "systematic persecution and expulsion of the Jews" from the medieval kingdoms, and of the frivolization to which this "innocent race" had been subjected by the interpreters of historicity, and about the allegations of the Koran against such a condition:

"If Allah had not decreed their expulsion, He would have punished them in every life."

In the middle of the philosophy of history class, whenever Professor Saez spoke to him about this subject he tried to avoid the approach, but Professor Saez insisted and told him:"Gibon, 'we should not be ashamed to talk about what God was not ashamed to create' Speaking about the persecution of the Jews, is like raining on wet, is like being trapped in the circle of repetition, 'although it is a painful and delicate case to discuss', without trying to justify anyone, for the Jews to get to where they are, they had to face that Karma, without the pretension of a masochist, you can understand that religion victimizes men even knowing that pain is the way to elevation, because, Jesus Christ couldn't have fulfilled his mission, We know that the limitation of man generates emotions of resentment and pain, and even many think that the persecution of the Jews was due to the karma that was contracted with the crucifixion of Jesus Christ, however it should not be forgotten that man chooses life before birth, and that that before the eyes of humanity seems a horrifying aberration, before the eyes of God, is nothing more than an experience of satisfaction, because each experience, promotes you to another step," Professor Saez explained with remarkable mastery.

"It is understandable professor, perhaps you mean to say that raining on the wet, is to remain in the past, and that in turn, to remain in the past is something like... crystallize?" Questioned Gibon.

"That's correct, Gibon, the past should only be used as a reference in history, and as a prelude to the present, to understand the evolutionary meaning of generational existences," said Professor Saez. While the students filled their notebooks with the notes they were writing down.

The classroom was impassable, that afternoon two sections of the same content had come together, so that both could witness the expository debate of Gibon and Professor Saez.

"Do you understand what the teacher is saying?" Gibon asked the students.

As they all responded in a single voice:

"Yes, Doctor, Gibon, everything is defined and understood."

"Very well," Gibon affirmed, and looking at Professor Saez, he added:

"Regardless of what Plato said 'that one can't compare two unhappy people, and then say that one is happier than the other', I think that each one endures according to their endurance, because the pain and suffering in the lines of humanity, even being a possible moral mockery, obey a cause, because there is no action, without justification to greater pain, greater elevation, and if not, see the case of Nelson Mandela, who after 27 years of imprisonment, was elevated from prison to the presidency, things do not happen to everyone, unless they are not assigned, or have not been chosen, but for this planet, each being brings an assignment, or a selection because if it were not so, all men would exercise the easy road, to get rich without effort, and clearly, that would not give then merit, however there is a large part of beings that in free will steal, plunder the public funds or seek to deceive those who have more, ignoring that there is no cause without effect, or action without justification, and that they are deceiving themselves" Gibon affirmed.

"That's right Gibon, everyone gets what they give, even if it doesn't seem like it," said Professor Saez.

"Yes, everything is defined, even with free will, the world is so well organized, 'that the grass that belongs to a donkey, is not eaten by another donkey"' Gibon affirmed, with full conviction.

Professor Saez, approached him with satisfaction, patting him on the shoulders, looked at the students who were astonished following the conversation open-mouthed and said to them:

"Time is up, write an opinion piece on this topic and bring it tomorrow, it will be scored, it will be worth five points," he said, while thanking Gibon:

"Thank you very much Gibon," he expressed.

"Thank you, professor," Gibon replied, as he left the room.

The students got up as a group and went to the corridor blocking his way, while Professor Saez was organizing his notes to change classrooms, they approached to greet Gibon.

A few months later, the students reached graduation, while Gibon went out into the world to rehearse pain.

During his journey, he would interact according to his philosophy, to understand, that it would not always be, what man believed, because life would induce him to tolerate what would affect him, however he went ahead, because he believed that each experience, would strengthen his conscience to apply justice.

And he saw something that impressed him, but he kept looking and discovered that "the more you live the more you learn", and he kept exploring along his path, and something extraordinary seemed surprising to him, but he reflected according to everything that brought impression to his spirit, until the time came to see and understand, many things that seemed to have no reason to be, but he was convinced that every man has an existential script, where what has to happen will always happen, and that the best way to live in peace, is not attracting the worry for what has to happen, because one should never mourn the death of a being that is not yet dying, and not even after their departure, because in this life, every mission that is chosen or assigned to man, somehow has to be fulfilled, and it is never more than what has to be.

But he never forgot Professor Saez, and the few times he returned to the Republic he met with him, and reminded him of those years when they worked in the audiovisual department of the state university, when Professor Saez gave him an assignment where he told him:

"Gibon, tomorrow I need the audio equipment and the slide projector, the Dean of Humanities needs them first thing in the morning in the conference room."

"Of course, Professor"

"No, no, no, no, no, not for my job position, no, you'd better do it for yours!" expressed Professor Saez, and after Gibon decoded the message he realized that it was nothing more than a joke that the professor was making to him based on the expression "of job position", and both laughed out loud, and Gibon for such condition, always remembered it.

That was Gibon's last dissertation, in front of Professor Saez, who was in fact a priest of the Jesuit order.

A few months later for personal reasons, Gibon had embarked on an indescribable adventure beyond his habitat, ignoring what would happen, he arrived at a place where it seemed that his life would crystallize, because the circumstances of destiny, had obstructed his way, and although he tried to return, life would hit him, years later he learned of the descent of Professor Saez, and this grieved him so much that he said to his disappointment: "Life is amalgam and candy, is to live it in hope and dismay."

CHAPTER 2

SOCIAL STATUS

It gave the impression that men had lost their condition of being, and were becoming a mass of deafening howls that disputed the scenario of survival, but somehow it would have to be, because in fact life was like a monotony and after being in it somehow would have to be exercised, Gibon knew that on the planet it was necessary to tolerate, especially when going through the temptations offered by free will, which never left a moment to breathe freely, without the mind being occupied by any concern and those temptations towards good or evil, or towards light or darkness, where the struggle of the opposite was located, on planet earth, would be represented by two entities that led the contextual conditions, to them the religions used to call God, who was the light that represented the good, and "the devil" who was the scab, the drastic darkness, that represented evil, although before, that which was named darkness, was once light, to make it aware of its transformation.

Each practice left an experience that would strengthen the conscience, each experience brought the understanding that would lead us to wisdom that is why "my people die for lack of knowledge", that is to say, knowledge saves, and wisdom liberates.

From the point of view of religions, God and the devil were two entities that were in constant belligerence, where one wanted to impose his condition on the other, and these tendencies exhausted all the time of humans, who without having other things to do, in the context of survival, sought answers to everything that was generated around them, and that God would deliver around their context something different to what they were used to seeing or dealing with, because somehow, they did not rest until they saw him succumb.

Gibon evolved like everyone else on the planet, with the difference that he was open- minded, in the aspect of thinking differently, and saw things differently, which made him qualify to be fatalized.

Gibon was called the Pastor of the Lord, because in everything he did he sought to apply justice, however some pastors of the time had progressed rapidly, some of them were described as "false prophets" and although Gibon sought to do things right, he did not escape the harassment of those who sold themselves as good, and they were in fact bad.

Everything obeyed that the dignity of humanity, had deteriorated when men superimposed their ambition over their condition, and as vile villains were offering gifts such as infamous villains, that without valuing the future condition of the represented generation, sowed the bad example as infected seed, in order that dishonesty reigned, so that the corruptness as a libertine Goddess, so that each one of its bites would infect societies, so that neither religious nor libertines would have the capacity to look each other in the eyes, without feeling the trembling that provoked the shame of others, that in globalization had become the remorse of all and the suffering of those who even without participating could not stop experiencing remorse, because they were not free of guilt for having appointed leaders of horrendous conditions, who taught their represented, the example of the aberration of corrupt societies, where chaos intensified, in some places, many voters sold their votes for seven cents, some of those called and the few elected, had erred the way, and many public administrations resorted to the use of resources and information, with the intention of obtaining economic or other benefits, ranging from passing information to front men who executed frauds against third parties, in exchange for gifts, promotions or sexual favors, but the natural kiss-ass, those who were nicknamed "toadies", bringing blindness in the soul, which prevented them from discerning adequately, worsened the condition.

Many lawyers called to defend the cause of the "innocent", sold out for money, aggravating the pain of their defendants, because the planet had lost the notion of honesty, and all or most, preferred to live in the brazenness and oppression, giving themselves to the highest bidder, such unworthy lawyers, had lost their minds, and began to disguise criminal cases with accidents, for the purpose of deceiving their clients, if they did not learn of the conspiracies in time, on such rails the world was on its troubled course.

Some prestigious law firms were stalling for time, seeking to cover up or justify the corruption of other law firms, such as Nona Shick, who had attempted to disguise an accident as a civil claim to justify the diversion of a victim's compensation benefits, and many of them were believed to have been involved in a conspiratorial ploy to defraud their client! What social chutzpah! Ethics had become a mere word, and as such lawyers were associated with judges who did not always respect themselves, and lacked the modesty to respect the law, they dared to sell the justice of a verdict for the complacency of villainy.

CHAPTER 3

THE BITES

This entire archetype rested on shameful bites (meaning bribes) that induced people to lose respect for the minority sectors, believing that they could do whatever they wanted with those who lacked the economic resources to pay, which is what many filled their mouths with saying:

"The monkey dances for the money."

Odebresch was an example of large and serious international bribes, so that from the smallest to the largest members of sick societies, could never rise from the shameless actions of corruption, where the lack of ethics would mark the condition of the investigation led by the Department of Justice of the United States, together with ten Latin American countries, which proved the degree of corruption to which the Brazilian construction company "Odebrecht" exposed the planet.

The millionaire Norberto Odebrecht, through his construction company, had brought to their knees those countries that tempted by ambition had allowed themselves to be disqualified from their ethical principles, by shamelessly accepting the bribes offered to their rulers, ranging from presidents to simple officials of Latin American governments, To the extent of having induced Alan

Garcia's suicide, former president of Peru, repentant for the pain of conscience and the turbulence of dignity, of the generality, although some Peruvians thought that the suicide was another cover-up tactic, to calm the claims of public opinion, while he kept enjoying the benefits somewhere on the planet, under another identity.

Odebrecht revealed the fragility before the temptation of ambition.

Even though Odebrecht had been established in Salvador, in the Brazilian state of Bahia, this didn't prevent its bribes from touching the big dogs in the different Latin American countries, where corruption or abuse of power was obvious and defined as a means to obtain personal benefits, ranging from illicit enrichment to acts of distortion of the policies and central functions of the states, allowing leaders to benefit at the expense of the common good, tearing the veil of corruption by requesting money to do or not to do something that by the nature of their functions they were obliged to do, or that by lacking ethics, and not having defined the concept of duty, they were appropriating the resources of the states, in an action of prevarication in embezzlement.

As I was saying, the world was going through a social distortion, to such a degree that in some Latin American countries voters were selling their votes for 7 cents of dollars, and most of those elected lacked the capacity and scruples to exercise their functions, without incurring in corruption, which most of the time consisted of a bribe to embezzlement, many were only interested in appearing in the package "not to serve the people, but to be serve from the people."

Many of the elected officials came funded by corporations, under the Mentoring commitment.

The chaos intensified, societies trembled, many public administrations resorted to use resources or information, with the intention of obtaining economic benefits, or other benefits, many times, some organizations used to infiltrate the public administration to use personal information of the clients of the state, to make frauds that harmed their persecuted, or used unscrupulous law firms to try to steal resources allocated to victims by way of compensation, without those who were called to be favored to get to know.

All these dubious services obeyed bribes and kickbacks, or in exchange for being promoted to a certain position; besides, some public or private institutions, whose policies allowed sexism and discrimination to prevail in their corporate policies, used to use women as a bribery mechanism, infiltrated them so that with their charms they could obtain information of corporate interest, and in other occasions, many of these women belonging to certain companies, only ascended to powerful positions, if they granted sexual favors to managers and administrators.

In all these frauds against the third party, the "toadies" stood out, "always ready to put in the spoon, but very little willing to help cook the soup."

Some lawyers of the main law firms both in New York and Latin America, had lost their minds, and disguised criminal cases as car accidents in order to deceive their clients, if they did not realize in time the conspiracies, and so the world was in its agitated course, humanity was moving towards crystallization, and decline.

Humans lived without knowing why they lived, the cybernetic era had replaced the effort of healthy thinking and behind every service many were waiting for the bite. Identity theft and cyber fraud were generated as if they were the dictates of the new societies.

The generation of public servants would no longer emulate Rabindranath Tagore when he said: "I slept and dreamed that enjoyment was life, I woke up and understood that life was service, I threw myself into action, and I have come to the conclusion that to serve is happiness".

Nobody was doing anything anymore, everybody was waiting for something, humanity had become dehumanized.

CHAPTER 4

TODY AND ESTRACE

A tender and pretty little couple, with their angelic faces could well have confused the most astute of mortals, Tody, seemingly the most conscious and innocent, was something like a Greek relic.

On the other hand, Estrace, who looked like she "didn't break a plate", "broke the whole set of dishes", because she was the most radical and calculating.

Before Gibon discovered the deal, they tried to make the others believe that he and they had known each other before, and that they were with Gibon with all the splendor of honor, supposedly they assumed to prove it by the disposition of the occult sect and the organization of evil. At least they made Gibon believe that Estrace had the money that was due to him, and they pretended and lied, they gave Gibon tests that after executing them were so disturbing to them that they upset their consciences, and lacking peace, when they looked at Gibon, out of repentance they uttered:

"I'm sorry."

And Gibon would look at them and without saying anything he would continue to study her.

But the interest of those women was that they, like others,

wanted the public to believe that Gibon was working for them in a cat company that they pretended to organize, well in fact they didn't pretend, Tody had a foundation that provided room and board for the cats, and since Gibon provided delivery services in Bulley, they thought it propitious to call him whenever they wanted to go hunting for homeless cats to house them, in order to justify the money they got from Gibon's compensation for being the homeless cat catchers, for being the lucky ones to "get" Gibon, among so many offers, to "accept" theirs, which brought the typical, smelly make-up of his felines.

Estrace in her delirium of businesswoman was always inviting him to dinner or lunch, so that the emissaries of the occult sect, and the organization of evil, would see them together, but she never told Gibon that they were trying to use him for the purpose of justifying resources that she had begun to claim on his behalf, making Gibon believe that she was aware of everything.

Well yes, one day in a fit of praising Estrace called him and informed him:

"We're going to give you a lot of money."

When the organization of evil asked her for some actions, she would act as if she was in emotional disarray, as if she had something to do with Gibon to see if he got angry, or lost control, one day Estrace started screaming to see Gibon's reaction, but seeing that he remained calm and did not pay much attention to her, she returned to behave normally, and Gibon told her:

"What happened, could it be that you studied dramatic arts

to fake such a lack of control, in that way if someone saw you they would think they were doing something to you, or that you were in a high emotional dilemma?" Gibon questioned.

Then she smiled and kept silent, but one day she said to him, looking him straight in the face:

"You need to get a job at a bank" Estrace said as if she was delirious.

Gibon looked at her in silence, while he thought: < <What Estrace wants to take me from a day laborer to a banker?>>, and she interrupted him, insisting, adding:

"I'll have to go with you when the money comes out."

Gibon listened to her in silence without insisting on anything, and understood that she was going through a radical economic obsession, but without ceasing to think about the condition of a Delilah in front of a Samson, they had their set up, Gibon followed their music, they believed they could deceive him and he in turn, made them believe that they could, the condition of naivety that he showed would make it easier for them to achieve their purpose, The thing was that Estrace was so convinced that Gibon would not know anything about the plot they had, that she fully believed that they could have control, to the extent that one day she told Gibon that Tody was a lesbian, anticipating that if Gibon tried to get involved with her he would stop, Gibon asked Tody, but she denied it, and said:

"Oh, Estrace is resorting to confusing you about me!" She said, and made a prolonged silence.

Then some of her friends, including Tody, told Gibon to be

careful with Estrace because she had a psychiatric certificate.

Gibon didn't know if they were right, or if they were telling him that with the intention of confusing him more.

Anyway, Estrace had her intentions, and would not stop inviting Gibon to dinner, she tried to make believe that the fraud they were setting up was due to actions authorized by Gibon, but one night Gibon went to bed early and the God of his being started to ask him: "What happened in '91?"

From that moment on, when he woke up, he knew that they were trying to defraud him, and began to spread it on social networks, in bilingual English and Spanish writings, which led certain sectors that were aware of what was occurring, to reconsider what was happening.

So from then on they changed tactics, Estrace would say one thing one day and another day she would say something else, she would invite Gibon to go somewhere, but she was followed by a dark-haired man who supervised her, and made her do things that perhaps she hadn't planned.

They were trying to justify the fraud mounted against Gibon, so that those who had engaged in the silent embezzlement would appear to be doing the right thing in the eyes of the government, leaving the impression that Gibon was on every action.

Many times in their conspiratorial eagerness, they wanted to act as if they really had delirium of madness, from Estrace, Mr. Pascualo and even Robert Wolff, who sometimes said one thing and then said another, Gibon did not know if they were buying time with the intention of evil or goodness.

The organization of evil had thrown its servants into the reiteration of the conspiracy.

Gibon would ask Estrace what she knew about the money, she would answer that it wasn't time to release it yet, that he was going to be surprised, and then when he brought up the subject she would act as if she was really an incoherent person, she would change the subject, or say that she had to call her mother, Gibon would look at her and continue studying her, and she in the middle of her delirium with all the splendor of her impudence would look for a reason to justify herself to Gibon, and another day she asked him:

"Would you like to start a jewelry store with me?"

Gibon looked at her and after a slight silence let her hear what she wanted to hear, and answered her:

"Yes, why not?"

And she happily looked calm and hopeful, and it was that many of the ruffians who sought to confuse Gibon were making plans with what was in it for him.

Then, since Gibon did not have a stated address that suited them, they offered to get him an apartment to rent close to where Estrace and her friend Mari lived, but since Gibon did not please them, they used an address where Gibon had once lived, pretending that Gibon was aware of what was going on, but Gibon did not know anything about it, and did not understand why. They would give him no information about anything, especially when the evilness was so great that they bribed and involved the lawyers to try to disguise a compensation claim that dated back to 1991, and was still pending, 29 years had passed, and they tried to disguise the amount accumulated since then, with the claim of a car accident that occurred in 2016.

They thought they could confuse Gibon, but when they were discovered they tried to gain time and pretended that everything was a test, always trying to hide the evil intention, in order to confuse Gibon.

There was one occasion when they went to Gibon's sister Lunch, and she asked him to forget about that claim, and Gibon answered her:

"Don't let those demons use you, how can they expect you to persuade me to forget about something that caused me so much suffering and of which by law I am the real beneficiary, I am not upset about the money, I am upset about the abuse, if I am a person who understands what my rights are, they have outraged me the way they have done it, what will happen to those who don't know what foot they are standing on? These acts of abuse and discrimination must stop anywhere in the world, wake up, don't let yourselves be used by a mafia that has oppressed those from below all their lives, and now they want to show themselves as saviors, when in truth they are nothing more than a group of hypocrites lacking coherent discernment" Gibon expressed.

CHAPTER 5

THE REASON

The compensation they were trying to cover up had been generated by a confusion they had had with Gibon a few months after he arrived in New York, that is, 29 years before, they had confused him with a drug dealer, and even though Gibon had his documents in order, they gave him a forced and racist sentence of one year for three years in the name of the person with whom they had confused him, in the beginning they offered him a probation that Gibon did not accept, because he had never been involved in criminal problems of any nature and he understood that he was innocent of what they were accusing him of, since he had never sold or consumed drugs, and they had even tried to add "felonies" of the real offender, without Gibon accepting, because of his innocence he never accepted any guilt, being forced to abort him at nine months, as someone whose turn it was to be born, despite the fact that Gibon gave his identity, they sent him to jail after an illegal sentence, and they had him under the name of another person, although they knew by the fingerprints that the other person was not him, and not being enough what they had done to him to the extent of destroying his life, at the time of justice, they had conspired again to make him believe that there was a fraud against him, because he had made an agreement to accept a job position, which they never gave him, in 2010, the justice department had reviewed the case and the conspirators, among which was the Scientology church, made a claim without telling Gibon, who was the real beneficiary, they introduced him papers to participate in a supposed seminar, making him believe that Gibon was aware of everything, and they received the money without informing him that they had it. In other words, they had let time pass without giving Gibon his due, they kept quiet because they found it was too much money to pay him, and pretended that Gibon worked for them, to justify withholding the money, then in 2016, they sent to cause a traffic accident to camouflage the amount of compensation, and there were still sectors that did not understand how in the United States, the country of "social justice and popular democracy", they could generate acts of such nature, especially after the Department of Justice had reviewed the case.

The conspirators carried their evil intentions to confuse Gibon, if he did not discover it, they would plunder him, but if he became aware of their tricks, they would pretend that everything they did to him, obeyed to simple tests to verify the condition of tolerance that Gibon could show, and for that purpose, they went and involved the most soulless and low sectors of society: mentally ill, drug addicts, prostitutes, and unconscious, making them believe that by requiring their services, they were of their interest, with pleasing and high importance, while granting them certain sporadic perks, while those ignored, that they had decided to use them and then discard them.

New York, lost control, the mafias planted dishonor, humiliate the men of value was the mission of their redemption, and when they addressed those whom they believed to be their subordinates, they did it with the intention of making them feel bad, to the extent of provoking a reaction of rebellion where justice sprouted by hand, generating violence, in order to justify their crimes and arbitrariness.

And Gibon often thought of those who were wicked, who disguised themselves as saints in religions, degenerate, perverse and merciless, who sought to destroy the path of good men, to bury them in abysmal tombs that appeared as common graves where great virtues were hindered.

However, it was understandable that since the country is so "Democratic", there would be some who in crazy positions would play the belt prejudging sectors of minorities, to see if their calculations of action were accommodated to their plans of darkness and evilness, so they tried to use Gibon, as a victim in the game of their purposes, ignoring that he would not allow it, and there were many involved to the degree that Scientology claimed, and the money was not delivered. Where did he keep it, that Gibon was not given it?

The evidence was so real that no one would doubt that those involved were obeying the requests of a deferred mob.

And some said they were testers, but others thought they were thieves.

They did not understand that they could not steal from Gibon, the Pastor of the Lord, because Gibon's allowance was generated by the Lord, and he was just a simple administrator, so trying to steal from Gibon was trying to steal from the Lord, and God would not allow it.

They were tests with more load of evilness and intimidation than a purpose of formation and salvation, were conspiring and were many involved, ambition, envy and evil had degenerated the patriarchs, those who for money killed even if it was not theirs, they believed that minorities had no rights even if they paid taxes, because those, they thought, that the minority classes, were their new slaves.

And, such a crude reality induced Gibon to think <To then express: "Neither hunger, nor prison have bent us, nor the persecutions of their gendarmes, have struck our spirits.">

It was time to wake up, for the sleeping people to become conscious, to not allow anyone to use them against their own people, to stop the abuses, the racism, the discrimination, and the police brutality, because at that time, they were "the force of order, that provoked disorder," becoming the only force paid by the poor, so that anywhere, they would act at the service of the mandate of the rich.

However, there were exceptions, and we could say that Captain Peter Gamboa and Officer Rodriguez, of the 50th Precinct, acted with justice, looking for everyone to receive what they deserved, showing the courtesy and professionalism that the institution deserved, nevertheless, some of the officers that were sent to Bulley's door were curious to know who Gibon really was, and on more than one occasion when Gibon went to the bathroom, he got inside and left through the front door and some would turn him around to exit through the door that was used to go out with the groceries, even though Gibon had nothing in his hands, but they did it as a simple act of provocation, trying to see if he would rebel or refuse, but as Gibon knew of their pretensions, he obeyed them and when he returned to climb the stairs in front of the door that had denied him the exit, Gibon discovered that they had incurred with him in discriminatory actions, because they were letting out other members of the club, through the door where they had not allowed him to go out, him, and he did not keep quiet and went and told the officer:

"Thanks for the exercise, you didn't let me out the front, and I see you are letting others out."

And the officer, knowing that what he had done was not right, took it as a joke and smiled.

For many years, New York struggled to be a model city, an example for other Cosmopolitan cities, but within its hard-working and dignified population, who as taxpayers had given their all, there had arisen a line that "disrupted with their feet, all that men and women of good will, did with their hands", the supporters of discrimination, were thoughtless, and many of those who believed themselves to be merciful, were often inclined to lie for manipulation, and condemnation, these were the standard bearers of chaos for oppression, many of them believed they knew better than others, and could confuse and use, the enforcers of change, they simply wanted to move the action of transformation to another line where they could disguise oppression, as redemption, with the support of the population, as if to say to them: <"come, put this rope around your neck to see how you stay.">

Regardless of contextual influences, the wicked would perish, no one was exempt from divine justice, each would receive the fruits of the tree they planted.

It was time to wake up; consciousness would blossom so that peace would grant freedom.

CHAPTER 6

THE CAT

An inclement motivation of her condition, a radical persecutor of Gibon, a false prophetess who offered liberation and in her actions imposed oppression, because the essence of her intention was to drag him to perdition.

The cat had made Estrace a kind of a thousand uses, she involved her in many things, which led to hitting Gibon, so that by her diligence, every day Gibon added a new enemy who came directly to provoke him, to make fun of him or to lead him to a place where he lost his equanimity.

For as I had already told you, occult sect and the organization of evil, they sought to make him sick, to defeat him, to drive him mad, to induce him to crime, to imprison him and then to disable him.

Gibon also thought that the city may have been involved in the conspiracy, giving the green light to the harassers to create parallel cases to divert the true origin of the compensation, and the truth is that the group authorized to follow up on that purpose also had members with criminal minds, a test to a human being whose rights have been violated, hiding the truth, was not called to include sabotage, like breaking two screws on one side of a rubber, and three on the other side for the rubber to come loose to see if the victim perished, not to pay, to all that baseness resorted to occult sect and the organization of evil, something like a crime of "lèse humanité."

They did not know that God was with Gibon, and therefore everything they planned against Gibon would backfire, so that every attempt against him would work in his favor.

So those were nothing but masters and drivers of ignorance and would not admit that every day, the spirit of God moved, and Gibon grew stronger.

Estrace was still being used by the Cat, the organization of evil and occult sect, to make Gibon believe that she had the money.

She, by disposition of The Cat, had formed a group of xenophobes, made up of parishioners of the Dominican degentium born and raised in New York who were dazzled when they saw her, and followed her instructions to the letter, to affect Gibon's interests in every way.

Without intending to reiterate it, Gibon did not like the abuses, and therefore expected justice, to such a degree that what he wanted was for them to make a mistake beyond what they had committed and for a lawyer to appear on their behalf whom they could not bribe, who would take the case and bring it before a judge, to see which of them would fall for being corrupt and malicious.

Gibon had pressured Robert Wolff to recommend a criminal

lawyer to throw down the evilness of the conspirators who were trying to withhold and divert compensation, but it appeared that Robert Wolff, too, was aligned with them.

So one day, Gibon called him and left him a message saying:

"I don't know why you prolong this case for more time, maybe you sold yourself or you are one of the conspirators and you haven't told me anything, tell me things as they are, that's why you are my lawyer," Gibon pointed out.

Half an hour after leaving the message, Robert Wolff called him to let him know that the pandemic court had been closed, that he was waiting to see if a judge would increase his offer, so Gibon told him it was okay, as a way of playing along, he knew he was buying time for whatever purpose, so he had devoted himself to lying to him.

So when ethics was lost on the planet, it touched all the lines, so that even some of the doctors were buried, so that when the organization of evil wanted to take someone out of circulation, they would send out to follow their victims wherever they moved, so that it was easy to find the whereabouts of key people who would do what they wanted, And in Gibon's case, his doctors would be of great help for what the organization was looking for, tempting some of them to manipulate Gibon's medical file, to prescribe him drugs with side effects, so that Gibon would feel sick, and agree to disable himself, thus facilitating their purpose.

Gibon was not violent, but there was a time when he wanted

to know who and where the ringleaders of such aberration were, to take justice into his own hands, because villains of such nature, he understood, could not be allowed to continue harming innocent people, and he thought that injustice and violence, walked hand in hand, because many times, injustice induced violence.

Let's see why the violence did not stop and how special was New York, so that people appeared so thoughtless that could well generate unexpected conditions in existence, so it was as in the major week or as they called it the holy week, unforeseen events happened that left dumbfounded many in the city, because they had chosen to gather in masses disobeying the mandate of social distancing, and although a large number of people had been vaccinated, violence continued to gain victims, and in different sectors of the city, did not stop generating shootings that affected many innocent people, while the pack continued to be active, without ceasing to rehearse their montage of evilness, which was that the pack agreed to try to get some to leave up to two times without taking turns, all with the intention of delaying Gibon on the waiting list.

They never tired of testing Gibon at the request of the occult sect and the organization of evil.

On April 3rd was Saturday, the day on which Gibon had to stay to close, and they took advantage of the occasion to try to make his existence difficult.

They had all left, and Petro, Goby and Gibon were left, Petro mounted a passenger, Goby left empty because it was close to closing time, and Gibon who believed that Petro would not return, did not erase him from the list, and thought to go down to the bathroom while the passenger was leaving.

While he was in the bathroom, Petro arrived and did not sign up, trying to get back on the horse before Gibon, claiming that he had not left, knowing that Gibon had just arrived, for this purpose, seeking to confuse Gibon, he began to provoke him and in the provocation he brought up a series of offenses telling Gibon that he was crazy, that he lived selling two dollar bills, that he suffered from delirium of persecution, that if a client came out he would not let him take him away.

Gibon asked him what it would be like if a passenger came out and he took him.

"Are you going to hit me?" He questioned.

"I've caught a lot more dangerous than you" Petro replied.

When he did not cease to speak what Gibon considered "baseness and boastfulness," interrupting him, he said:

"Engaging me in a discussion like this, simply demeans me, but do not take it in the wrong way, I know techniques that allow me to bring down donkeys like you. From this moment on, the correct and healthy thing would be for you not to address me again, it is clear that you are not a friend of anyone and you are only interested in money, you are a Cali or spy of a occult sect that you think you are going to lead me to your land, you are so malicious that you cannot pretend envy, for the same reason, we have nothing to talk about, so be content that you tolerate yourself, and do not respond as you deserve that I do."

"Oh, if you put your hand on me, there's a camera here," he said.

"We have nothing to talk about, from this moment I withdraw my friendship, you want act as if you're a trusting person, and everyone is who they are, and how they are, I do not wish ill to anyone, but none of those who have been with me has behave well with me."

Petro kept silent, no one had gone out, and a few minutes later Nicole came up to say that there was no one left in the store and that they were about to close.

Each one walked towards the street and boarded their vehicle without saying anything or saying goodbye, they went in different directions, the night was freezing, from the alleys of the skyscrapers, you could hear the meowing of cats, freely roaming, away from Estrace's cages.

Such was the pack with motive and surprises every day, and as Gibon kept to himself, they often looked for a reason to throw him into the middle.

The street titans knew that New York was the real cathedral that taught them to war, where whoever seemed to be a friend sold you or betrayed you, where whoever pretended to help, did it to exploit, neither family nor friendship spoke to you with the truth, everyone loved money, the cause of inequality.

For a few coins, you could be crucified.

Money was the love, which you induced them to tolerate, carrion graveyard, which the world wanted to inhabit.

At that time Gibon, had been so discriminated, persecuted and vilified, that some tried to alter the life he had chosen before he was born, and threatened to pass on to his children what by law they were called to give to him, they did not stop mocking and manipulating, those victimizers persisted in violating the law against him, as if each being, even if they were family, did not bring different lives.

He had already told them about such arbitrariness, but yes, they tried to make him sick to disable him by force, there was so much evil in those hearts that they feared that Gibon with power would give them a drink of his medicine, so he used to say that the wicked were cowards because they liked to do to others what they did not want to be done to them.

However, Gibon was different from all, and in the land at that time, it was said that the "thief judged by his conditions", and that the one who "kills with iron, may die with iron".

He believed that the men of eternity should never give up, and he kept waiting for what was bound to come, so he never doubted that triumph was behind him, and that at any moment it would come.

Although at that time we were going through, as I had already told you, the apocalyptic era, where mankind was waiting for two shocking events: the second coming of Jesus Christ, and a global disaster that would make man turn his face to God, because in reality it was living a radical struggle of all against all, because the prophecy was fulfilled that "would be taken from those who had less to give to those who had more", the money did not reach the minority families, because the cost of living, every day was rising, and had to pay the price set by the distributor of the market unless they did not want to suffer hunger.

As the man expected such exemplary events, whenever a storm was announced, the people of New York City, believing that the world would end, would go out shopping and places like Bulley would become impassable and the members of the club would go out with large purchases, and many of the pack would take advantage and ask for transportation for a large sum of money, The one who charged the least was Gibon who used to make long journeys for less money and sometimes, when the pack had a hundred, he used to have a hundred and fifty, and those in their ignorance would sneer, while Gibon was still satisfied thanking the Lord and said to the pack, "You think you earn more than I do, but I earn more, because while you are waiting, I am on the move, and at the same time I am helping to balance the budget of the needy, the money is more profitable for me, because my needs are less" He said, and the pack became irritated, almost ready to bark.

At that moment Mario the elder reappeared, one of the pack that had retired to implement a night frying, which worked for more than two years, but then decided to approach the pack, some of those who did not know him wanted to make opposition, but Rene Cariño who was aware of the reappearance specified that Mario the sauce had been absent but that he belonged to the group and that no one was called to prevent him from working.

Then after a few days, Mario the sauce with his patience and his firmness made them quiet, and the pack stopped barking, and Mario the sauce began to dance, and many laughed to the roof of their mouths.

CHAPTER 7

THE PACK

Consecrated animal pack, they pursued a reason every day, to justify their courage to bark, if in their arbitrariness let you bite, they generated rage, because they were dogs that did not always feed the soul, their goal was to produce to live, to carry a passenger bowed taking off his hat, many were barbers and masons, but Bulley, was changing his style of eating, and survival, all accountable to him.

In spite of being so suspicious, he did not always discriminate, so some uninhibited and unattached people showed up, Romualdo, a manly girl, Burdock's devoted friend, in love and conflictive, had been admitted.

In the beginning, he was tolerated but then, on one occasion when he went to war with Wing the manager, and threatened to sue him for gender discrimination, everyone came down on him and he was forced to leave the stage.

As a santero, he threatened many people with enslavement through sorcery, and if he fucked someone, if they didn't kiss him, they would run him off,

One day Gibon was walking with his daughter Queen, Romualdo saw that he was a passenger taking her in the front seat, and because of that, she tried to call the police, then the next day he was wearing white pants and it seems that he had scratched himself hard causing lacerations and had bled soiling his pants in the back, and Burdock, who was not even a friend of the mother who had given birth to him, started to shake and approached Gibon, to murmur about the dirty trousers he was wearing, and Gibon made the mistake of commenting in front of Burdock, that Romualdo looked like a woman with menstruation, and Burdock, in a malicious way commented it to Romualdo, causing her to insult Gibon in an inconsiderate way, anyway, Gibon ignored him and went to take a passenger and when he returned, the pack combined with Mark, Wing's assistant, who at that time still did not admit in the kingdom of his heaven to the whole pack, taking the opportunity to test Gibon, induced Romualdo to lend him a drama, and she, like a resentful woman, jumped on him saying:

"The next time you start talking about me, you'll see what I'm going to do to you."

Gibon surprised blocked the blow and grabbed her fist and retreated back:

"Be careful, don't fall and get hurt."

"The one I'm going to hurt is you" Romualdo said.

"I'm going to let you go, be careful if you fall," warned Gibon.

Then he let her go, and he lost her balance and fell, and Burdock was shaking him so that Romualdo called the police, and filed a complaint against Gibon, for "domestic violence and gender discrimination".

However, Romualdo on that occasion did not dare, and specified that Gibon did not knock him down, that he was the one who fell, and that Gibon even warned her that she was going to let him go.

And his arrogance expanded some time after his friend Gladiolo died, he took a vacation to Cuba and there he met a guajiro [1]from Santa Clara who had suffered all the hungers that had generated the American blockade to Fidel Castro's regime, and that used to hunt witches, one night he went to Copacabana with a white trousers of what the padrotes used to wear (pimp), tight to where there was meat, and Romualdo as perverse at the end, he saw the zipper, and in a passing fantasy, he thought that more than traditional cable was a hanging hose, because he wanted to be killed by him, and he was so inspired, that the Santa Clara pimp, without knowing how the hell he would do it, was whispering to him kissing the cup of his ears, until he put him to sleep, as he was used to do with the "jineteras" (prostitutes) of Havana, and got five hundred dollars out of him, He warmed him up and did nothing to him, with the promise that he would see him the next day in the hotel room, where Romualdo was staying, because that night he was a little tired, and it turned out that at the time they had agreed upon, nor at any other time, he appeared, and Romualdo did not want to be satisfied with having been knocked down in the most vile way, and in his anger he cursed him in the name of the infernal legion, all for having been ironed without being clothes, all that generated a night of discomfort for him, and in his santero condition, the next day which was Saturday, he went to a

[1] Peasant

botanical to remove a Saint Lazarus statue that he had paid in advance, and left in the establishment, since he had no space to keep it in the hotel room, and the next day Sunday would fly to U.S. ports, so when he arrived he told the administrator of the Botanical to save the Saint Lazarus so that it could reach American soil without breaking.

Before that allegation, the administrator explained that he had not told her that it was for shipment and that therefore he had to pay two hundred dollars more, to complete the four hundred dollars required for the packing abroad.

Romualdo was so upset that he could not control his anger that he punched the wall, which was obviously made of boards, while a splinter of wood was introduced between his fists, while the impact reached the head of Saint Lazarus, who put it to fly through the air, shattering it, the splinter in his fist caused him to bruise his hand with fingers and all, so he had to go to the emergency room of the hospital "Havana", where he was kept until he arrived in Miami, but when he arrived, he changed to the plane bound for New York, and went to the Presbyterian, where he was told that in the condition in which he was, he had to go home and call an ambulance from there to take him to the emergency room, and as he was instructed he did so, but as he was diabetic, the bruises on his fist and wrist turned black, causing gangrene, during the trip to the hospital he had been sedated, and remained sleeping for long hours, it was a life or death factor, and as he had arrived sleeping without waking up, When he woke up he tried to plead but they told him that what happened had been generated in an effort to save his life, then he thanked the hospital for their decision, and then he thanked the hospital for their decision, and then he appeared in the pack with his arm cut off, and Burdock reminded him that this was paying Jochelo for what he had done to him before.

It turned out that Jochelo had sold him some natural products that he paid for with a credit card, and then he called customer service and told them that his card had been stolen and that Jochelo had charged him $196, then the company that Jochelo worked for called him and told him: "someone is accusing you of charging your card without your authorization, because we know who you are, we assigned the company's lawyers to represent you before the credit bureau and an FBI investigative commission" Jochelo swallowed dryly, hearing such a bitter dissertation that turned into disappointment, then he showed up to a meeting where they questioned him and asked him if he had sold some products in the period in which Romualdo alleged that his card had been charged.

Jochelo said yes, and in whose name the charge had been made, and detailed the products that had been charged, they told him that they would call Romualdo three ways, Jochelo agreed authorizing the action and made the call, Romualdo was asked if he had called alleging that his card had been stolen, he denied that it had been stolen, and alleged that Jochelo had charged his card for some products that he had returned it, in that conversation the company, the FBI, and the credit bureau had already realized that Romualdo was lying, and Jochelo who was on one of the lines listening to the conversation denied it saying that he had not returned any products.

From that moment on, Romualdo's credit cards were cancelled, they had to make a public apology to Jochelo by giving him a double refund, the FBI asked him if he wanted to charge Romualdo for perjury, damages and prejudice, but Jochelo refused and that's why they didn't arrest him.

From that moment when Romualdo lost his arm, those who didn't know him began to call him "the armless" and he was sharpening his hatred against people, to the extent that he was plotting things in order to take revenge even on the innocent, and many of the members of the club, They no longer wanted to go with him because they thought it was a risk to ride with someone who drove with only one arm, and as he was one of Garget's people, accustomed to charging overprices, one day he rode a Mexican and told him that he would charge him 25 dollars for the trip and when they arrived he blackmailed him and said :

"What happened, armless? That was not the deal, you told me it was twenty-five dollars." Alleged the Mexican.

"You'd better pay me, it's 30 for the trip and five for the tip, and if you don't pay me I'm going to call immigration."

Faced with a threat of that caliber, the Mexican felt intimidated and paid him what he demanded, but then went and denounced him to the pack, which never kept quiet about anything, on the contrary, exaggerated, so that some used to say "God save me from the sticks of my mother and the barking of the pack".

That's how Burdock, who wanted to get rid of him, agitated Rene Cariño to put him in bad with the administrator, so Wing told him he didn't want him there, and

Romualdo wanted to sue him for gender discrimination, until the pack barked for him to leave.

"God is not deceived by anyone, he is wise and powerful, he is the cause of this beautiful world, I understand you to the full; all divine grace is granted only by you." Gibon praised.

He understood that if there was justice to imprison the poor, there had to be justice to make sure that those with white collars did not escape punishment.

But the radicalization of the occult sect and the organization of evil had already exhausted all the mechanisms and events that could affect Gibon, first they had bribed Celeste Castellano to disappear with her son Marquet, and then they were looking for a way to get him out of his equanimity, because they were following him, and they were going around with emissaries whom they were relegating to do the dirty work.

One afternoon Gibon had gone to One Hundred and Eightieth and Souther Boulevard to drop off a passenger, and on his return he pulled over to the side of the road, and they sent one of the dirty workmen and that one opening the car door on the passenger side, had stood in front of Gibon, asking him as If he had been in front of the counter of a Market:

"Give me a fifty."

Gibon stared at him as he said:

"What are you talking about? I'm from the police, you want to go to jail?"

"Close that door and you're out"   He said.

The passerby was surprised by the way Gibon spoke to him and said: "Police?"

He closed the door without a word and walked away with quick steps, occult sect had had another failed coup, trying to destroy Gibon.

"To prevent the truth from being spread;

It would be like trying to cover up,

the rays of the sun with one finger".

CHAPTER 8

RIVALITIES

"That Burdock is getting on my nerves", said Witches in one of those explosive outbursts, as he took off his cap, and shook it violently on his right knee.

Look at the last thing he says, that he doesn't mind wearing the same pair of pants for a week that he changes them so that the troublemakers can rest their eyes.

Gibon looked at him without saying anything, as if he questioned him, but after an interval he added:

"Ignorance is the blindness of the soul, they do what they do because they ignore that at the moment of divine justice, we will see each other face to face, because they will not be able to cover up, nor will there be a place where they can hide, it is better that the mockery, the abuses cease, because if those who have power persist in abusing it, they could bother God, and we must avoid making Him angry, because God's anger would lead the wicked to crawl like snakes," he concluded.

It was that the natural reptiles, were cynical and passionless, crawled on their chests on their shell, were always studying how to betray, for walking on excrement, lacked compassion, their evilness and wickedness slowed down their evolution, and even had no reflection, for liberation.

The problem was that Burdock was not mature, one day he would make everyone believe that he was going to change, and while he was given credibility, in that pause he would take energy to continue his rudeness, and one could hear him utter great "expletives", such obscene words that one did not know how they could fit in his mouth without getting stuck when pronouncing them.

"Well, what's to be done? Actually, old parrot doesn't learn to how to talk, and for that one, only the grave fixes it," added witches.

"It seems to be so, Witches, that's why there is no other for me, more suitable than God, because God is the essence of my being, I am God in me, and God dwells in you, God is, the one who is for me to be the one I am, we are the interpellation of the I am, in the being, I am health, wisdom and youth, and God said, you will be my ear, and you will be my voice, you will execute what I say, I will obey, and as he said, so I will do it" said Gibon.

In the pack it was difficult to trust anyone, because they mostly gave more honor to money than to man, if someone went out and did not pay what they asked for, they would not take him and would take him to Gibon, who, full of love, would travel extensive roads to take the people for what they could pay.

Witches on the other hand was the typical individual who halfway through the journey shouted to be noted, and was watching to see who hesitated to retain his turn to take the passenger, on one occasion while it was Gibon's turn, he took some gentlemen that he knew and whom he had ridden before, and spoke to him and said: "Don't you remember me? I had taken you before, you were going with Cholinfe and then you went with me," He said, until he convinced him to stop going with Gibon and go with him.

In the face of such radical impudence, Gibon complained and said to him:

"I didn't like what you did."

Turning back he faced Gibon, giving him the murderous look and asked him:

"What do you want?" he said.

"Take me to the gentlemen, because it's my turn" Gibon reiterated.

"No, that is not going to be possible, I know them and I have taken them before, so they are going with me," He specified.

Gibon self-controlled himself so that there would be no physical friction between them, because of his act of abuse he told him:

"That's why you don't progress, because you're selfish."

Witches, knowing Gibon, kept silent and kept walking pulling the cart of the gentlemen who finally ended up leaving with him.

Those who were there at the time, who witnessed what happened, began to murmur behind his back, censuring the attitude of that while Gibon waved to see if he got into trouble with him, however, when Witches returned from leaving the gentlemen approached Gibon and told him:

"I am your friend, Gibon. Then Gibon specified:

"With friends like you, I don't need enemies." He said.

Witches again, kept silent, because even though he knew he had done wrong, there was no way to make it right.

In reality, after God, money was the dearest love on earth, and many were unaware that if they had not chosen the opulent life before they were born, even if they earned it to survive, they could not have it as their fortune, however, what they with faith asked God for, they already had it allotted to them before they were born, however as they ignored it, God gave it to them in free will as a miracle of faith, but only those who chose it before they were born, would receive it in abundance before they abandoned the exercise of experimentation in the earthly life and many of them reciprocated the bribe gifts that the occult sect and the organization of evil offered to shamelessly give Gibon a hard time, and acted like hypocrites pretending friendship.

But the voice of integrity used to whisper to Gibon:

"You are a torch of the Lord, they have wanted to make it difficult for you, but God has not allowed it, in every step you take, he leads you to happiness, on your way he shows you the light, you will not be blinded, you are the light that he makes shine."

I want to understand by love, what many in their obstinacy refuse to understand, the sacrifice for redemption, which today prevents us from the yoke of pain.

CHAPTER 9

FANATICS AND MERCENARIES

Gibon had already gone through what he had not been assigned, on one occasion, they sent a woman with a girl, to occupy their transportation services to be followed by a cyclist, which would end up causing a scene of violence, regardless of the presence of the infant, seeking to test the patience of Gibon, and check his reaction, if he responded with violence, that the woman would become a witness to such a reaction, the cyclist was at the time when Gibon was preparing to dismount the woman, he approached the vehicle with a mitten in his left hand and without speaking began to hit the front window with the intention of disabling it, seeking to provoke anger in Gibon, however, he went out and stood at the door of the driver's side, watching what the cyclist was doing, who seeing that Gibon was looking at him became adrenalized, and accelerated the blows with the mitten on the glass, when the glass was already cracked and he saw that Gibon did not react violently, he was disappointed.

Then Gibon said to him:

"It was not necessary for you to destroy that crystal, to seek my reaction, I am who I am, and whoever sent you has no power over me."

That one like a crazed satyr kept rolling on his bike and rode away, the woman who was hired to witness the scene looked at Gibon silently, and he said to her:

"If that young man doesn't change his attitude, they're going to kill him, because violence begets violence."

"Yes, he might be on drugs," said the client, Gibon, without saying anything, proceeded to take down the woman's groceries, when he had finished, he went back thinking that everything was due to an intimidating cause, he called Estrace and told her what had happened.

Estrace said nonchalantly "Don't worry about it."

Before that prerogative, Gibon understood that they were trying to intimidate him, and knowing him, who understood that in good times he was a honeycomb, but in bad times he was like burning steel, he published a radical response on social networks:

ILL-BRED OR ILL-MANNERED?"

"Domestic terrorists are like poor children with expensive toys, sort of natural boors, with nothing else in mind but evil, manipulation and intimidation, and violence, they don't yet understand that they cannot manipulate and intimidate those of us who have been polished like steel.

Those troglodytes accustomed to plunder, to manipulation, to illicit enrichment by embezzlement of funds, who, not being their own, seek ways to make others believe that they have a familiarity and a closeness and a bond of friendship with the victims, to justify retaining what belongs to those who bring it assigned to them, and that it has nothing to do with them.

That is the style of manipulation they resort to, laws are laws, and they should not be violated because of racism, to favor and tolerate acts of criminal actions, harming the innocent because two or three want it to be so.

On Friday, April 3rd, they sent a minor on a bicycle to vandalize with a mitten, the front window of the vehicle in which I was being transported that day, I was waiting for the light to change, while the cyclist in an act of provocation, began to hit the glass until it was damaged, they sent him to provoke me in the hope that I would react with violence to justify themselves, but those "mentepollos[2]" have to know that they can't always be smarter than their victims, we have put up with many, because we know that this is the way they resort to drive them crazy, and make their victims lose control, but it's good for them to know:

"A thousand and ten thousand shall fall at my right hand, but they shall not come to me, for I am the one who I am".

In reality, the magic of the expression that motivated Gibon, was to see a wall where he could pay all that abuser, who for some reason, defied his lord; for him, God was the alpha and the omega, conjugated in the beginning and the end.

And it said:

Those satraps do not understand that the planet is in mourning with the thousands of dead that the corona virus and its evil have generated."

---

[2] Stupid people, dumb people.

"Stop your abuses, because when nature portrays you and begins to murder you, for your deeds and wickedness, there will be no money that will be of any use to you." He said.

After that publication, Gibon informed Mr. Pascualo of what had happened, who after communicating with emissaries of occult sect, called Gibon and told him:

"Every cloud has a silver lining', I know it's not your fault, so I'll assume the costs to fix the glass" he said.

Occult sect financed the double standards of Mr. Pascualo, to test Gibon, he sent to carry out the sabotages, and paid him for the repairs, of each thousand dollars Mr. Pascualo took six hundred and gave Gibon four hundred for the repairs, every day a new sabotage arose, but Gibon assumed it with patience, without clinging to anything, he knew that occult sect and the organization of evil, were trying to make him sick to intern him, For the same reason, he was looking for a way to resist without getting upset, it was a fight of good against evil, so he was aware that whatever happened, they would not get away with it, and he reflected on the insensitivity of those who only honored the tenancies and sexuality, and again he understood that all that obeyed the apocalyptic mark that was the opposite of what was sensible, and the clear and pure discernment of existence.

The case was that Mr. Pascualo had sold the car to Gibon, so that he could pay him in installments, and he did not want him to pay in advance, because he had agreed with the occult sect to give evidence about Gibon through the car, in a period of time, and many times when the harassers wanted to open the car to do internal sabotage, he facilitated the access with the key copy that he kept, in one occasion when Gibon owed him eighteen hundred dollars, he told him:

"You don't have to pay me what you owe of the car if you help me move out of the place where I live."

He had said it with a concern, which Gibon had been obliged to answer:

"What's going on? Is there some apartment assigned to me and I have to be near you, to justify the fraud?"

Then Mr. Pascualo kept silent and said:

"The only thing I know is that I have to help you" he said, while Gibon pondered silently:

"I hope your pretensions are not to help me sink" he murmured as a whisper.

"What, did you say something?"

"No, I was talking to my other self."

"Oh... It's that sometimes, even your silence communicates something" added Mr. Pascualo, as they walked.

Gibon had always suspected that Mr. Pascualo was aware of what was going on, and although he hinted at it, he didn't tell him clearly what it was about.

It was a silent trick that the occult sect and the organization of evil had resorted to where everyone knew what was happening, except the victim, who felt that they were evil, but the accomplices understood that the evil was feigned and that they were "patriotic" vindicators who wanted to make sure that they were not wrong to put in the hands of Gibon, part of the treasure of the city.

In any case, "no one was free from guilt to cast the first stone, and who tied the cow's legs was as much a thief as who stole the cow."

Two or three weeks after the breaking of the glass, the organization of evil and the occult sect in their eagerness to get Gibon out of Bulley, resorted to all the mechanisms to tire him and make him abandon that job, they already had the money they had claimed in his name, and they needed to justify it or the moment would come when they would have to return it, and they were not in that, So they sent Rodo to provoke an accident, in the way that, when Gibon was leaving a parking lot, when he was about to leave, a car stopped unexpectedly in front of where Gibon was going and Rodo was unexpectedly entering the hole that Gibon was leaving, hitting the back of his van with the back of Gibon's Jeep:

Gibon commented:

"Don't come here acting wise, you wanted to bump me because you thought you were going to take advantage, but you were wrong."

Rodo kept silent and playing the victim, started asking for money, blackmailing and manipulating and extorting and saying he was going to call the police.

However, when Gibon showed him a patrol car that was watching in Bulley, and told him to make the report, he refused, then Gibon told him to talk to Mr. Pascualo, who was the owner of the car, he was surprised, because they were looking for a pretext, with something that would bring him closer to Gibon, but as the car was in the name of Mr. Pascualo, first they asked him for five hundred dollars, then three hundred, and finally two hundred.

Mr. Pascualo went ahead and filed an insurance report, and it turned out that the state farm insurance company had already sponsored a fraud against Gibon, trying to allow the Shick to disguise as a car accident compensation money from a mistaken identity dating back to the twentieth century, The City's compensation award to Gibon was still pending and withheld for all those years, because the City had never honored an offer of employment it had made to Gibon in return, and Gibon had been prosecuted in many ways in violation of the law and some constitutional provisions, and to justify their fraudulent actions the emissaries of the organization of evil and occult sect had sent to provoke a crash to a car that although it was almost Gibon's, it was still in Mr. Pascualo's name; occult sect that had paid Mr. Pascualo to facilitate the car to continue testing Gibon, admonished him for having made a claim without consulting them, so Mr. Pascualo called Gibon telling him that "Alma" one of the agents of the state farm insurance company had called him informing him that a witness had told him that Gibon was backing up and hit Rodo's car, while it was parked, and that he was going to withdraw the claim, that he should take the car to another place to have it fixed; that he was going to pay for the repair.

Gibon explained to him that it was a conspiracy of occult sect, and the organization of evil, and that the state farm insurance company, was an accomplice of them, because they allowed the lawyer Nona Shick, to try to disguise the compensation money of 1991, with a car accident generated in 2016, certainly, everything obeyed a conspiratorial action, that they insisted on having mounted, where there were several "fat fishes" involved, in that dance of corruption.

Later, they made Rodo believe that they would make him a millionaire, and in the midst of such hallucination Rodo began to get drunk, they sent him a girl who exhibited some tattoos that induced romance, who drove the van, and who went with him wherever he moved, and in his hallucination of millionaire, wherever he arrived he left generous tips, the wife in a fit of jealousy threw him into the street, he was surrounded by guards, suckers and toadies, and only realized his reality, when the card revoked, from there he began to experience the shame of having everything, and suddenly discover that he had nothing.

Occult sect and the organization of evil, created the illusion and the mechanism of looting, because even to have money intelligence was needed, because the envious wanted to steal from you even before the money was in your hands, or some lawyers forced their clients to take loans they did not need and then at the time of the lawsuit or compensation to give two or three pesos to the beneficiary and they kept most of it, claiming that the interest on that loan had consumed much of what was due, and it was that in New York, more than anywhere else, the mafias and gangsters, believed that they had more opportunities to cheat without the laws would generate long sentences, and therefore, they wanted to have the victimized sectors, in the midst of ignorance, which in fact continued to be the mother of all evils.

From the very moment they realized that Rodo had spent

what was his, and what he borrowed from those who thought he still had to pay, from that instant, in the blink of an eye: girls, back guards and suckers, had vanished.

In the pack, those who called him boss, to give him the impression of greatness, laughed and made fun of him behind his back, and even Kinkin, when it was time to get drunk, made sure not to go wherever he went, so as not to have to share his rum with him, because he was one of those who thought that "gifted rum was bad for you".

Time went by and life passed unnoticed, and Mr. Pascualo Alcanforado, accused the ghosts of the system of having flooded him with radiation, and accused them of the discomfort that caused him pain in his back and limbs, and when he stretched he would let out a cry similar to that of Tarzan of the monkeys, in the middle of the jungle.

All this led those who knew him many years before to think that he embarked on the clouds of time, sailed through the air and the storms, and then was shipwrecked in a stormy sea.

We were all ignorant of how he appeared, but some knew how he came, occult sect sent him.

A November 31, 2018, appeared in Bulley, as if driven by the breeze, some thought rightly, that his target was Gibon with whom he had moved from that first day, leaving the impression that they met to be friends, the first three weeks Mr. Pascualo supplied him with evidence of the reason for his presence, He would put him in conversations that seemed strange, he would throw him hints about the consumption of certain pills, to see how he would react, but Gibon, knowing what he wanted, would go along with him and tell him so that, when the moment of truth came, he would not be surprised.

Then two years after his appearance when he was about to conclude his mission with Gibon, he behaved in an irreverent way, when he saw that Gibon greeted one of the neighbors of the building where Mr. Pascualo lived, he said to him:

"You're a hypocrite. How come knowing that guy broke my arm you're saluting him?"

Gibon, who had not expected such an attitude from him, was surprised.

"No, because it wasn't you that got your arm broken, that's why you don't give me the reason, if I had a gun I would kill him" He said, while insisting "Get me a gun to kill him, look, those boys are his sons, and they are making fun of me, if they want to do something I will defend myself" he said while looking at the man's sons who were distracted talking on the cell phone.

"It's not like that, Mr. Pascualo, the first thing is that even if I could get you a gun, I wouldn't do it because I would be getting you in trouble, because if you kill someone you will go to jail, and the second thing is that those boys have just arrived from Africa and they have nothing to do with what you are insinuating, I believe in justice and I know that they are not doing what you think they are doing, if that man broke your arm as you are telling me, then go to the police and file a complaint."

"No, I don't have proof," he expressed curtly.

"Then keep quiet, those accusations are imaginary and boys of your age often like to rave."

"If you help those people, then we are not going to be friends, don't come looking for me anymore."

"Mr. Pascualo, calm down, you are the one who is looking for me, because you want me to help you, actually I know you more than those people, they saw me in Bulley one day, he was short for transportation because nobody wanted to ride him because of the amount they had and I brought him, that's why they greet me when they see me as a way of thanking me, but I have nothing to do with them."

"No, because since Arnulfo put the key in your eyebrows I haven't spoken to him again."

"That's wrong for you, my life is not his life, I would not be angry at any time if you have friendship with him, the problem was between him and me, and I forgave him, why would I be angry if you have friendship with him?"

"With Arnulfo?"

"Yes, with him, we are talking about him, I am different from the others, for the same reason I don't have to think or act like the others, besides, how is it that being a reader of the Bible, a follower of God, you could think that way and talk about killing? There is a reflexive incoherence in your procedure, so much for our conversation, good night, Mr. Pascualo" He added.

"Hey. Is that how you make friends?" asked Mr. Pascualo.

"Yes," Gibon answered.

"Hey, you've got something I haven't told you," added

Pascualo.

"Good evening, I can't talk to you any longer," Gibon specified to him, as he left.

Some time passed without Gibon and Mr. Pascualo Alcanforado communicating, he was waiting for the Department of Motor Vehicles to send him the license plates and the registration in his name, so that he could return his, but since they were late in arriving, he tried to communicate with Mr. Pascualo Alcanforado, but all the numbers he used did not work, so he waited some more time, and when they arrived he decided to go to the place where he lived, he went to his house, he knocked on the door, but Mr. Pascualo did not open it:

"Who is it?"

"Hello, Mr. Pascualo, it's me Gibon, who came to bring you the plates and to give you the two hundred dollars I owe you,"

"I can't open it now; leave it there on the floor in front of the door."

"But you need to sign that you received your two hundred dollars" replied Gibon.

"You can bring me a money order," he said.

Letting it be understood that he had done something behind Gibon's back that might have induced him to violence against him.

It was obvious that such an action would lead one to think that the wicked are cowards.

"I am sorry Mr. Pascualo, although you are being bribed by those who want to sink me, you do not have to fear me, when we did that business, it was face to face and in full agreement, I do not know the reason why now you are running away, but it is necessary that you change your condition, and pray for deliverance, your life can be better, when you get the hatred out of your heart" Gibon answered.

Mr. Pascualo kept silent and Gibon left, a little later Mr. Pascualo called him, with a unlisted number, but Gibon had left his cellphone at home and could not answer him, but when he arrived he saw that Mr. Pascualo had left five messages telling him to send him by mail the receipt he wanted him to sign, but Gibon did not pay attention to him, because sending him a letter by mail was facilitating the way of justification, Nobody was free of guilt to throw the first stone, and none of the misdeeds of the occult sect and the organization of evil could affect Gibon, Mr. Pascualo was one more of them, who had tried to swim in troubled waters, a few years later he found out that they were no longer in the same place, the city had removed them, he was 77 years old and his mother 94, they were two old men alone, who could not do much for each other.

Gibon was looking for the way that any business transaction that he made with Mr. Pascualo, was documented, because according to his convenience, he resorted to momentary Alzheimer's, said things that later he claimed not to have said it, or not to remember that he said it.

Saddened was the heart of God, he shed a tear for his great

understanding, he wanted us to learn in him, but we did not listen and we were struck by a collapse, and when we went to experience, we felt his pain, then we understood that God is the source of love, and redemption.

For without God, there is no cause, no love and no deception, he is the essence of love honor and understanding.

In it we polish ourselves like steel, to become the sword of the warrior.

The universe is, by his love first, without that could be seen, turned into form, what is now seen, from what was not seen made what is being looked at, and let us feel the love and the pain.

The light of the universe is harmony, and its great colorfulness is joy, what is seen in it is philosophy, which becomes patience and harmony.

Time shows us what we are, storms of glory and unlove, letting us understand with clarity, what war shows and peace generates.

And when the inclemency in the weather becomes radical, I am there to help, I am the source of love, with great honor, says the Lord.

You are my heart, who redeems in time the cause of love, you are the hope, you are the great cause, you are the Lord of salvation, you are the goodness, who bestows honor, you are the cause and glory of salvation.

Hallelujah, Hallelujah, Hallelujah, glory to God, all splendor is reborn, as I ponder.

Gibon never imagined that he would be persecuted like any other Jew, nor that they would resort to the lowest souls in the context, but that was life, no one knew what was coming next.

CHAPTER 10

ARROGANCE

On October first, a Thursday, Rodo had sold some rims to Gibon, which were exchanged for Petro in Bulley, obviously, Gibon checked that everything was ok, because he still didn't trust anyone of the pack, and that night they followed him to where he parked the car and broke two screws on the left side, then the next day, it was Friday, October 2nd and dawned cloudy, and again they had broken three on the right side and although the noise that began to produce did not notice Gibon to take action in time, He was forced to live the test of sabotage, because on the slope of Bruce in Yonkers a tire came loose and ran down the hill without control, moving from one side to the other on the way, throwing away the cars he could overtake, until, like a tired old woman, he collapsed on a sidewalk without damaging any of the cars that were parked, and suddenly people that Gibon didn't know and didn't expect appeared from one side to the other looking to help him, and some called a tow truck while others diverted the traffic.

An hour before, Estrace called to find out, but she was silent when she heard Gibon's voice, she couldn't find anything to say, but Gibon knew it was her, because the caller ID showed her number, and she was forced to talk to him and the first thing she said was, that she needed him to take her to Fulton, in lower Manhattan, as Gibon knew she was using a strategy to get information out of him, he played along and asked her if she would be willing to give him gas, as he didn't have a penny for that, she replied that she could only give him twenty dollars, while he warned her, twenty was not enough, she replied that she was going to give him the twenty dollars to take her to Broadway and from there on she would take the train, he played along and said yes, she asked how soon she would be at Bulley, since she was across the street, Gibon replied that in ten minutes, but when he arrived and called she was not there.

At the moment of Estrace's call still the rubber had not come off and she was calling to find out indirectly, how it had affected the sabotage where she was directly or indirectly involved.

That day Gibon was unable to work because the mechanic who had been contacted by them, extended the time to fix the car, which had been moved by crane to his workshop, which was two corners away.

After the reparation he approached Bulley, but as Gibon did not speak to Cholinfe, who stretched out his ear to listen to what Gibon said to the Pack, his face was full of joy, and as he silently celebrated the evil that had befallen Gibon, and as he noticed how happy Cholinfe was about the evil that had befallen him, Gibon raised his voice so that he could hear him:

"I don't need money like others, who drown themselves to earn two or three pesos, and the more they drown, the less they have, but for me, God turns everything that seems bad into good."

When he had heard that, his smile faded and he moved from where he was, lest Gibon should be angry with him.

Certainly, Cholinfe admired Gibon so much that he wished to be equal to him, and in a fit of envy he scoffed and said:

"We brutes are stealing the blessings of those who think they are smart, because we earn more."

When an intelligent person wants to theorize about the moon, we brutes simply point a finger at it, and we have the explanation.

He wanted to provoke him, but Gibon did not listen to him and left him talking to himself, because he perceived that Cholinfe had a high level of emotional decontrol to the point of needing psychological and possibly psychiatric help. The occult sect and the organization of evil had led him to that level of acceleration, those who made a pact with the occult sect, even when they were young, mysteriously assumed a face of aging and decontrol, many of them began to smoke as a refuge from the natural stress they assumed.

Some beings were born for thoughtlessness and bipolarity, Cholinfe was one of them, a lunatic person who easily clashed with anyone because he lacked the goodness to be respectful, assiduously appeared giving opinions without being asked for them and participating uninvited in what he was not supposed to care about and often used to make passes at women he did not know, who were irritated by him threatening to call the police or to go down and lodge a complaint with Bulley's administration.

Burdock had already lost the tinge of the villain, Cholinfe had surpassed him, everything he expressed was by raising his voice like a loudspeaker, and many members of the club thought it was a foolish condition of "Nazism", which he could not get rid of, and the craziness of his expression, annoyed the ears of those who passed near him, and there were many who wanted to hit him, many did not do it out of respect for the police, who often used to wait for something to happen, to cage the aggressor.

Cholinfe had developed evilness that he used to mistake for wisdom, sometimes when he had a client that he didn't want to ride because of the amount he was offering, he would move him away from the door and pretend to negotiate trying to get him to pay more, and for not passing him to the next one on the list, especially if it was Gibon, he would send a text message to one of his brotherhood, one of those who had come from Garget with him, and he would say: "Chamo, come over to where I am, this client is going to 187th and Crotona, pay $20, you ride him, I'm not riding him."

That's how they used to do it, and when Bulley's people, or the one who was behind them noticed and wanted to protest, it was too late, there was no way to complain, because the client was already outside, that way they had set a precedent of survival, and many times, Plutarco Rene Cariño, who was the defender of the pack, would scold him and Cholinfe would raise his voice, as if he was going to eat him, and they would get involved in a dispute until someone approached and calmed them down.

On one of those many occasions, Cholinfe was on duty, and some women came out whom he tried to charge forty-five dollars to take her groceries to southern Boulevard 183, the women offered him twenty-five dollars, and as he never sacrificed his prices, he held them because behind him was Donko, who had discarded them, and as Gibon followed Donko, he could not pass them on to another because Gibon was watching every action, and when he let her go, Gibon approached her and said:

"I'll take her for what you pay" and the women agreed to pay thirty to him, and as they assembled the purchase Gibon spoke aloud, to be heard:

"They go with me because I am the advocate for minorities."

The women burst out laughing, and went away congratulating Gibon. When Cholinfe arrived with his batteries on, the pack barked because he did not get tired, one day when he had not took his pills, he arrived accompanied by some children, one of those girls who did not go unnoticed, he looked at her, and graciously told her:

"Hey, mami, are you married? Or are you applying for a stepfather for those kids? Because if you are, you don't have to go far, I'm here, and I'll take your application." he said, with the utmost definition of disrespect.

Before speaking, the woman looked at him and was moved to answer him:

"But I'd have to be crazy to have a stepfather like you for my kids," she said.

"But are you married or single?" insisted Cholinfe.

"I'm married, so stop bothering me." Cholinfe kept silent, and the woman walked away.

At that moment another woman appeared asking for Gibon:

"Where's the papi chulo? One who is polite and speaks well."

Cholinfe was like a horse without a bridle, who often used to get in front and meddle in everything even if he wasn't called, he couldn't keep quiet, so his intrusion became imminent:

"Are you talking about me? Here there is no other that comes close to me, they call me papi waist, I have tuned the ball box, those who have tried me call me daddy. How do I serve you my dear?"

"She is looking for the pastor," said Fredesvindo interrupting.

Just at that moment Gibon appeared, she saw him and said to him.

"I'm looking for you sweetheart, come and take me" she said.

"But it's my turn, I'm the one who will take you" said Cholinfe.

"But it's my money, I'm not going with you, even if you take me for free, for being fresh, trusting, and smiling," he said while they went with the groceries to where Gibon was parked, when they got out Burdock who was another one who always had amplified ears, commented:

"Take that, Cholinfe, they didn't want stuffing, eat egg, if you don't know people, don't get fresh, one day you're going to find yourself in big trouble."

"Hey Burdock, now you come to get agitated?" He questioned, as a woman came out to whom he said:

"Taxi?"

The woman nodded her head and he pulled her away from the group to ask for an exorbitant sum, the woman refused to pay the price he demanded and said walking away from the woman:

"Which one is next for me?" Fredesvindo, who was next on the list, showed up and took her for twenty dollars to 181st and St. Nicholas in Manhattan, Cholinfe required a payment of $30.

There he was waiting for more than an hour, until someone came out who would pay what he required, the people he moved with had to be programmed to pay twenty or he didn't take them, one came out who paid fifteen dollars, but he refused, Witches went and he passed it to Rocko Vulcan, Witches got upset and tried to growl, but Cholinfe raised his voice at him, like when a father wants to hit a disobedient son and they got into an argument, while Rocko went away and left them insulting and threatening each other.

Cholinfe barked, in a tone that overcame Burdock, he lacked

emotional control and customers who heard him walked away and asked for private services.

Certainly, there was everything in "the Lord's vineyard," so there was no lack of applicants for the service who demanded like rich men, and paid like poor men, just as there was no lack of those who looked down on those poor devils who often lacked discernment, and often by such actions as Burdock used to do, wanted to get them all into the same coffin.

Because in their conception of discrimination, they believed in a false perception, that dogs and cats were the same, they could not distinguish, that some barked, and others meowed.

The administration, who checked from the cameras, sometimes thought they were going to hit each other and had the police officers who served in the store come up, but then they returned without any details, seeing that they were just barking dogs that didn't bite.

Anyway the hectic course of everyday life in Bulley, made the pack a whistle or a tune, every day generated something new, occult sect and the organization of evil, tried by many means to control the pack in the same way they were controlling the machine shops, and all the small businesses that were within their reach, but the pack took the money, they did the drama and finally acted as it suited their interests.

Gibon moved independently of what the pack decided, so whenever they wanted to involve him in a leadership position he said:

"I prefer to operate independently, I'm not used to being ruled by gangs or groups of morons, who smile at you from the front and when you turn your back they want to stab you, sorry, I'm not interested in any position" he said.

That night the cat was in the area, two provocations had been designed exclusively for Gibon, while he was making a purchase; he had been approached by an emissary of an occult sect of those who followed him in any direction, and he was in a white car and went straight to provoke him and told him:

"Hey old pooper, move your car so the others can park" He said with an eminently malicious grin.

Gibon, seeing that he was making a cruel joke, followed his line and answered him: "That's why they shoot you and leave you lying on the road."

The man in the white car, not expecting a surprise response of that nature, felt fear and his tires lifted the autumn leaves they found, and he disappeared like an evil spirit.

A little later, a white van passed by with the Cat and one of her servants, they passed by the other end of the street because the Cat was avoiding being seen by Gibon, and she shouted:

"Eeeeh, Gibon."

But Gibon didn't know who it was and answered:

"Yes, Gibon here, tough nut to crack, the mice don't know what to do anymore" she said, and the driver didn't stop.

It was one of the ways they used to tease Gibon, they needed a reason to tease him, but Gibon trained by life did not to let himself be led where they wanted him to go.

So he took refuge in divine grace and said: "In profundi":

What is the fire that I carry in my feet, to move to where I found you, what is the reason for the bonfire, for that warmth that I generated in you to ignite me and walk where I will be taken.

I want a real reason for my existence and my walk, I want a non-casual reason to reflect.

In you, there is always hope, the cause of living for each day, you are the grace and glory of souls, who cry out at every moment for your harmony.

That is why our heart beats, waiting to define the profile, in each pattern and step of your future.

You are, you are and always will be, you are the nuance of humanity.

You are the living and eternal grace, in every line, in every pardon, and in every beat of my heart.

CHAPTER 11

MISCHIEF

I can't discriminate,

and anyone who hides anything,

I have to report them.

At that time, the Dominicans had begun to stand out in the action of North America, and wherever there was a review of what they were doing, so some foreigners sought shelter under the umbrella of those and many times, pretending to be one of them. Galy Buchi was one of those who loved to interact with that Caribbean species, he was from Arabia, but his family lived in the Holy Land, in Jerusalem.

He had been overconfident, and whenever he found an opportunity to annoy Gibon, he resorted to a ruse suggested by emissaries of occult sect, in that way, on more than one occasion he had taken upon himself the task of helping Gibon to lose his equanimity, making him uneasy, trying to make him angry, sneering like a sick sadist at those who took pleasure in the pain of others.

Many times when the passengers were leaving slowly, Galy Buchi used to go down to the store and check some of the members of the club who were shopping, asking where they were going, offering them a balanced price, so that when they left, they would go directly to him, who, looking at the person on duty, would tell him:

"Mine, staff." And he took him, jumping over everyone in front of him.

In the pack if one did not fly then ran, and everyone had their own history, and occult sect, and the organization of evil knew it, and that is why they resorted to various ways of using and manipulating such souls, to make their presence known to Gibon, who for them was the target and the center of attention.

They used to send a couple of emissaries to bribe some of the pack, so that they would make Gibon believe that they wanted to be his friends and when Gibon agreed to treat him as such, then they would tease him so hard to make Gibon angry, and Galy Buchi who had incurred in such a condition, at the first carelessness of Gibon and with the greatest impudence he would erase him from the list so that someone else would go on his turn, and he would be forced to sign up again so that he would be last, but Gibon, who used to check the list frequently, would not let himself, and as he knew who he was behind he would protest and put himself next to where he was erased and regain his turn.

Galy Buchi did such evil deeds in complicity with Burdock, who was always trying to use and take advantage of those who were ready in the pack, to do the dirty work, and then, to share the bribe gifts.

On December 3rd, two emissaries of the occult sect appeared

ready to make it difficult for Gibon, because it was cold, he got into the car to warm up, while it was his turn, which Galy Buchi took advantage to erase his name, then insisted that Gibon had left, although at no time he moved the car from where he had parked it, and Galy knew it, so Gibon taking a defiant stance told him:

"Galy Buchí, trust is the shortest way to make a mistake, respect me, you are from Arabia and I am from America, you can not come here, to make things difficult for me, 'do not do to your neighbor what you do not want them to do to you', I am going to take my passenger, and if you think I am not the one who is going, try to take him away from me to see how we play."

The Arab before such a reality, kept silent because "it was not the same to call the Devil, than to see him arrive".

The Arab before such a reality, kept silent because "it was not the same to call the Devil, than to see him arrive".

As Plutarco Rene Cariño was the mediator before the Pack's conflicts, Gibon raised him a complaint about the Arab's behavior, that René promised to solve, but when Gibon went to ride someone, Rene Cariño took advantage and claimed to the Arab, Burdock and Galy Buchí were justified with that it was an order of the organization, as occult sect had delivered a bribe for that purpose, he was forced to do so.

They had to deal with Plutarco Rene Cariño, who upon his arrival told to Gibon:

"I investigated and more than five told me that your name

was erased because you were gone" said Plutarco Rene Cariño.

Gibon, who had understood what had happened, answered him:

"Equals pursue each other, criminals understand each other" he said, while warning Galy Buchí that if he persisted in disrespecting him, they were going to have problems, and reiterated that he had done the same thing twice before, and that since he was trying to use him for his own benefit he preferred that he did not speak to him; that was the way Gibon used to keep the pack away from him.

The Arab kept silent, then a few days later he had reflected on how he would treat Gibon from now on, and he changed his style and began to respect him by taking care of the way he would address him.

A few months later, Galy Buchí, suffered a great disappointment, he had been absent from the pack for about three days, which Burdock took advantage of to collect money alleging that he was in prison and that they needed to grant a bail under the assumption that the FBI, had arrested him for questioning in relation to two rebel emissaries of occult sect that had tried to attempt to attack American properties in New York, As the Arab was friendly and sympathetic to all members of the pack, with the seriousness with which Burdock expressed it, no one hesitated to cooperate, and they collected one thousand and five hundred dollars that three days later he could not justify, because the Arab had appeared denying Burdock's lie.

They threatened to call the police on him, but he didn't flinch, and claimed that they couldn't accuse him with the police because there was no proof, and since the pack knew the man's character, they left him the money.

And Galy Buchi did not speak to him for some time because of that "cruel joke". Then once he had reacted regarding Burdock, he only opened his mouth to tell him:

"Now you just showed me two new bad habits... "You're a liar and a thief"

Burdock looked at him, without saying anything, while showing a fake smile that confirmed Galy's statement, he didn't mind being insulted, he had lost his shame, the greater the insult, the greater the cynicism. He was a case study, so Gibon didn't understand, how "an animal, that was supposedly rational, was indeed so irrational."

CHAPTER 12

EVERYDAY LIFE

Life in New York, not always defined as people thought, everyone was focused on survival, if there was no production or a relative to provide the stay was a bitter melody.

Some sects in the name of their religion sought ways to harass Gibon, because such harassment gave him satisfaction, and many had an alarming envy against the Jews, and insisted that the Jews had killed Jesus Christ and that behind every test in the spirit, were they, so the organization of evil and occult sect sought ways to discredit all who showed a minimum sympathy for the Jewish people.

Occult sect and the organization of evil, were institutions integrated by fanatics, pious and religious, obviously, some would appear among them, that after committing a sin or something that they considered sinful, or whipped themselves, or took turns to whip each other with a rope of cabuya[3], and then moved ramping on their chest like soldiers in training, because they could not lie on their backs, and all that was because they believed that, thus, they made up for their faults.

The leaders of such organizations had the full certainty that Gibon had been chosen by God to participate in the changes that

---

[3] Fiber

would generate the planet in the new era and therefore they needed to prove it in every way to be sure that they were not wrong in their assessments, but their evidence exceeded the evils, so they bordered on fanaticism.

Burdock, was a kind of contact that they had in the pack, but as that libertine spirit did not believe even in his mother, some in the pack considered him as "a raised abortion", because without being of the brotherhood of the occult sect and the organization of evil, he took bribes and acted like a madman, and he had a penchant for pederasty, and when he went to the Republic, he would send pictures to his friends in the pack showing them his new conquests of children and young boys with whom he used to fuck, so "Ojitos, Y Frank" the ones who picked up the shopping carts, used to call him the "dirty one".

After the incident with Arnulfo and Gibon, Burdock having arrived from his trip from the Republic, the pack informed him in detail the events, and the latter, seeking to provoke Gibon, dropped a hint consisting of the following expression:

"Anything you need, call Arnulfo."

As Gibon knew their games and pretensions, he let it pass that first time, but the second time he told the same little joke, Gibon stopped him in his tracks and said:

"You just arrived, stop agitating, Arnulfo is not broken because I don't want him to be" Gibon expressed, which induced Burdock to emit a guttural chuckle, walking five steps further, from where Gibon was, who added nothing, and remained silent.

Sporadically the pack suffered moments of tension, mainly when Burdock appeared, who, because of his depraved way of expressing himself, did not respect the presence of anyone, when he felt the urge to let loose his string of obscenities, like a real madman.

When that happened, Gibon kept his distance, so as not to be confused, and the pack had qualified Burdock as the group breaker, because every time he did such an action, the pack would disperse with a roar of murmurings, which were usually conjugated in phrases and sentences limited to expressions such as "dustbin, garbage can," etc., which was a joke for him, who shamelessly made fun of those, because they would sing his tune, and the real dogs would be wary of being confused, dump, etc., which was a grace for him, who shamelessly mocked them, because they sang his melody, and the real dogs were wary of being confused by him, so often when it was his turn to move close to where Burdock was, they emitted a guttural growl, which turned to be in howls of wolves, because sometimes they coincided in that one was passing with its owner on the sidewalk and Burdock, by that condition of mental derangement, let out an anal burp, as happened when a woman was leaving with her purchase to request the transportation service, the car was crowded but at the precise moment she was approaching was surprised by a chemical air and expressed being heard by all:

"Fo[4], how fucking low", she said with some nervousness, to the extent that in her eagerness to get away from the door, part of the groceries fell out of the cart and the other

---

[4] Expression that's used when something smells bad.

members of the pack had to help her pick it up.

A Spanish blessed woman, who was confidentially walking with her dog, suddenly noticed a sudden change in her pet, he was stagnant without being able to move, and he barked and growled at the same time.

The nauseating smell of Burdock's gluteal roar induced him to bark, and the dog-walker, who was in the habit of picking up the feces of the barker, thought that he was celebrating his doggy air with a shriek, but when she saw that everyone was running away, she fled from there without knowing what was going on and without any desire to investigate.

The blessed one, who had not yet inhaled the chemical, expressed with uneasiness,

"Hey, tío[5], but what is happening?" suddenly she noticed that Petro was holding his nose and was making signs indicating Burdock as the generator of the bad smell.

"What?... get that thing out of there" she said with some nervousness referring to Burdock, and added "run, Bobi, run, before that demon spawn suffocates us," she said and ran, almost dragging the dog, because the ambient air of the context had given it the aroma of a rotten cat, so the environmental office, on more than one occasion prowled around the place, looking for the real target of the stench, and some members of the Pack told him when that happened:

"Run, Burdock, before it's too late, there goes environment and "sanitation".

------

[5] Spanish word to say "dude", used most commonly in Spain

On the other hand, the Spanish Blessed in her eagerness to escape the stench, was going so fast that she was about to be hit by a car with a license plate from another state that was running at 35 when the speed should not exceed 15 miles, and when suddenly braking turned into a U-turn, remaining prostrate in the same place, the Blessed was so nervous that she could only say, Saint Alejo, "take us away".

All these exasperations had generated Burdock, in his lack of control.

"Hey, Burdock, what did you eat, dead mouse or rotten cat?" Petro asked, but Burdock didn't answer.

"Be careful, Estrace could hear you" Vilinsky said.

"Who is Estrace?" asked Petro.

"Don't tell me you don't know who Gibon's girlfriend is?... The cat lady," he affirmed while letting out a laugh.

The smell of rotting cat had turned into a powdery odor, as if an explosive had been discharged, prompting the police to patrol the area as well.

Suddenly everything had dissipated, the woman who had left with the cart full of groceries, had started to call a base to send her a taxi, but when she saw that Gibon, who stayed away from the pack, approached her and asked her if he could transport her, Gibon said yes, and she dropped the call, while he spoke to her.

"We are here to be useful lady, tell me where are we going?"

"Yes, I was going to call a taxi."

"I understand ma'am, but that purchase will not fit in a taxi, they do not have space for large purchases, we do delivery and we have where to accommodate your purchase so that you and it, arrive on time, and safe.

"Okay, how much is it going to be?"

"The same as you always pay."

"I always pay 25 from here to 135th Street."

"Okay, let's ride you."

They set off for their destination and on the way the woman commented on Burdock: "How can you have such an undesirable person around you?"

"Ma'am, nothing is casual, and it seems that we are called to experience a test with that individual," Gibon said, the lady kept silent, while admiring the panoramic view of the western highway.

When they arrived. Gibon put the groceries on the cart, she handed him thirty dollars and said:

"Keep the change, you are very kind."

"Thank you very much," Gibon said.

"Give me your number so I can call you when I get back and you can bring me back." The woman added.

Gibon handed her a card with his number on it, said goodbye, and the lady's children went out to bring up the groceries.

The neighborhood where the lady was going to, there were some houses of nuanced colors and adapted to the Latinized tastes, and many of those houses were inhabited by whites, of which it was murmured in the community, that they possessed the best houses, because the existential history of the planet established advantages in favor of those, that had in America the first black servants, that had gone through a series of vicissitudes that consisted of whippings, raping and humiliations typical of the racism of the egos of that time, inflated by the condition of masters that inhabited in the mansions, while the black in their condition of peons, occupied the corrals, giving to understand, that the history of the earth, apparently was a history of social injustices, while that stamp of the time had remained crystallized, in the enslaved souls, where many of those beings, even with the passage of time, remained with a grudge against their fellow man, and even with a thirst for revenge, all because they ignored that the man before being born, chose the life they were going to live, because if it were not so, everyone would have abandoned the burden of suffering that went through without knowing that he had assumed it.

But they used to say that time healed the wounds, and those years of obscurantism were left behind, now was the twenty-first century, and the generation showed its progress through its technology, although many in their dissertations accused technology of radicalizing and confusing the sanity of those who inhabited the planet, and even humanity was approaching great acts of misunderstanding, and some commented:

"If in two thousand years the wicked did not assimilate the teachings of Ben Joseph (Jesus Christ), not to do to others, what they did not want to be done to them, as the essence of justice", now come the time of transformation, anyone who in the free will, would use a whip to whip, would also be whipped, to experience the pain of their neighbor, because if Christ had already died for all, no one would die for anyone, and everyone would be responsible for their deeds, and no one would go beyond the sacrifice for those who did not deserve it.

I must remind you that at that time, man loved money more than God, and in their free will they did not spare themselves in the sin of repentance, and when someone appeared who with their mouth pronounced to be a Christian, and with their actions showed the contrary, with a certain modesty Gibon would say to them:

"You, only imitate Jesus, in the beard, but in your heart corruption is contained, you are one of those who crucified him and that for this era together with your friends reincarnated, to show themselves as false prophets, trying to deceive and confuse the people of God."

Then, they looked at each other, and kept silent.

It was true, the apocalyptic era had been channeled into forced changes, America was no longer the springtime of sunshine and greenery.

It gave the impression that capitalism was returning to the primary stage of barbarism, an apparent return to socialism, each movement was a row, and the time that was divided into several actions during the day, at that time was only enough for a single reflection without the intention of advancing to more than one line.

In the twentieth century, New York was no exception to the pain, for during the 70's and 80's, from 145th Street to 172nd Street, when in Manhattan you didn't need a permit for anything and drugs were sold on a tray like sugar or rice, and firearms including a nine millimeter, Smith and Watson, 38, 380, were sold like high caliber toys from hand to hand for 150 dollars, whose sales were under the control of the darkies, the "after hours" in the subways, after midnight, assumed their hegemony, the nocturnal vampires represented by drug trafficking, alcohol and prostitution, took control of everything, spreading terror, violence had increased, and daily one or two dead people appeared in the dumpsters, and if a day passed without anyone dying, then, two days later, six dead people appeared, replacing those of the previous days.

That is to say, the history of darkness in the city, brought a high price to all those who longed for riches, and every Latin American nation that granted the dead, emanating from the heart of the ambition that induced them to gamble their belts, were forced to mourn with tears of blood to their fallen, who finally happened to be deported in coffins.

At that time the police were careful not to get visibly involved against the masters of the streets who obeyed the dictates of the mafias of those times, who opted to move the business to the Latin America backyards from where they would export the poison to the streets of North America:

New York was still the scene of pain, and the confusion was so drastic that fear induced detectives and police officers to make blunders.

So was New York until Mayor Rudolf Giuliani, Italian descendant, from 1993 to 2002, took the streets away from organized crime, and the quality of life in New York City regained its dignity, while the cemeteries of Latin America gave burials to the fallen in New York, in the drug war.

From New York, glory and pain departed, many believed that New York was the promised land, where God ruled for the oppressed people, but confusion degenerated the honor, the devil was in control, and false prophets wanted men of God, to demonize them.

Money was the bait that induced them to take the bait, the prophet struggled, until he turned us back to the hand of God, all of this immured the organization of evil, and they wanted to add us many obstacles, to prevent us from occupying our pedestal.

Democracy had become oppressive, because those who moved within it, confused it with debauchery, the city had become populated by motorized rats, who used to follow their victims to where they parked, and once they moved away from the vehicle, they broke the windows, if such an aberration continued, the time would come when it would be necessary to go around with insecticide ready to fumigate, so that the rats would be reduced for the peace of men of good will.

The earth had no righteousness and those who still hoped in a higher source, cried out for God's righteousness, because wickedness had become a disease.

Most of the men, had begun to depend on the technology that generated the machine, that kept all the thoughts, and the man had become addicted to the machine, and incurred in doing thoughtless things that came generating a radical social condition, which induced it to control without the ability of self-control.

They said that the Pharaoh's gang had its center of operation in New Jersey, from where they emanated orders of pardon or condemnation, the case was that there the beans were cooked, and for the same reason from there came out stampedes of carriers that traveled the streets of New York, doing and undoing, under the guidelines of the occult sect and the organization of evil and used to provoke accidents programmed to give a crumb to the victims and they retained most of it, which was distributed among doctors, therapists, and mainly those who did the dirty work that included lawyers, paralegals, police secretaries, and why not, also for the personal masseur of the boss among others.

On June 26th something similar happened while Gibon was driving to drop off a purchase, he found that an accident had been staged on a closed street, it had all happened on Park Avenue between 183rd and 184th Streets, and as Gibon was driving towards the vicinity of the scene of the crime, an ambulance and seven police cars suddenly appeared, The forward traffic had become impossible, and Gibon was forced to reverse back to 184th Street and Park Avenue, to continue to Bathgate Street, to descend to 182nd Street, where he would end up dismantling the delivery, and then return to Bulley, the pharaoh's carriers were looking for volunteers to crash or be crashed, in exchange for a pitiful bribe.

So was the world, the planet was in turmoil, in many places there were no pedestals, and where they existed was attackable.

In relation to the pack, everything that was agreed to be corrected, was repeated, Mazambula wrote it down and Arnulfo erased it, which induced Mazambula to rub his face in the presence of everyone, that he was "a butter maker", who inserted syringes between his veins, He was forced to refer him to methadone, whose speech dragged Arnulfo to violence, who under no circumstances accepted that his past should be touched. That day they fought until they bled, and the pack pressured Mazambula to leave the place, and he was forced to return to Garget.

As the day dawned, the pack was still howling, their business depended on the Bulley Club members, whose action served as an umbrella of survivors, Bulley, as a corporation freely contributed to the poor for them to generate the focus of survival, where many parents, looking for bread for their children, where many took the initiative to become managers of their small businesses while working for themselves, whether self-employed or motivated by the support of Smart Business Administration, all those men and women had taken advantage of the tolerance of the club's servants to grow as human beings.

In a cooperative exchange, the unit at 184 West 237th Street in the Marbel Hill area had been of great benefit to those who honored the opportunity to grow with ample freedom to understand that God designed the greatness of growth for the expansion of many.

There, inside Bulley operated a team that served with vehemence, the club members, all ready to give the best of them, highlighting some tender visibilities who named Mery

Ann, Amber, Beatrice and Katy, and Schenequa among others.

Beatrice and Schenequa, sporadically, came to be transported by Gibon, who in turn, wished to investigate Mary Ann's Hermeticism, admired her in silence in an indecipherable Platonism, he loved the moderate and silent style that she assumed at the moment of a conversation, leaving the impression that no one should doubt what she said.

Amber was the definition of understanding, being an assistant administrator, she did not hesitate to serve from her position for the edification, she loved her neighbor as herself, becoming one of the best servants of the entire Bulley, ready to protect the investment, and in every action inside, she raised the quality of the service, impregnating satisfaction to the heart of the consumer.

Katy, assuming a posture that showed her little given to talk to the pack, nevertheless she used to request the Jochelo's transport services, who used to see her as a heroine, and told the pack:

"Katy defends us, whenever the issue of removing us from the front has been brought up, she is the first to say "they are a great help to us, they give people information about the store, and they don't let the cars pile up outside, because they always help us, bringing them in".

And thus, in such a way, Jochelo defined the impression of the interior.

When Gibon arrived where he lived, he wrote a hint to Estrace, who was acting as a Zombie managed by puppeteers, and it said:

"To the criminal mind, fear makes it tremble, the third party errand boys, today they are so confused, that they fear their destiny, with sabotage they will not succeed, my natural force will bring them down, I am, the one I am, that I show love, if something is for me, no criminal will be able to divert it, there is no more foundation, their torment arrives, those who have conspired will have their concern."

Later in the evening, Estrace went on social media and greeted him, as if nothing had happened, she said:

"Hello!"

Before that audacity Gibon answered:

"Hi, the sabotage didn't affect me, I'm still alive".

But Estrace kept silent. The next day was Wednesday, Estrace was leaving Bulley's when Gibon met her, she went ahead of him and told him:

"I have ten dollars for a ride to Hillman Avenue."

Gibon took two bags she was carrying in a shopping cart, without making any allegations, put them in his transportation, and they drove to the scene.

The street they were headed to was located in the "<Amalgamated>" cooperative housing complex on the outskirts of Bulley, where to buy an apartment at that time, it was necessary to wait ten years on an acceptance list.

There was a prolonged silence, until the angelic blonde broke the ice to tell him:

"Find yourself a job in a bank."

Gibon looked at her in silence, and thought that she was a soul throwing claws, to see what she caught between her nails because she acted as if she had something to do with him, however Gibon understood that no matter how crazy she was, she could not go beyond that, because if she did she would have to suffer, since fear, more than facts, was destroying the perverse ones.

However, she wouldn't stop, three days later she called him again to take her to the yard where she used to hunt the cats.

On the way Gibon told her that he had met a girl who might be a suitable partner, Estrace asked him if it was her, Gibon said no, wanting to see her reaction, he told him she was an Irish girl who was working as the receptionist for his new lawyer.

Estrace didn't think the comment was in good taste, she was somewhat attached to money, and whether she kept it or pretended to have it, she didn't like to bring it up, and when Gibon questioned her about it, she got a headache, or looked for a way to excuse herself.

When they arrived at the yard located in the vicinity of Grand Concourse and Ryerd, she wanted Gibon to take a key and open the front door for her to make those behind them believe that Gibon was her employee, but Gibon refused and left.

The next day they met in front of Bulley, Gibon greeted her and could see that she was depressed, he said to her in a voice like a whisper:

"I'll call you," he expressed, and they each continued walking in different directions.

Then on another occasion she called him again to leave her in the yard, she insisted on justifying herself by letting herself be seen with Gibon, and again in the yard, she wanted him to help her open the door but Gibon told her:

"I can't do anything like that, I am avoiding being used by foxes and bitches, if they see me helping you they will think that I work for you, and you are going to take the money they give you, and you are not going to give me anything, actually, when I bring you, they give you twenty to pay me, and you only give me ten" said Gibon.

She kept silent but insisted:

"I'll give you twenty if you come get me and take me to Tody's."

"If you wish, when the time comes for you to leave, call me and I will come." specified Gibon to her, but she only wanted to try it once more, so when it was time to leave she didn't call him and one of her friends from the motorcycle gang had passed by her.

CHAPTER 13

HOSTIGANTS

Gibon, in fact, was a strategist who knew the tactics of combat, he had grown in a condition of ambivalence, interacting with those above and living with those below, his wars began at school between a forced learning between rules and boards, when he did not respond as the teacher wanted to hear, since childhood he was admired in the club of the great, because he did not lack the courage to stand up to abuse and bullies.

He was a long-suffering man, because he dared to face alone, the gangs that dared to spread terror to those, who fled from the problems.

Very seldom did he distinguish between tension and joy, he was always ready for whatever came, if he was thrown, he blocked, that's why he never succumbed, and if life brought him a lemon, with great feeling aspect he would make a lemonade with love.

SSome thought he was made of iron because he seemed not to suffer, and from the pain, he made a melody, and many saw him as the community paladin, fighter against the urban guerrilla, that's why it was easy for him to face and defeat the evil of the minions and emissaries of the occult sect and the organization of evil; who did not cease in their harassment, whether it was by making him a ticket with policemen at their disposition as they had done with officers like Kom, whom they had sent behind him, and he went on one side and Gibon on the other, and when he saw that Gibon was going from south to north, and he from north to south, he supposed that he didn't have his seatbelt on, or he focused on making a ticket in that direction, the thing was that he turned the patrol car where he was going as he was used to do and turned back to follow Gibon, and as he saw through the mirror that he was being followed, he stopped and when the officer approached the window, Gibon before the officer spoke asked him why he was being ordered to stop, and the officer Kom answered him:

"When you passed by me, I didn't see your belt."

"I see officer, you were sent to look for confrontation, as you can see, you looked but you looked wrongly, you are looking I have my belt on, I am going to give you my license no problem but whatever comes out, it is going to be your word against mine, you guys when you want to fabricate a ticket or a case with a person, you will use any pretext."

Officer Kom was silent as he caught the license between his fingertips, and immediately returned with a ticket that said belt.

Officer Kom handed it into his hands telling him:

"You have 15 days to resolve that contravention," Gibon kept silent and accelerated and left, that was the first time that Gibon and Kom argued, before his descent.

More those who were consciously grateful expressed themselves, with a voice of velvet and with satisfied longings:

"Thank you Lord for allowing me to laugh when others cry, thank you Lord for being the light of Eden that many long for, thank you Lord for making me a conscious reflection of your being, thank you Lord for being the cause of dawn.

It is pleasant to experience, your glorious awakening, which redeems the prize I am to win, you are the light of dawn, and you are the cause of power.

You are the feeling of awakening, in each being of rebirth.

You are the serenity of a slow gaze, where the water flowed without you batting an eyelid.

You are the movement of silence, where water moves without being agitated.

You are the pure essence of the crystal, of a real cause, to be carried.

The silent water wanted to fall in love and a thirsty palate, tasted it again, and God, looked and smiled."

Already the organization of evil with their gangs, had resorted to everything, they were trying to destroy Gibon's nerves, because the members of the organization of evil, were of an inclement nature, depraved and unconscious, beings designed for evil, and testing Gibon was their obsession, and they wanted to intimidate him by resorting to the Taxi and Limousine commission, and their emissary whispered in officer Maykol's ear:

"You try to provoke him, to see his reaction, that kind of calmness can not be true."

Officer Maykol smiled shyly.

They had sent a woman from the church to solicit Gibon's services, and they followed him from 237th Street, from Bulley to 193rd and Wadsworth terra in Manhattan, but as there were people watching they did not show themselves to him until Gibon had left the woman, who asked him:

"How much is it?"

"The same as you always pay," said Gibon.

"I always pay 15," she clarified.

"All right," Gibon said.

She handed him twenty dollars, he handed her back five and when he left they followed him and half a mile later, when Gibon stopped to check the mailbox, at the Broadway post office where Pitt, an informant for the organization of evil, worked, the T&LC emissaries showed up. They were colored men, they had gone up to Gibon, as if they were engaged in a narcotics operation, they did not identify themselves and pretending to be private detectives, they had tried to intimidate Gibon; so Gibon was annoyed, because while the woman was with him they did not approach him, and then they went to weave him an intimidating story without an eyewitness, which induced Gibon to answer them:

"You are wrong about me if you think you are going to intimidate me, I am not a taxi driver, therefore you have no power over me, I am going to change this city, eradicating the abuses you have against minorities, you are slave holders, ignoring that your ancestors were chained."

They are handing you a quota of power so that you can do the dirty work, believing yourselves to be oligarchs when in reality you have been sent to do what they lack the courage to do.

They have loosened your chains so that you can tighten them, and then justify themselves by saying, we gave you freedom, but you did not know how to appreciate it, because as the wicked do, for a few coins you sell your honor," he said.

Officer Maykol and his cliques, kept silent, the key fell inside the car, one of the officers bent and looked for it, taking possession of the vehicle, so Gibon called 911, and denounced what was happening, a policeman went to the scene of the event that only said with a mischievous smile between his lips:

"You have to let them do their job," the officer said.

"But what is their job, if I'm not a taxi driver, they don't have to go after me, I just do delivery in Bulley, as a motivated entrepreneur with small business management, I pay my taxes, they are in the wrong place," added Gibon.

In reality, they were all combined, they simply wanted to give Gibon one more test in everyday life, they wanted to see his reaction.

They took the vehicle to the police parking lot for doing him wrong, then told him to go there to pick it up, although they gave him a ticket to go see a judge in a court named OAS, which the system had set up for that type of operation, Gibon did not pay the fine, and did not go to any court.

Two days later he picked up the vehicle, he was charged a reduced parking fee, and then gave that and another vehicle to the 'Hope for Children' Foundation.

Gibon's life, with so much harassment, had not been a sweet one.

The Taxis and Limousines commission had assumed a kind of shameless harassment against some sectors, so they were referred by an emissary of the organization of evil, to test Gibon, they tried to charge him a bill generated by a fabricated case, where some "sick" money lovers were involved, who in any line were looking to find a slave to put him to pay, either by fabricating a ticket or making a case to penalize him and make the victim spend what he didn't have, and everything was done as an illogical revenge, generated by the abuse of power, acting as cretins disguised as benefactors, because by that time, all the actions of existence, generated taxes, to such a degree that the only thing that was saved from the tax was breath, because it was subordinated to the divine nature of God, and even they wanted to put a price on breathing, so they were inclined to create the COVID-19, that although its diffusion came to life in 2020, the scheme of action had been mounted already since the year 2017 in different points of the planet.

CHAPTER 14

THE PANDEMY

The time came when the corona virus had hit everyone, and the pack stopped caring about what was happening, which took advantage of Plutarco René Cariño, to establish himself as a landowner who would sow new members, to make Bulley's stop, the place of "friends who were friends of friends", occult sect and the organization of evil were looking for those to form a kind of association with directive, believing that in that way they would have control of Gibon, and Rene Cariño, took his brother and his nephew, and related and friends, from that moment, the wait to take a passenger was longer and the supply began to fall, but Gibon was fine, because he transported people for what they paid.

The corona Virus, marked its path and through codes had been defined purposes and destination contained in a document of the world bank that had somehow leaked, the document spoke of purchased products codes, the code for shipments for the year 2017 was 300215, and for those of 2018, indicated the 902780, that is, everything had been forged two years earlier, in 2017, to be propagated in 2020.

The leaked document contained 70 pages, spoke of the World Bank, under the title "COVID-19 strategic preparedness and response program" labeled "for official use only".

The document referred to all export records of COVID-19 diagnostic testing instruments and devices shipped in 2017, whose destination countries listed in order of total dollar amount were: China Switzerland, Germany, the European union, the United States, Ireland, and the Netherlands, and with a slight expansion in the destination geography for 2018, where the European union, Germany, France, the United Kingdom, the Netherlands, Switzerland, the United States, Japan, Singapore, China, and Hong Kong appeared again.

And the public's question was: What would be the purpose of all this?

And the answer was money, power and control, the ambition of man in all times, had been to measure force between spirit and matter, and to expand the trial of their planetary practice of:

Controlling the population on a global scale to the levels of enslaving it in its totality, through the permanent tracking, and imposition of cryptocurrencies, that would allow to control what each one spent, in what they spent and what was the amount of economic accumulation of each inhabitant of the planet, where they moved?, what they did? And even, many considered that in addition to the economic purpose the vaccines would be a tracking mechanism to introduce a remote information microchip program whose reading would be facilitated by the 5G program.

All these conditions led to results of possible biological

warfare against the human population, to impose the purpose of their ambitions, a sovereign who would rule the world.

The fact is that nothing was casual and after the ascension of Jesus Christ, there arose a character that religions named "the Devil", and after fulfilled the two thousand years of the interaction of Jesus Christ and the holy spirit in the lives of the inhabitants of the earth, appeared the organization of evil, which represented the devil, always ready to sponsor the wickedness of the wicked on earth, looking for ways to damage the nerves of the men of God, since they knew that the power of God would sooner or later prevail over all their wickedness, and therefore they would receive double what they gave as a cup of their own medicine.

They wanted to divert Gibon's attention, to keep him busy in another direction, looking for a way to make him forget something that corresponded to him and that they had it fresh despite the passage of the years, so they sought to justify the amount to be paid, that someone had in his hands and did not want to release, and they had created a series of fictitious accidents to disguise the case, because they loved to commit social injustices, but they were not interested in public opinion to know about such injustices, because they did not want to question their honesty, because they were conservative and hypocritical, so they spent large sums of money to spread their virtues, not their evils, and when someone rebelled, they refused to accept their patterns of behavior, and sought ways to discredit or destroy them to the extent that they could never raise their head in society.

And many times they managed to impose their patterns of evilness, because within the communities there were sectors that had a reduced conception of value, and as they did not value themselves, they did not have the understanding to value others, so they end up believing all the lies generated about a victim, by those who could pay the bribe.

However, fighting against Gibon was like fighting against God, because when God saw the wickedness that Gibon's free will imposed on his heart and soul, he over-guarded it, strengthening it with splendor, and Gibon was rejuvenated and greater energies were born in him to the point of being invincible.

It added to the evils of the organization of evil and occult sect, having conspired to take his son, Market, away from Gibon, having bribed his mother Celeste, arranging custody in a Yonkers court and making her disappear for over 13 years, so that Gibon could not enjoy his son's childhood, the last time he saw him, Market was only 6 years old, it was a way to hit Gibon, in the plan of evil and conspiracy.

A day earlier, Gibon had told Market:

"My dear son, if for some reason we stopped seeing each other, it wasn't because I abandoned you, it's because there is a conspiracy to take you away from me," he said, while Market with six years old answered him:

"Don't worry daddy, I know that everything I get comes from you," he affirmed, as he hugged his father.

The next day the Yonkers court gave custody to her without summoning Gibon, who also once again, had his rights violated and forcibly prevented him from seeing his son grow up, and when he realized what had happened and tried to claim his right to visitation he was told that Celeste Capellan, had left the address he had given to the court and that therefore, they had nowhere to serve him the papers, and in such a condition they could do nothing.

As we have seen, and as its name indicated, the organization of evil fed on evil, and had infiltrated men into the various lines, who sought to control those above them.

As the occult sect was composed of hypocrites, thieves and mockers, they presented themselves as kind, but they were eminently malicious.

The persecution of Gibon did not stop at the simple, because they had resorted to everything in order to make it difficult for him, and even so, occult sect and the organization of evil, had not been able to break Gibon's patience, and they began to bribe employees of the motor vehicles department who had been infiltrated for that purpose and once again Balzac's expression was confirmed: "bureaucracy was still a giant run by dwarfs" and as such they began to make it difficult for Gibon and when it came to renewing the driver's license they delayed the process by resending and asking for documents that they could ask for once, they were asking for up to five times each time with a new suggestion, and with all the evilness of criminals with power, which on their own merit they could not overcome.

Racism and discrimination were cards to the highest bidder, giving merit to the skeleton but ignoring the spirit, making the villain saintly and condemning the kind.

The pandemic had led the states to lose funds and New York

was no exception, many wanting to contribute were hindered and many became criminals being innocent because thousands of men were driving with expired or suspended licenses many times for violations or manufactured tickets that later, the Motor Vehicles Department itself obstructed them to solve it leaving phone lines that no human answered. And when they did, a robotic machine appeared that did not always provide a solution, making the process difficult, causing people to spend the time of the appearance being innocent and were forced to pay such violations in order to recover the active status of their licenses, which in many cases had been suspended.

On one occasion, from 2018, a city official combined with a police officer went shopping at Bulley, at the conclusion she made sure Gibon was the one who ride her, the police officer followed them and when they were close to arriving he approached and alleged that Gibon had turned improperly, and on such pretext fabricated a ticket for him which was forwarded for administrative convenience from 2018, was forwarded to 2019, and then to 2020, and later to 2021, when the Department of Motor Vehicle was still closed, it was a contravention to which Gibon from the outset pleaded not guilty, and the Department claimed that "because he had not said whether he was guilty or not guilty" he would be given a license suspension, Gibon moved, he got in line but when he thought he was going to get in, they made him waste the day claiming that he had to call a number that they gave him; a number that no one answered, and then he got another general information number and when he got through he thought they would make him an appointment because he had sent the notice to Albany, they tried again to give him another website, so Gibon said:

"the truth is that Balzac always had his reasons when he said that "The bureaucracy was a giant managed by dwarfs", I do not understand how the administrators of these matters, who are supposed to facilitate the way to the service users in the middle of this crisis, prefer to create more difficulties, because I understand that you are paid to serve, not to obstruct. I have been persecuted in every line, but I have never doubted the justice that will lead to repentance," he said.

"I'm sorry, I apologize for everything that happened," the employee replied.

"Do not worry, nothing of what happened has been designed by you, everything is typical of a criminal mind, which with such measures seeks to induce civil disobedience, and then justify the repressive actions."

"I understand; do you have anything else I can help you with?"

"No, that's it, I called to find adequate response to the ticket and suspension and you don't have it, goodbye."

"I'm sorry, have a good day."

They hung up the phone and he thought:

"The crop of cretins and evildoers does not stop; they will always be born to harass the innocent and try to involve them in their criminal peripeteias."

Anyway, the system was designed to collect, and make them pay.

So he paid the ticket to have his license suspension removed, the days passed and he learned not to worry about anything, because what was bound to happen, would always happen.

Many of them were aware that these practices of difficulties and impossibilities for the drivers were not the most appropriate, but being a supporter of sadism and cynicism, they lent themselves to whatever was necessary in order to satisfy the requests of the occult sect and the organization of evil. That they did not rest in their eagerness, to subdue treacherously those whom they persecuted.

In Gibon's case, a chemical potion had been injected into him, to intensify his pains by running through all areas of his body, and finally concentrating on his feet, seeking to reduce his ability to move in such a way that he would become disabled in order to disable him and remove him from circulation.

However, they were unaware that the spirit of God was in and with Gibon, and although he felt pain, they could not paralyze him, Gibon before the Pandemic had received a spiritual injection that had immunized him from all types of infections; it was like an antidote against all the evil and treachery that tried against him.

CHAPTER 15

EVENTUALITIES

Rocko Vulcano, came directly from the countryside to the city, without processing or schooling, however a fifth grade would come to support him, because it showed him how to sign his name, but no training of civility could tolerate it.

Like many others in the pack, he wanted to impose himself by force, shouting loudly, seeking to intimidate in order to control, without any real success, for he always generated responses as violent and aggressive as his own.

When that one arrived in the pack he had shown a humility that was embarrassing, somewhat distant from the pack that had put him in stripes without allowing him to approach, but some time after the occult sect and the organization of evil perverted him, he had assumed an arrogant arrogance that induced him to believe that everyone in the pack fit in his mouth, at the time of a confrontation, perhaps because he lacked argument, he tended to raise his voice like a greengrocer in the market, inducing those who heard him to shout at him that he was ill-educated.

He often used to walk around with pornographic pictures on his cellphone, showing them and commenting on them to those in his brotherhood who interacted and thought like him.

He wore a mask in his vehicle so that when the organization of evil assigned him a dirty job he would cover his face so that no one would recognize him.

On more than one occasion he had had frictions with Rony almost to the point of aggression, although Rony very rarely had encounters with members of the pack, but when he was invaded by the pride of bipolarism he put, whoever was, in their place, and used to resort to a sarcastic game that seemed mockery, many did not pay attention to him, but others did not like his style of proceeding. Many in the pack spent weeks and months at odds with him, or anyone else, and when that condition began to worsen, Rosalba, his wife appeared to mediate, and accompany him so that he would not be alone, he would sign up on the list of the pack and take his turn, there were those who wanted to protest but that did not stop him from going ahead, and one day Cholinfe tried to confront her and went to the 50th precinct and made a police report.

Then Rony began to argue that if Plutarco Rene had his brother and nephew there, why couldn't he have his wife?

And his presence became noticeable precisely because of the confrontation that had arisen between Rocko Vulcan and him, and the misunderstanding became so sharp that Rony no longer referred to him by his name, and when he was going to name him, he spoke of "the pussy".

Rocko, on the other hand, sought to impose himself and control the others, which generated another conflict with Gibon, for trying to incur in prefabricated evilness such as leaving with a purchase and if nobody erased him, he would come back and try to leave again in the same shift, pretending that he was registered and that he had not left, and he had already made a habit of it and being on Gibon's shift, he tried to do something similar and Gibon stopped him in his tracks, told him not to be so dishonest, and that's when the disagreement and argument started, which Rocko took on with threats, expletives, shouting, etc.

He, like so many others in the pack wanted to be confident and believed that they could outwit everyone, ignoring that "confidence was the shortest way to make a mistake", and in his assembly of complacency to occult sect, he combined with Cholinfe and other servants of the organization of evil, trying to annoy Gibon, trying to threaten him with violent threats such as "break his mouth, or burn him alive" claiming that he had a street, however, Gibon discovered that such expressions surrounded by noises, was nothing more than a way to cover up his cowardice.

While he was ranting, Gibon experienced that inner peace which God bestows on his children, and seeing that such an aggrieved voice led only to annoy the ear, and to vex the spirit, he was obliged to withdraw his friendship so he said to him:

"The simple fact of arguing with you lowers my human condition, when you arrived here you did it like a scared kitten, and you can't pretend to pass over me, I'm here before you arrived, and before your violent condition, it's not pleasant to infect me, for the same reason, I'm going to ask you not to talk to me ever again."

And it so happened that one day Rocko had left his vehicle

parked and left in a vehicle of one of the members of the organization of evil, and at the time of his return at approximately 11:30 at night, a gang that at that time was moving to the west of Jerome, assaulted him, beat him and sodomized him, leaving him lying, until one of the inhabitants of the sector found him unconscious, and called the 911 emergency line, transporting him to Montefiore Hospital.

While he was in the hospital he was visited by Rene Cariño, Burdock, and other occult sect followers.

Then, while the pack was on duty, Burdock, who never shut up, took advantage of the situation to make comments with more inclination to foolishness than to a solution:

"I have always said that around the pastor moves a terrible mystery, and that is that no one escapes the wrath of God, and anyone who dares to defy him, something happens to him."

"I have always said that around the pastor moves a terrible mystery, and that is that no one escapes the wrath of God, and anyone who dares to defy him, something happens to him." Burdock said.

"Oh, but, with the children of God, no one is prone, Gibon does not bother anyone, but no one should bother him, because whoever does it, somehow regrets it," commented Rodo.

Rodo, was one of the pack of little barking, Gibon and he exchanged very few words and when he addressed Gibon it was to tell him that he was first on the duty roster.

She gossiped more than a woman in the neighborhood, but

quietly, with little noise, Gibon was a silent subject of his conversations, and he talked without Gibon hearing about whether he dressed well, where he got the clothes he wore, and so on.

That figure had a big head, a broad back, a protruding chest, and eyes like a toad, in short, he was a character that Cholinfe could not face without being exposed, and as such, many times the organization of evil and the occult sect used to use him to test Gibon, which he tolerated because he knew that the organization of evil used everything and anyone to expose him.

However, Gibon's condition as a strategist allowed him to survive without having to fall into the games generated by those who were always ready to give an answer when talking about survival.

CHAPTER 16

DRUNKEN KINKIN

Let's see how the events happened, to that group of survivors, who were always ready to give their best, as did Jochelo, who in his pilgrimage, had met Kinkin, a drunkard who offered him a hundred dollars to take him home, and when Jochelo asked him for the address, he answered him:

"Come here, that's your problem, if I knew the address, do you think I would be offering you a hundred dollars?"

"Are you taking advantage of the fact that you're drunk to relax me?" he said, "I'm not."

Drunken Kinkin kept silent and into the car he went, and as he sat down he sang to him:

"It is that I am an adventurer, that I don't deserve consolation, because I solve the sorrows that come with money".

Jochelo got into the car and said "If so, I'll take you anywhere."

Kinkin drunkenly nodded, at that instant handed him $20, and after three corners when he thought to stay Kinkin drunkenly questioned him:

"Did I pay you?"

"Yes, obviously you paid me," Jochelo said.

114

"No, I didn't pay you, I did the drill and you think I paid you," he told him, as he handed him twenty dollars more, as he left the car wobbling as it moved.

When Jochelo saw him walking away, full of satisfaction, he shouted to him:

"They take advantage of you because you're drunk"

"Yes, you're right, but that's not my case, I drink the rum, but I leave the bottle, the forty dollars I gave you, are not real dollars, they are fake bills, I had no originals and I thought that would serve me something even if it was to make you get closer to my house," lied Kinkin, looking for Jochelo not to get away with his, the bills were real.

Jochelo saw little stars when Kinkin confessed, and he felt that the rascal had easily fooled him, he was driven to run after him and hit him, for having made him lose the chance to transport someone who could pay him with real money, he thought, but he restrained himself in the attempt, because he knew that many of those drunks, when they lost control, wandered in illusion,

When he came to the pack his tongue betrayed him, and he told Burdock about it, the teasing went on for three days and the lesson was learned.

Kinkin pretended to play with him, the money was real, and a week later, he was able to prove it.

Drunken Kinkin had a strange logic that many did not understand, he said that there were such naive and innocent people, whose condition attracted death, while there were others so evil and radical that they should give up, however, those did not find those who would kill them.

Many thought that the conscious limitation did not allow them to discern nor to reflect in adequacy, but others in their reflection affirmed and pondered that the best expressions, were proper of children and drunkards who expressed the truth, without fear and freedom. Kinkin, above all, was something like that, like one of those that the neighborhood chose to make fun, of those who were snooty, and the people of the neighborhood loved him for his grace when he got drunk, having fun with him, on more than one occasion the neighborhood had already laughed loudly, and had seen him satirize many, mainly those times when in "Your House Restaurant" those popular events were presented, sponsored by the community program "Cultural Dialogue", where the animator was jocular and very cocky, and that night when he began to call the girls participating in the contest Girl Spanish New York, he with all the splendor mentioned with pleasure the contestants, and said:

"Ladies and Gentlemen, I have the honor to present Miss Colombia," and that beauty appeared on the catwalk, showing herself like a gazelle, when everyone had just applauded and there was silence, you could hear the roar of Kinkin's voice saying:

"What a crap!" But Rando the entertainer, in order not to damage the event, pretended not to hear, and continued announcing the contestants and again he said:

"Now with you, Miss United States"

And again Kinkin would show his recklessness and say "What a crap".

"We continue with the essential fragrance of Miss Venezuela," said Rando.

"Uh, Uh, that's crap" Kinkin persisted in replying.

Already Rando was getting angry, but when he announced Miss Puerto Rico, and he showed his recklessness, Rando wanted to get him out, but the doorman told him:

"It's better to avoid a scandal, let me talk to him."

Then Rando announced Miss Dominican Republic, and Kinkin showed his appreciation, supporting the beauty, then Rando approached him cautiously and said:

"If you come back with your recklessness and don't keep quiet, I'm going to take you out myself, even if I have to carry you," he warned him.

"Hey kid, what a disappointment, that you didn't understand me, what I wanted to tell you was: "what a crap, the one I have in my house," Expressed Kinkin, and those who managed to listen, almost lost the box by the laughter generated, the doorman who was his friend, invited him to a glass of milk, and kept him away until the event passed.

On another occasion when he had been drinking and he could not stand up, he was taken to alcoholic anonymous, and after three days an evangelical pastor appeared to make a conference and to try to persuade him, he took a glass of water and threw a worm in front of all those who attended the conference, they saw that the worm swam in the water, and then he took it out fresh and healthy, he showed it to the drunks and then he threw the worm in a container with alcohol, and immediately, the worm stretched its leg, and the pastor satisfied with the demonstration asked who could explain what happened, and as nobody answered, Kinkin stood up and bravely exclaimed "Pastor, that has only one meaning."

"Let's see, say it Kinkin," suggested the pastor.

Then Kinkin, half staggering, answered:

"Pastor, that means that he who drinks rum, has no worm," he expressed.

The pastor was so disappointed that he suggested that they make sure that the next time Kinkin attended an orientation they made sure he was sober, because he didn't want him drunk.

Kinkin always used to get involved in the affairs of the neighborhood, so when Petro wanted to be taught the "Hungarian" and protested about the loss of the twenty dollars, Kinkin, who at that moment was in the vicinity of where he was passing by, interrupted him:

"Ah, ha ha, speaking alone, to God, look at him, shouting for nothing, men should not cry for a bad move, I'm surprised that you go around lamenting that the Chapi have laid you with twenty"

"Oh yeah, if they were yours you'd care, right?," said Petro.

"And what's twenty dollars, in fact, take them and stop shouting," Kinkin told him.

"I wouldn't even take that stuff you have to light a cigarette" argued Petro.

"Well, it will not be you, who dares to address me with such impertinence?" said Kinkin.

"Do you think that I don't know that you lay on Jochelo with forty?" Petro affirmed.

"On the contrary, he wanted to knock me down, and as "thief who steals from a thief, you have a hundred years of forgiveness", we owe him nothing, he sent me three blocks, and I gave him fort dollars, which he assumed were false, these that I now offer you are real money, that for doubtful and without faith, you have just lost it, That's for you to see, that everything is paid on this earth, unless you have assumed the opposite before you were born, you think I didn't know that Chamo and you stole 55 dollars from Gibon, what the Chapí took from you, is what you took from Gibon, the others will pay separately what they owe him."

"Stop, I don't want anything to do with drunk," said Petro.

"I may be a drunk, but if so, then you're a drunk" added Kinkin.

Petro swallowed dryly, kept silent, and walked on.

CHAPTER 17

BARKING AND SNORING

Galy Buchí, with a big head and square jaw, robotic machine body, Frankenstein shoulders, Turkish nose, embedded in his galactic face, bushy beard like a Bedouin, was the owner of a natural stress, induced by the need to produce resources to help him support his family, he used to pretend friendship to Gibon, who because of his diplomatic condition made him believe that he was unaware of his hypocrisy, until one day Gibon arrived before others, which Galy took advantage of to register the last ones before Gibon, which induced Gibon to review the list and tear it up in front of his eyes, and since Galy Buchí was something like that, like the ears of Plutarco René Cariño, Gibon took advantage of it and commented to him:

"Go and tell Rene, how I reacted, he will know that I am demanding respect even from those who do not respect themselves," Gibon said.

Galy Buchi said nothing, and without further ado a passenger came out and grabbed him and took him away.

When the pandemic was announced, and was gaining ground, like everyone in the pack, Galy Buchí had also disappeared. Only Gibon covered the ground and kept on offering transport service to the club members in times of hardship.

The absence of all gave rise to the appearance of carriers from other lines, and among them, those of Gargets, the first of the newcomers to clash with Gibon, was one who was called Anjo, Plutarco René Cariño's nephew, who from the moment he arrived had begun to throw hints seeking to provoke Gibon, and trying to attract attention:

He said addressing Gibon with a note of provocation, "If you, had done to me, what you did to Rodo who crashed into him and then wouldn't give him the two hundred dollars he asked for, I would have broken you."

Gibon, with all the splendor of his patience, answered him:

"Actually, I would like you not to talk, but to come and break me, I'm not violent, but I'm used to taking blows. Because of your condition and your origins, you are disrespectful and trusting, so that if you have been sent by an occult sect, or by the organization of evil, to provoke or cause unrest, here, a war will be waged that will teach the sheep, lackeys, macaques and cockatrices that I must be respected."

AnJo kept silent, but he couldn't fake his mischievousness it was his turn and he found a passenger and left, but his goal was simply, to annoy Gibon.

A while after the arrival of Rosalba, Rony's wife, there was a cross of words between them because she had taken a passenger, ignoring that it was his turn, and the next day was Friday, it seemed that the pack would attract demons, Witches, Rosalba's brother made some comments in Anjo's favor and those who had arrived from Garget, so Rosalba complained, but even being brothers Witches rejected her claims telling her:

"Get me out of there, you and I have nothing to talk about," said Witches.

Rosalba insisting reaffirmed. "It's not like that either, have a little respect for me.

"If you don't respect yourself, how do you demand respect from me?" Witches weighed in.

It turned out that at that moment Rony who was listening to what was happening, confronted Witches, who had reacted violently, they had thrown some blows without touching each other, because the other members of the pack prevented them from hitting each other, when it was believed that everything had happened, Rony's daughter's boyfriend arrived and without much thought he gave Witches an punch in the left eye, sending him to the hospital.

The event prompted the police to show up, and some of the pack, saying they would not accept them back in that way.

A family quarrel had broken out between uncle, brother and brother-in-law, where everyone was affected.

For many days the pack kept commenting, and they talked their heads off and said that Rony had thrown his vehicle at Witches, and that he should sue his sister to make a living off him, and they talked and talked until their throats were dry.

They let some time pass until all was forgotten, and reappeared a few months later.

Days passed, and on another occasion, Gibon, was talking on the phone with a section of prebisterian emergency payment collection, to which the insurance had not paid the debt that generated the key that Arnulfo introduced between the eyebrows.

And as far as was known, Galy Buchí, and Arnulfo, was one of those who got along best with Plutarco René Cariño, but Galy, perhaps because of his Arab origin, often sought to be on good terms with him, and for that he said:

"The only one who is related to the affairs of the office is René Cariño, therefore, you have to listen to him"

Fredesvindo who was following the conversation of that one, interrupted him and commented:

"From what I can see, the Arab likes to get in bed with the bosses."

"What boss are you talking about? I don't have a boss, you could have a boss but not me, and that Arab is nothing more than a tremendous toadies," expressed Donko.

Fredesvindo laughed and shouted:

"Galy Buchí, shake Plutarco René Cariño's shoulders."

They all laughed, as Galy Buchi looked confused.

It had snowed the night before, and the snow blocked the sidewalks, Rene Cariño following up on his beliefs went down to get some shovels that Mery Ann had given him, and they took turns clearing the front that remained blocked, and in less than an hour, it was sparkling.

Later MeryAnn was passing in front and Plutarco Rene

Cariño stepped forward looking to get the credit before her:

"We cleaned all that up ourselves," he said.

Mery Ann scanned behind the silence of a glance and replied:

"Oh yeah?.... Thank you!," she said, as she walked to her car.

CHAPTER 18

PRESENCE AND COMPLACENCY

Sometime later Rene Cariño had undergone an eye operation and limited his activities at Bulley for a period of time, sometimes going on to supervise the pack's behavior and to admonish those under his brotherhood who did not do what he thought was right to do, and his aim was simply to keep the occult sect satisfied, and to fulfill the requirements of the assignment.

Occult sect and the organization of evil, were in the argot of desperation and had decided to find a way to control Gibon under any circumstances, and knocked on Claudy's door, and manipulated her so that she in turn, manipulated the children and they in turn tried to control Gibon, for this occult sect and the organization of evil, began to make a claim to the city, for suffering to Gibon's family, and while doing so they tried to use those to harm him.

Claudy was sent a lover to keep her numb, and drive her to alcoholism, and Frankely, the second of her children, was sent a friend to induce him to smoke marijuana, who in turn would find a way to suggest to Claudy how she should handle things with May and Queen so that in Gibon's presence, they would overreact, and make him spend money on things they often didn't need, and Claudy would disappear many of the clothes and toys Gibon brought them, and she told the children that she had donated them to charitable organizations, but the real objective was to keep Gibon in debt, paying credit cards, or ruined so that he would accept loans from them in coordination with their allies so that when it was time to deliver the corresponding resources, they could justify their debt and deliver what they wanted, however, no matter how hard they tried, they couldn't do it.

Then one day Gibon went to drop May off late at night and he brought up a television receiver that Gibon had bought her and Claudy felt so grateful that she went down the steps and hugged and kissed him who, without flinching, reciprocated the action as she commented:

"If you're kissing me, it must be for a reason," he said.

"Actually, it's because I love you very much, even though sometimes we argue," she turned away from him, with a mock smile, as she replied:

"Take care of yourself, the street is dangerous," he said.

"Don't worry, it will only happen to me, what is going to happen, nobody dies a day before, nor a day after; everything is coordinated in the universe, and each soul brings its own script inside, life is theater and dream," he said and left, but after walking a few blocks he received a call where she asked him to return because May had forgotten the gym bag in the Jeep.

Gibon went back to drop off the bag, and from that day on, for a long time Claudy was nowhere to be seen.

God had strengthened Gibon so that they could not overcome him in their attempts.

The organization of evil and occult sect, used to be related to the destruction, and although they controlled and influenced some sectors of the police, everything was relative since the presence of that one intimidated some, and infuriated others, everything was defined in the struggle of the opposite with the following expression: "Peace and happiness on the planet was fleeting, man could not always do what they wanted to do, and the frequent concern was the award of the decoration of the one who lacked the power of reflection."

And although Gibon had been mistaken, he had never been on such a path, but life allowed him to be cast as a victim whose human rights had been violated, making him a candidate for vilification, harassed for many years.

The case was that the city and its minions, believed him to be a peasant, in a car that made noise, that was honking, alerting the neighbor to let them know that after riding donkeys, they moved in Limousine, and many who were taxi drivers, became electricians, Cholinfe crazy and without judgment, continued to do his own thing, disrespected Gibon, He became the evil that they wanted to eradicate, he was the subject of attention, and they prayed that he would leave, some were afraid to beat him for not wasting time in court, and his presence in Bulley had become a bitter pill to swallow, but something sad happened that the pack barked at him, someone crazier than him, became angry and killed him.

Emiliano Federé, the jail saw him grow, violence created him, and sent him to jail, five years later, he conquered Pamela;

his cousin introduced him and she gave him her number, she spoke to him on the phone, until he left, he walked everywhere and went to Bulley to grow, Cholinfe without understanding, Pamela complimented him, and Emiliano Federé killed him out of courage, he kept so much mistrust, he even forgot about God.

It all happened when Pamela was leaving Bulley's, with a cart full of purchases, and Cholinfe, who didn't notice that she was accompanied, because of his impudence, ignored that Emiliano was coming behind, and like a runaway horse, he said:

"Mami, here's papi waist, to make you tasty, let me give you tenderness, and explore your plain," he said.

"Oh, so that's so, if you offer her tenderness, and you want to walk on the plain you're going to offer me?"

"I have nothing for you, I don't eat donkey's meat," said Cholinfe, full of mockery and pride.

"You are a bold and disrespectful and that will bring you consequences," he said. Emiliano walked away, and silently returned, a shot in the heart, he shot Cholinfe, that's how he killed him, the place got hot and the police arrived, all the transporters on the other side were located, and the Garteans left, and no one else returned.

"Fuck, for those guys to leave, one of them had to be killed," Burdock said between regretful and scared.

In reality, he was always giving his opinion, even if he didn't contribute anything.

Certainly, those who knew the truth understood that dogs did not always bite as they barked, but the pack did not respect each other, and on one occasion Rocko Vulcano had gone out to the republic and the first to spread the word that he had sold his vehicle to go and marry a man was Burdock, who with an ominous voice expressed such an unworthy comment and in the midst of his murmuring said:

"I knew that even if it was a postcard to a male would claim," While Rony who was playing the game responded:

"It's just that when I saw him arrive with that little flowered shirt, like the blouses that women wear, and those pants tighter than Mari-Luz's, he left me no room to think otherwise."

"The one who does dress like a man is Gibon," Jochelo said.

"Oh, Gibon is a dish from another table..." Said Donko who was arriving at that moment but could hear what they were saying about Gibon, he was carrying a dessert that tempted everyone to try it, except Rony who said he had finished eating.

And the delicacy looked so succulent, that it led one to think that just as the alcoholic knew that he should not swallow liquor, and the diabetic that he should not give sugar to the pancreas, Jochelo had become aware of his condition and as he had been tempted before by the dessert of tres leches6, he was tempted by that milk flan, and breaking the norm he justified himself in the middle of a sermon he said with a deep voice that only competed Gary and Kinkin's voices:

"Let's follow the parameters of the master Jesus Christ: "It's

---

6 Latin American cake that's soaked in evaporated milk, sweetened condensed milk, and whole milk.

not what goes into the mouth that hurts, but what comes out of it", and as what doesn't kill makes you fat, never look a gift horse in the mouth, let's make a party out of what costs us nothing," he said at the time of taking a bite in his mouth, but when he tried to have the second one he was stopped by Burdock who was salivating like Pablo's dog when he heard the bells ringing, for the conditioned reflex.

"Now, give me mine here, I don't go to eat it all."

"Eat that there is enough for everyone, I have one more piece in the car," Donko said.

I should add to better understand the situation, Donko was a man of small stature with such a big soul that did not bend to the impossibilities, always inclined to solidarity, always went around buying things to distribute among the pack, and sporadically when he realized that it was someone's birthday he made a sign with the name of that person wishing happy birthday, or welcoming him who had gone on a trip and was returning.

His motto could be defined in the following statement that Gibon used to sing with fire in his heart:

"Dates a refreshment of hopes, in every glory and longing, that virtue is brought by light, and goodness thou hast.

You are beauty and truth, which induces to create peace, you are wisdom that gives, fullness and sweet virtue.

I am clear in my path, that I always walk with you, you are the glory and the light, you are the divine reflection.

Keep on being blessed God, keep on being blessed God, hallelujah glory to the father, glory for salvation, that in heaven and earth the Lord is my shepherd, hallelujah, hallelujah, hallelujah, thank you for redemption."

CHAPTER 19

THE TRAJECTORY

Gibon had no way of appearing different from what he was, because wherever he went he was called according to how the spirit showed him, for more than 29 years he had been watched without him knowing it, a conspiracy was running in his way, to the extent that he thought that a fatality was chasing him, the organization of evil did not let him breathe, and even a job he was looking for, brought the supervision of the organization of evil, which always watched him from a distance, to be aware of what the victim was doing, and many times, they did not allow Gibon to stay long in a job, because when they realized that he was working, they made an offer to the administrator of the place, so that he would find a reason to justify his dismissal.

Thus, in their plans to discredit their persecuted, they said that those people were unstable and therefore, lacked the conditions to be accredited.

The organization of evil, despite being anti-psychiatrists, did not hesitate to drive those who rebelled against them crazy, so they made sure that their associates kept an eye on each other.

Many times they would find relatives of their persecuted,

they would bribe them and ask them to make a proposal to their victims that they agree to go to see a psychiatrist, if the victim accepted and went, they would bribe the doctor, to use that record to disqualify him, and thus justify their purpose.

But Gibon believed that God's blessing was better than man's favor, for what God allotted by inheritance, no one could embezzle.

But as a function of his reflection, Gibon used to question himself about how Joshua Ben Josephs (Alias Jesus) life would have been, if instead of having risen at the age of 33, he would have had to live a little longer, enduring an ungrateful neighbor, especially if he had lasted the time that Gibon had already been on earth, seeing and experiencing everything, and self-controlling his equanimity, exercising patience, adjusting his discernment, because the human in his free will, did not understand nor wanted to understand, why it was necessary to be patient and tolerant.

On planet earth life was a falling and rising, it was a kind of constant instability, because there was always something that obstructed, a problem was solved and another appeared, and even if you ran away from what had to happen, it always happened.

Despite all that had happened, humanity was beginning to awaken, and spoke silently of a quantum leap, the human collective began to rise par excellence, while the organization of evil did not rest in producing and involving the unconscious in their games of slavery, and conspired frequently to make believe that those who had managed to expand their vibration and looked like masters, different from traditional man, and who did not submit to obey the program of evil that they, in the dullness of their blindness, had designed, were dangerous people, and they sought ways to drive them crazy, sell them as madmen, or discredit them for being and looking different from them and those who were in their service.

Already the organization of evil was determined to increase the wave of violence on the planet, that is why they sent to provoke the peaceful ones, through sabotage to their property or through physical attacks, that is why when they practiced violence, and were answered with violence, they were strengthened, because they were dragging to their ground those who responded as they expected, in order to confuse them, and make them lose the essence of their purpose, the liberation of souls.

For every blow that was given, another would be received, and this whole condition tended to retard the evolutionary ascent.

Gibon had overcome all the evils of the organization of evil, because although they knew that the city had to compensate him, they, as criminals invested with power, were constantly looking for ways to make him fall, and although it was not stipulated that he would be going through the vicissitudes of earth, he touched the ground and ended up in a shelter, he wanted to experience and he did it and he saw how life was lived in that place, how the being was humiliated, how the minorities survived under the dictatorship and the harassment of those above, and after so much sacrifice, if they gave him a program that helped him to overcome, in what way the harassers conspired so that a few months later they would lose him, so that those affected, if they lacked strategies, would return to experience the pain of their hunger.

In any circumstance, the inner strength would bend the ghosts of darkness, because the light, always could more, because perhaps those seeking to gain merit with the city, to go around bothering the men of peace, had chosen to abuse, so he hoped that someday, they would have to recant, because if they were not willing to be accountable to men, death would ask for explanations.

CHAPTER 20

DEFINITION

The tinge of discrimination was notable in New York, which despite being one of the sanctuary states, where there was greater mercy for minorities, for many years Gibon had been mistreated, the rulers had acted on a larger scale favoring the wealthy.

The whites had the best housing for less money, and when he thought he was outclassed and tried to leave the room, the mafia assigned to turn his life upside down prevented him by going ahead and bribing the property owners to discriminate against him in housing, as they did before at work.

Anyone who pretended to be Gibon's friend could be an informer for the occult sect or organization of evil, to report if he had been employed somewhere, to bribe the manager on duty to fire him.

But social justice and the management of political actions had fallen to the lowest levels of their conditions, giving rise to a disproportionate lack of control in the increase of rent, with the clear intention of favoring the owners, to the extent of ruining the working class, putting them to pay high prices in rents, which in fact was contributing to impoverish the taxpayers, who often lacked wages, or income that would allow them to live with dignity, pay rent and eat satisfactorily.

So many fell to the levels of being unable to afford housing, with four, five and more family members having to join together to pay for a one- or two-room apartment at a rent that regularly began to exceed a man's salary, while the landlords got richer.

In the case of Gibon, unusual matters were generated, he remained single, waiting for the promised wife to appear, while the organization of evil, did not cease to pursue him, to the extent that he was absent, and on his return they kept him the surprise, that they had closed the apartment where he lived, in absentia, even being up to date with the rent, so he was forced to collect some important documents and some clothes. In the middle of the chase, one night the organization of evil opened his vehicle and took his computer and some certificates of ownership, among other belongings, and although he complained to the police, they ignored him, claiming that there were no cameras in that place, so they had nothing to do.

Then on one occasion he met the Jewish owner of the building where they closed his apartment, and he pretended to be very worried about what had happened to him and said:

"I'm so sorry about what happened, why didn't you talk to me before that happened?" he said.

"I didn't think, that something like that would happen in my absence, but, I usually don't regret it, so as not to be pitied, anyway thank you very much," he said while thinking about the apocalypse expression again:

"It will be taken from those who have the least to give to those who have the most."

Then the building manager would call him, and leave him a voice message, pressing him:

"Gibon, come and get all your crap," he said. Gibon listened to it in silence, until he realized that those had violated his rights, the lease was expiring a year later, in addition, they had entered a concubine of the manager, following all in Gibon's name, while the super and the manager, had divided the belongings of that one, and such actions had been made in function of a conspiracy."

And Gibon answered: "I am the magic circle of protection, around me, which is invincible, which repels all disturbing elements, and all dangers that try to interact to harm me, I am perfection in my world of health, abundance and youth, in the perfection of my body, which is the vehicle that covers my spirit".

The prophecies were fulfilled, and the government of the "beast" persisted in stamping out all those who slept, because those who were caught sleeping would be incorporated into the zombie sector, because they would be constituted as an enslaved force.

Gibon was unaware that the organization of evil was after his bones, and from the shelter, they sent him to a program called "Back to Work", and for nine months as a useless man they had him making history, refusing to give him a job according to his ability, until finally, they chose to employ him in an industrial laundry, where he spent three years throwing towels on a belt that steamed them and then packaged them for distribution to the various hotels in the nation.

That without first telling him, that such criminals invested with power, intentionally followed him, managing his progress, bribing an emissary of those who claimed to be friends of Gibon, to keep them informed of his steps, conspiring with the citizenship of Gibon and manipulating his career, trying to fabricate cases to discredit him and prevent him from receiving his blessings and a job of dignity, managed by him, but ignoring that against God you can not, and that no one could mess with the children of God, because all evil, God turned it into good, everything they did to him as evil, God turned it into good, and accommodated it in his favor, so that those evil, God turned it into good, and God accommodated it in his favor, so that those racist, malicious and treacherous officials, understood that "the world was wide and had an owner", and although some believed themselves to be possessors, we were all passing through, and that even in the free will, they could not prevent what had been assumed since before birth, because what was called happen, would always happen.

Three years of agony, pouring through his pores the sweat emanating from an unmotivated salary, but to which, because of necessity and the obligations of survival, he was obliged to do honor.

From the moment he arrived there, he stopped calling himself Gibon so that he could be called a pastor.

And as some of you may know, there are voices that sound like shrieks, sometimes annoying to the ear.

While he was in the industrial laundry, he was followed and watched, and escorted to the bathroom, by crossovers experimenting on unwanted bodies, something like a man living in a woman's body, or a woman inhabiting a man's body, they were beings infiltrated by the organization of evil, naturally, with the supervisors bought to report even the way Gibon breathed in that place.

There was one called Janina, who had her eye on him, provoked him and told him.

"You have a nuance that induces; it is a nuance of attraction that moves to temptation."

But Gibon listened to her and said nothing, because he understood that behind those words, there was a snake ready to tempt him and corner him.

And it was in such a way that she was stalking him, he was dissimulating, she was sneaking around, wanting to tell him something, she was insinuating and insisting, "you have a nuance that induces."

"How so?" he said her.

"It is a shade that attracts me, that moves me to temptation, that provokes illusion in me, that leads me to love," replied Janina.

"I understand your expression, and it even calms my pain, but I know your condition and I share your concern, but there are missions that are not understood, however when you wake up and see the light, you will understand the glorification of my pain, because the tears of this earth, are the pearls of the heavens" said Gibon in verses.

"Uh, that's why I like it, for that tender expression of your heart, for being a poet of love and emotion." Janina answered him.

"If you provoke me to tell you, I will be inspired and tell you that you are a beautiful garment, with whom I will go out to eat," Gibon replied.

"I like your verses Gibon; they light up the hopes of my love" Janina, who resorted to all the mechanisms of her honor, a woman trained by the organization to hunt males, some Dominicans called her "chapeadora[7]".

Gibon, who understood the language of what she wanted, said mischievously:

"The little tempest, sooner or later it will be, without paco the dog coming out, believing that he will bark. Possessed of such inspiration," Gibon replied.

"Can I affirm that you are taking me to the cinema?" asked Janina.

"It could be, perseverance is the mother of results, and although hopes don't fill the belly, at least they keep the mood up," he said, just when Jocelyn, the supervisor interrupted them, alerting them:

"You are running out of time for lunch, stop talking, and get to eating," she said as she took a plate out of a bowl and put it to warm in a microwave.

---

[7] Woman only interested in money

CHAPTER 21

HISTORICITY

From the beginning of its founding, the American nation had been overrun by adventurers bent on seeking prefabricated well-being, regardless of the condition that it was generated people more inclined to evil than good, and those same people used whatever they could to lift up or overthrow those on their billboard.

Gibon was not a person who liked these kinds of spectacles, which lacerated the dignity of being, so he seemed more like a kind of redeemer, in the prison of indifference, he thought that when he cried out for justice to the one who acted as judge and executioner, he had to have God close to him, so as not to be harassed.

And it was that Gibon had been subjected to all the trials and humiliations, generated by the organization of evil, which devised all kinds of conspiracies, ranging from antagonizing relatives, discrediting victims, stealing benefits and believing that they could enslave those who opposed them.

However, Gibon understood that the earth was a stage set for various scenes, therefore, these monsters of evil, by their shameless condition used to realize that they had the necessary funds to defend themselves in court if for some reasons they had been forced to respond, they could only operate in "democratic" societies, because in a society of force, they would not hesitate to shoot them as a way to eradicate their wickedness, as it happened in Sodom, which in some episode of history, had been destroyed by the intolerance of impudence.

Now, those incarnated beings had returned.

They were shown as good and they were bad, they were the picture of hypocrisy in a carnivalesque society, where the drama behind the abuse prevailed.

They took refuge in religions to show themselves in society as the merciful misunderstood, but behind such a facade, they dismembered all those who dared to oppose them.

Everything had to change, the truth had to come out, and Gibon determined to make a difference chanted a mantra of hope, which would change the world naturally and he said:

"I am the will of reason, I am the understanding of why I am, I am the I am, I am the light of the sun, I am health, I am opulence, I am youth, I am love, I am the I am, I am, I am, I am, I am splendor, I am brilliance, I am attraction, I am the I am, I am in control, I am attraction, I generate love."

In reality there were many anecdotes of the pack members, some wanted to be crooked, but others acted like they were macho and heroes, on one occasion of those times when Plutarco Rene Cariño was inclined to crime, in his apparent good times, he had traveled to France, in one of those summer excursions, and he found that in the Eiffel Tower, someone was trying to commit suicide, she had tried to throw himself from the reception floor, and although there were several people, everyone was cautious, but Plutarco Rene Cariño who was a conqueror, when he saw that woman, he approached her with love, talking to her with passion, and he said to her:

"Love, precious pearl, how is it that a beauty of your nature, an entity made woman is going to commit suicide, leaving so many admirers with a melted heart," he said.

The one with the paralyzed heart looked at him and smiled, at the same time she answered:

"Oh God, there are still heartful men."

Rene, fondly seeing he was being reciprocated, added:

"Yes, my dear, there are still some of us, and seeing that there are still ladies of your category, we will be strong for you, why do you want to commit suicide? Why don't you better give to a human that which you pretend to let be eaten by worms? Come on love, come down from there and kiss me here," he said showing her the good side of his face.

The woman gave him her hand, coming down from the place where she intended to jump at the same time that she gave a passionate kiss to Rene, in full mouth and without breath, those who were looking at them began to applaud, and the woman only spoke to tell him:

"My parents, because of their religion, refuse to let me dress as a woman, and they don't want me to have a sex change operation."

All those who heard suddenly ran, but Rene Cariño, who had understood, led him to where a group of paramedics were waiting for him, and he never mentioned it again, until prison induced him to tolerate it.

Upon his return to New York, he wanted to run a drug trafficking operation, then he was arrested and sentenced to ten years, during this time he was forced to rub the backs of some of the strongest people who didn't want to soap themselves.

After leaving, he was in parole, and besieged by immigration, until he reached Bulley, where he began to apply his skills and malice to gain control on others, and impose himself as leader, trying to use the splendor of his smile to get noticed, and slandering according to his interests anyone he thought he could discredit, he accepted bribes from occult sects, to conspire to get Gibon out of Bulley.

Before the corona virus quarantine was decreed in New York, he had taken a customer who knew Gibon, and who had seen Gibon a few minutes before the purchase was on Mr. Cariño's car, and on seeing him she greeted him with much appreciation, but as Rene Cariño felt a natural jealousy against Gibon, and concealed it, the customer asked him.

"And Gibon, since when is he in that place?"

He replied:

"Gibon has been there for a few months, he is camouflaging himself, because he stole money from a foundation."

"How can it be? That's not true, I know him, and I've even been to his house, and he's not that kind of guy," she clarified.

René Cariño kept silence, and, on his arrival, dismounting the purchase with the awful clatter of a despairing, quickening his pace, returned to Bulley, with some disappointment, because he could not persuade her to turn against Gibon as was his purpose as the occult sect had asked him to do, in their usual intention of discrediting Gibon, and alienating him from all those whom he knew.

A few days later, the Chachi, which was the name of the young woman who had defended Gibon against Plutarco René Cariño, met him again, and as soon as she saw him she greeted him and told him:

"Gibon, love, be careful with that man, he envies you, and he wanted to convince me to doubt you, but I told him not to insist, because I know you."

Gibon thanked her, and took the precaution, so that Plutarco René Cariño would not conspire against him, and when he had to face his evilness, he resorted to a photograph that he kept in the photo library of his cell phone, where Gibon appeared dictating a lecture of literary analogy, to some American citizens of Anglo-Saxon origin, after looking at it, he showed it to René Cariño, asking him:

"Who is this person you see giving this lecture?"

"But, that's you," replied Rene affectionately.

"Indeed, that means that you have no reason or condition, to lie about me, trying to damage my reputation. Do you know why? Because I have contributed to the cultural development of the citizens of this nation, I have paid my taxes, and although the organization of evil or occult sect, have contacted you so that in the blurry of your ignorance, in deep turbulence slander me, and make fun of me, because the ignorant by their condition of unconsciousness, are always ready to pay obeisance to the satraps."

"Hey, Gibon, you're insulting me you're mistaken," replied Rene honey.

"No, the one who is mistaken is you, and all those who act in frequent conspiratorial action, as an entity without foundation, those who have contributed nothing or very little to the development of this nation, and who live watching the makers of development to disable them with the obstacles of their envy, precisely like you who in your years of drug dealer obstructed everything and gave nothing in return...."

Gibon was rudely interrupted by René Cariño:

"Stop that there, I already paid my debt to society," replied Plutarco René Cariño with all the splendor of his arrogance.

Then Gibon, not allowing himself to be diverted from what he was saying, returned to the subject:

"What is done is done, but remorse lingers in the sensitivity of conscience, when the trajectory of youth has been lacerated, and although before being born they chose to be destroyed, in your free will the ego was inflated so that your evilness remained, and even so, the after-effects are still inflated, because you live forging how to make your neighbor stumble, you have insisted on selling me for a few coins, you feel important and your ego is inflated when you make fun of me at the request of the occult sect and the organization of evil; Ten years in prison did not teach you to understand that 'who kills with iron, dies with iron,' and as far as I can see, the trials brought into your life, instead of correcting you, made you more inclement"

"You hear, devil shepherd, what you are doing is deceiving people, so leave your sermons for those who believe you, and don't try to confuse me," said Rene.

"René Cariño, stop defending yourself like a cat upside down, and stop slandering me that I have contributed more to society than you, because even in your good times, your unwashed income, not being taxable, was nothing significant to the treasury of this nation, so stop playing dumb with me," said Gibon.

René Cariño kept silent, turned his gaze to the floor, and walked away from Gibon, giddily.

A few months had passed since that day, when the pack was notified that René Cariño had had a heart attack; it was like a warning from God.

CHAPTER 22

EVENTS

A few days later, Nicanor appeared and commented to Burdock.

"Well Burdock, I think it's true what they say that "a bad weed never die", because cariñito had a heart attack, and yet he "survived.""

"Hey, Nicanor, stop talking nonsense, don't let them hear you, you know that gossip is formed here for anything, if he survived it was because it wasn't his time yet," said Burdock.

Nicanor swallowed the raccoon smile, which he was showing at that moment, and kept silent as Burdock suggested.

In reality they had a formidable mechanism of communication, they had managed to develop a kind of brotherhood, which allowed them to understand each other in a pack language, typical of their animalistic condition, although Nicanor was already more reformed, in the past he and Burdock got along wonderfully, since those times when they were unified for the extortion and manipulation of those who tried to approach Bulley to make delivery, without first confessing to them and licking their hands with that metal that the Phoenicians had invented thousands of years ago, yes, with that metal that they called "currency".

"It's not that we are radicals, it's that everyone who wants to work with us, has to contribute for the horse's food," said Nicanor, referring to the fact that it was necessary to pay him to buy his marijuana, and he said it looking at Burdock with a surprising camaraderie, because Burdock shook his head in affirmation, but leaving the impression that he had nothing to do with it, but since they collected the money from the aspirant to join the pack, they immediately distributed it, without the others knowing what was happening.

Every day and in a funeral procession, hope gave way to death, the crack of survival, the atheists cried out for God, the parishioners continued to wait for Christ.

The generation lived day by day, without saying goodbye to the cause, because life had become monotony, to exist and die, was a lottery for the highest bidder, no one wanted to be graced with death, because everyone ignored the reason for their stay on earth.

Many kings refused to let go of the throne, because ruling became a habit.

And in the face of death many felt confused, and their affection was that death would remove them from the kingdoms they had built, giving way to "moths to corrupt their earthly riches", so that beauty and lovelessness pretended to love each other to keep up appearances, and between tender glances they declared their love.

But it happened that many, in their vanity let themselves be confused by an unknown tool that granted death, and it happened that corona virus possessed them, and there was no sanity or rebellion, poetry was a hope, but the cremation erased their forms, the families would never be able to claim, the sphinx had to return, where they once thought they had their home, the spirit had to fly, no longer having a body to inhabit.

The pack was alarmed, nothing was known about Crispin, his family said that he had been admitted to a hospital, but Moraima, his beloved consort, when she was kissed she remembered Judas, without knowing how, she embraced the contagion, his tender consort, when she got free, she could not get close, through the camera she saw him breathing, with the pipe, which supported him, supplying him with the air that he would long for!

Fear invaded those who murmured that they would not be afraid, and life was decorated with fear, which, becoming a sword built with air, would prevent them from taking up again what they had lived, and seeing me alive, I was forced to show them the way, which gave hope for each day, and God told them:

"Fear nothing to be with me, for I am the key that will unlock destiny."

Then I saw that death was riding on the ambulances, the sirens swelled the heart with pain, every day more infected were reported, and the fearful institutions hid their dead in clandestine vans, which then denounced the fetid odors.

The generation was transforming, sorrow saddened, souls, pain corrupted, but I, seeking to give strength to existence, expressed myself with an air of conscience, to force the force to show all its nobility:

"You are the annunciation of my prediction, you have become my ideal made woman, you are the essential rock of my path, and I am your breathing without virus crown!

Now I am the triumph of your destiny, because God has entrusted me to be with you, and my silhouette is your best friend, is your light my virtue, and my spirit your light.

In you God gave me the suitability of being, you are my flower of the sun, you are my dawn, today you are the illusion, which makes you virtue, you are truth and light.

Glorified in the path to walk, you are health, virtue, light and welfare.

God has been the essence that guides my journey, making you the peace of my happiness.

Today you make me find strength and security, because when you become peace, you are like faith, which brings harmony and the great guarantee that life is a melody that reactivates the being in every dawn.

Being in you, I turn to God, who is the source of love, and being in God, we value the source of light.

To be in God eliminates pain, God is the guarantee of each day, and through your being in each dawn, my love is reborn.

Life is reintegrated for a better world, pride is lacerated, redemption is here, your arms give me calm, and God gives me love, he is the eternal flame of forgiveness."

The pack didn't know what to do, they crossed themselves

at dawn, it was a way of blackmailing God, they wanted easy money, and they thought that getting it was difficult, but in truth, they didn't care about dignity, nor did they know what conscience was, they ignored the meaning, and there was no dictionary within their reach to define it.

Nature would provide a form of justice that would give the cretins their place, so that the man of peace and good will could work without ties.

Many of the enlisted had been radically affected by the corona virus, COVID-19, had swept away a high percentage of the wicked, the pious and the kind.

To the evil, the tooth of death appeared to them in a merciless way, and all their money, was of no use, their money, taken from the people, could not help them. Many of them died as heretics wishing the cross, but they could not buy health, despite the money, all were killed in similarity, without fanfare of history, they left as scum because the money did not grant him glory, because to avoid contagion, many were cremated, and others, were thrown off a cliff, in an unpredictable crack of confusion, that sharpened suffering and pain, by melted bodies that made emotion a dismay, by love, they felt pain behind the mass grave, the families regretted not looking at each other in their gazes, not being able to say goodbye and feeling the universe snatched the scales of time's embrace, and the pain that remained was music without concert.

Many people expressed their sorrow: "By the profile of your blue gaze, I can define, that it brings your heart, imposing eyes, and smiling lips, let me understand that you are still my love.

And the nightingale who understood what was happening, stood frightened at his window and sang with glory and hope his dawn: "You are the love, that when I wake up turns me into alarm, that howls on the threshold, and I hear the melody that brings your memory, making me live, full of comfort."

Then, everyone had understood, that the COVID -19, had already been defined before its fate, so a leaked information in a 70-page document referring to the world bank, entitled: "COVID-19 strategic response and preparedness program" and labeled in the expression "for official use only", whose date dates from 2017 and 2018, two years before the pandemic was made public, was the burning sample of what was forged before it was disseminated had emerged as a conspiracy theory that had escaped from the hands of its proponents, which in turn, had generated the participation of a public opinion that made its judgments based on what appeared every day where measures were taken to deal with the mini-crisis that would generate the disintegration of the pandemic.

Codes from the archives of the World Bank 300215 902780 and such codes were the keys to the export of materials to Switzerland, Germany, USA, Holland, Japan and Hong Kong. In the "instruments and apparatus for the COVID -19" world bank archive, where the purpose of the creation of such a radical disease was split, was aimed to enslave the population, restricting their movements, to impose a vaccine that eventually to travel would require proof that travelers had been applied, and could generate a catatonic state, linked to 5G technology experiment qualified as a possible biological attack, which would serve the purpose of the NOM: (New World Order) that consisted of reducing the population and canceling the reflective thought of the human being, to the degree of zoning it to control it.

CHAPTER 23

POSSIBILITIES

But, let's go back to the pack scenario, and see what happens:

Life on earth, was like an ungrateful surprise, Mark and the pack used to get along with sort of distance, but Plutarco Rene Cariño, in his eagerness to be noticed, was always in front making him feel like the prince and how his entourage, and many times Mark, as an administrative assistant in order that the pack did not ignore his condition, when he asked for a favor, he used to ask for it with a certain radicalism, which made some of the members of the pack feel uncomfortable, and when they saw him walking away, they did not control their egocentric condition to express behind his back certain racial expletives such as:

"I don't know what that coconut-eating nigger is deprived of," said Burdock then he was interrupted by Plutarco Rene Cariño who faced him saying:

"Burdock... Mark is a good man, he's just stressed out."

"I understand, Cariño, but that does not give him the right to believe that we are his poplars, we don't get paid to get into the cars, we do it voluntarily, so he should be more polite," alleged Burdock.

"All right, I'm going to talk to him to calm him down" said

Cariño, playing the "fire and brimstone" or rather the conciliatory and relatable one.

Plutarco Rene Cariño often had his antenna up to listen to what they were talking or what they were silent, without ceasing to conspire he showed himself as the defender of what was convenient for him, so that some saw him as a kind of the worst hypocrites, they also believed that he was servile and "toady", and they believed him to be an uneducated soul, despite having read several books in prison, but as "in the land of the blind the one-eyed man is king", after Gibon, Donko and Fredesvindo, he was one of the most skilled in the pack, because Burdock was simply the most malicious.

Plutarco Rene Cariño, often used to get irritated with Gibon, especially when he accepted a gift from occult sect to provoke him and Gibon, on the other hand, ignored him with silence, and Cariño got so irritated that it seemed that such an attitude raised his blood sugar, and he could be heard to cluck, raising his voice, shouting, manipulating and making everyone else believe that they all fit in his mouth, because he kept going up and down, carrying and bringing, running errands for the store's administrators.

At the time that he let his condition of merciful flow, and to gain the favor of the pack, he used to take food and distribute it among his followers, or buy coffee or sodas, but such actions were part of his strategy to ponder himself, he was very ready to seek "enllavadura[8]" telling gossip to the administrator or his assistant, of what was happening in the

---

[8] To sponsor someone through friendship or political influence in order to obtain a position or job for them.

pack, but above all, putting in bad to those who disagreed with him, to take advantage and make himself look as the good one.

He had been marked by prison, and there he had learned to obey, and to run errands for the bosses, with ten years in a maximum security prison, he learned to cook for others, in exchange for various favors, and when he got out, he could stop identifying with evilness as a form of survival, and he used to give the image of a fiasco, a kind of false prophet of those who wanted to fish in troubled waters.

That was only an isolated case because the pack, always had an idiosyncratic reason to act, on Tuesday 13th, Rocko Vulcan snatched the list from Gibon, so he with all his calmness told him:

"Man, if you see that I have the list, don't take it from me, ask my permission out of politeness" said him, but Rocko stammered in an effort to justify himself, and spoke unintelligible words, without saying anything close to an apology.

"Disgusting, what a guy, he didn't even apologize" expressed Galy Buchí, with the intention of irritating Gibon.

Gibon kept silent, thinking that they were assuming a conspiracy to disrupt his patience, since they had all somehow accepted bribes from the organization of evil, which had an army of minions at its service, and often used them for dirty work.

At that moment a brunette with four cute and calm little children like herself, moved outside, it was apparent that she was a lady bringing a battered mass origin, but at that moment in her Muslim disguise, she gave the impression of being besieged by a disturbing concern, on reaching 90th and Broadway she said her uncle would pay, then said Gibon had gone past where she was going, Gibon ride and skirted back to the right down Broadway to re-enter 90th Street, and the supposed uncle, who at that moment appeared at 90th and Broadway in a belligerent attitude, first yelled at his supposed niece to go into the restaurant where she would leave the cake, and she obligingly obeyed him, the uncle didn't want his niece to know what he was going to do.

When she left, the uncle asked Gibon if he had change for a hundred dollars, to which Gibon replied:

"It depends."

The guy kept quiet and started counting a roll of money trying to impress Gibon, the street was narrow and full of confrontation.

Gibon wanted to move fast, but the intention of the uncle, was to delay and humiliate him by order of occult sect, so that the cars that were behind him without being able to move, came into conflict with him, so Gibon trying to win time told him that it was free, so he could forget about the money, while the uncle, with all the splendor of an offended executive told him:

"I don't need anything for free," said while throwing a twenty-dollar bill into the car, which had a half-open window, as he stumbled away like a zombie.

At such an attitude Gibon looked at him and commented:

"I feel shame for you." but the brunette didn't turn around or add anything else, while in his steps you could see the disappointment of someone who had been forced to do a dirty job, they were testing Gibon, and they had resorted to all sorts of ways.

Gibon commented to himself, however:

"Poor misguided soul, 'the monkey even dressed in silk, stays monkey'" He thought, and sought to find a reason to justify the action of arrogance of that strange character.

Then he came to the conclusion that those beings, could not hide their condition of minions when they assumed a position of command and dragged the complex that generational masters had instilled in their ancestors, who in times of servitude, had kept them in the pens, abused and sleeping on the floor, and although time had passed; by the narratives of history, some descendants wanted to take revenge on all those whose physiognomy seemed different from theirs, because some brought the generational trauma, and had not managed to overcome that condition even understanding that the chains had been broken, and that there was no reason to be crystallized by the whipping of bitterness of the experimental existence stages.

Gibon also thought that day had been chosen for him, he went back locally on Riverside Avenue and at the 167th Street level got onto the westbound freeway, and when he tried to get off at Exit 17, he found a highway patrolman went after him, he didn't stop until he was near Dyckman and Broadway.

When he realized she was behind him he stopped, the officer approached him and Gibon who still didn't know what was going on asked him:

"What's going on?"

The officer answered with the confidence of the one who had the pan from the handle.

"I told you to stop twice and you didn't listen to me," said her exaggerating. "You have a burned out brake light, give me your license and registration."

Without saying anything, Gibon followed her order, handed over the required documentation, the officer returned to the patrol car, and she reappeared telling him,

"I have two news, one good and the other I don't know how you'll take it, everything is fine, but I'm going to give you a ticket, you have 24 hours to solve it, go fix the light, and then you go to the nearest precinct, there they will verify if you really fixed it and then they will give you a signed paper that you will immediately send to Albany, and in the procedure they will take the ticket away... where are you going now?" she asked.

Before answering that question Gibon entered into camaraderie with Officer Cepeda and before answering he asked her:

"What is your name?"

"Officer Cepeda" she answered.

"Thank you, officer, the first thing I'll do is go to solve the light problem, then I'll go to the nearest precinct and then, to Bulley," answered Gibon.

"To Bulley?" questioned the officer.

"Yes, I have some work to do there, thank you again, and God bless you, may I shake your hand?" he asked.

The officer nodded her head as she held out her hand.

Gibon reciprocated the gesture by shaking her hand and saying goodbye.

Gibon took advantage of the circumstance, approached 202nd Street, where in less than five minutes they repaired the light, and handed him the accreditation paper, which he immediately took to the 34th Precinct, where the officer on duty with high courtesy after shaking his hand and congratulating him for some notes that Gibon had spread on social networks, and that Officer Grand had read.

Then the officer asked him to approach the car where he could verify that the light had indeed been repaired, because once verified he signed the form. Gibon ten minutes later, had deposited in the mail, bound for Albany.

Then, as he had told Officer Cepeda, he returned to Bulley, where he found chaotic anarchy.

The organization of evil, had laid the groundwork so that from moment to moment Cholinfe and Burdock showed off their barking, and with unbridled voice started a discussion that people actually thought it was a war to death that they were holding, since, as we had commented the organization of evil was dedicated to oppress and harass men in the world and where they had followers of their cause, there was not always peace, their carriers kept going in and out of a parking lot to enter another, seeking to delay traffic or cause accidents.

The organization of evil and occult sect were global organizations that played the Satan's role on earth, were the global harassers, integrated by beings of globalization, with office in New York.

CHAPTER 24

COMPETENCE

Even if you run away from me, my memories will follow you, because prudently the glow of your scent, will emit the murmur of my voice, that in the silence defined you, clarifying the existence, in every clarity that induces the awakening, in that Bilingualism, of clouded gazes, that in their internal music decreed the sorrows.

Actually, for Gibon, doing the deliveries was a thrill, Teresa came out with her purchase, asked Rocko to ride her for ten, Rocko refused and passed her to Gibon, who expressed it in an introductory way:

"I was telling the carriers why they refused to take you, because you are a fine woman, and fine women tip."

Teresa was so impressed that she laughed, Gibon, without adding anything else, rode her, and for such an attitude Teresa increased the amount, instead of ten, she paid fifteen, and Gibon was also impressed, because he was always ready to take those who were less able to pay.

Suddenly Burdock approached, with the full certainty of the splendor of all his evilness, stretching out his ear to show that he was more malicious than good people, always looking closely to light the fuse at the slightest movement made by his neighbor, so that he could slander him with his filthy tongue of a playground agitator, of a masculine little woman with a face of apparent innocence.

His arrival in the United States had been full of traumas, he had left Miches, one of the Dominican beaches, looking for Puerto Rico as his destination, but life from the first moment of his escape hit him at sea, the crew that accompanied him perished, the boat that transported him broke in two, and in his shipwreck he ended up in luquillo on the side where loneliness reigned, but nevertheless luck in his misfortune assisted him, the devil was indebted to God, who saved his demon, and Burdock, with Gladíolo and Romualdo met, they were two reincarnated sodomites who had not overcome the condition of crossover, and since they saw him they gloried, Gladiolo, he said to Romualdo:

"It's mine."

"Hey kid, but how can you be yours if I saw it first," replied Romualdo.

"Now, let's stop this, let's take the tiger to cure him, and then let him decide."

"I like with your humanitarian reflection."

The first thing Gladiolo did was to get on top of him, and practice mouth to mouth breathing, when he realized that he had removed the water he had swallowed, between the two got him inside a car that they called "brush" which was owned by Gladiolo, left the beach and went to Rio Piedras, where they lived.

When he was out of danger they began to flirt with him, but

Gladiolo reminded Romualdo that his return to New York was already confirmed, in three days he would leave, and that he didn't want him to deceive someone who had suffered so much, so he reiterated, "that it wasn't wise for him to go about disqualifying another man" and also let him know that when he returned to New York, then he would take care of Burdock and help him, but that even though they both liked the man, "he should leave his selfishness behind". Even though they had argued over the male, like two females in heat, Romualdo understood, and three days later he returned to New York. His friendship with Gladiolo was of many years, they had known each other since they were very young, and they had even rehearsed together how to learn to kiss, since they had attended elementary school together in Puerto Rico.

Romualdo was Cuban with a Puerto Rican mother and an Italian father, he was born in Cuba during a vacation his mother took, and although he was registered as Cuban, his mother processed with the representative of Cuban affairs of the chancellery, and they took him to Puerto Rico a month after he was born.

Gladiolo, a native of Puerto Rico, although Romualdo had emigrated with his parents to New York, kept in touch with him, and during vacation time, one year Gladiolo would go to New York, and the other, Romualdo would travel to Puerto Rico.

But that encounter had changed the monotony process of their lives. Burdock married Gladiolo and made his residency, the first two years they lived happily, but on one occasion they went together to the rainbow party, where Gladiolo caught Burdock flirting with Yeyé, and from that moment the relationship became strendous, Gladiolo got jealous, and four years after Burdock got permanent residency, he contacted Romualdo to receive him in New York, Romualdo received him, but three weeks later, pressured by Gladiolo, he threw him to the street, Burdock slept in the trains for a week, until he met Guga, a girlfriend he had in Sabana de la Mar, in the Dominican Republic, she picked him up and helped him to get a taxi driver license, and he stayed with Guga.

A steamy divorce from Gladiolus definitely pull him away, Gladiolus went into depression, so an over-dose killed him.

In a brief expression, his fate defined, Burdock, arrived in a Yola, which had broken in two, all had already perished, his boat was wrecked, Gladiolo rescued him and took him to his home, before convalescence, Burdock looked his face, and Gladiolo in love his the heart trembled, And so it was that Burdock married Gladiolo, who gave him documents and legalized Burdock, in a fit of jealousy, Gladiolo got angry, and Burdock, disappointed, fled to New York, Romualdo, who lived there, lodged him for a few days, and three weeks later, pressured by Gladiolo, threw him out into the street.

Burdock's destiny was marked by life to harass, and be harassed, and there he was at Bulley.

He had been hired by the organization of evil, to denounce the slightest error that Gibon assumed, so that the fuse of pride would induce the pack to bark against him, however, Gibon, man of God, a hard nut to crack, in full cover of the

Lord, was far from the failed attempts that those against him made, all lacked power over him.

"I am that I am, I change in my favor everything related to health, youth, opulence and love, I am that I am, because everything that is seen, was made from what is not seen, I induce the invisible force that does justice, to not allow any injustice to me and mine".

Burdock as his name indicated, was not only brazen and shameless, but was always forging one of those evilness own of his condition, as expected he arrived and did not sign up on the waiting list that defined the shifts of those who would go out to make the deliveries, and giving it the majority businessman, expanded his ego and claimed that he had opened that business for having been the first to have started making deliveries when the Bulley club began its services in the area. Under this pretext and under inconsiderate and abusive forms, he would take away the turn of the one who preceded him, believing himself more of a dog than dogs.

With Gibon it was different, he didn't allow him his doggy actions, when he tried to bark, Gibon would confront him to the point of putting him down and reducing him to growls:

"Hai, hai, hai, hai, hai, hai."

And so on and so forth, because he spoke like a loud speaker, almost shouting to manipulate and intimidate.

After the Gibon's arrival, things were changing, but before, whoever wanted to start working doing deliveries in Bulley had to pay an amount that oscillated between 300 and

1000 dollars, everything depended on who it was, and that money was distributed by Burdock and Nicanor, another bird of his nest, as good people as he was, since both barked with the same howls, always ready to manipulate and intimidate the inexperienced, but in the case of Gibon, they did not dare to oppose him, but they warned him that they had raised that point, and therefore he also had to pay, if he wanted them to let him start.

Whoever rebelled and did not pay, suffered from sabotage and disappointment ranging from three and two slashed tires when the incumbent was careless.

Gibon, who knew the idiosyncrasy of the people of such kind, showing his agreement told them that yes, he would pay but they had to let him start, because he had lost the job, they accepted and agreed to charge him 245 dollars, and then they told him that with that amount would be enough, without paying more, and Gibon, to seal the conflict, decided to obey them, to make them believe that from now on they would be the bosses, because as I said, if someone dared not to pay, and they would come down on him, in any carelessness they would crack the tires of the car, Gibon decided to obey them, to make him believe that from now on they would be the bosses, because as they told, if someone dared not to pay, and they would fall on him, in any carelessness they would slash the tires of his car with knives, or they would put nails or spikes, they practiced domestic terrorism, through such unworthy sabotage.

In the beginning they tolerated Gibon, but as Gibon gained

a foothold, difficulties began to arise, the organization of evil, figuring out ways to loot him, bribed Burdock and the whole pack to make it difficult for Gibon, They needed him to give up willingly the delivery job on Bulley to justify a fraud by making it look like Gibon worked for them, so they could withhold the compensation money to underpay Gibon and keep the pile for themselves.

CHAPTER 25

THE FRAUDULENT

Perhaps you are a little incredulous because you believe that in these times of "false prophets" we are all the same.

It is not like that, we are not the same, I know the history of Gibon, and what I say is as a testimony to God.

It turned out that the city and its cliques 29 years ago had violated the rights of the aforementioned, imprisoning him instead of another, Gibon fought from jail and instead they offered him to change his case for a job, and although Gibon accepted, they never gave him the promised job, the years went by and the money accumulated, scientology, an organization in the area dedicated to the "defense of human rights" had contacted Gibon. They invited him to participate in some seminars that he accepted, among the student paperwork, they introduced some documents for Gibon to sign, but they did not tell him that they were claiming the compensation with the intention of distributing it to him, by that time they had used the services of a French fraud expert who was called Pierre Duluc, who after Gibon signed the documents said "With a dotation of 25,000, it will be enough, but nothing about suing the city, nor the government of the United States" added that one, without Gibon understanding the reason that induced him to express himself in that way, but Gibon automatically replied:

"I don't think your request can be arranged," said Gibon, the Frenchman, kept silent and withdrew.

Gibon never accepted the accusation, and he was never given the job he was offered, many years had passed since he had not fulfilled the agreement he had made, which amounted to a large sum of money.

Then, a few days after Gibon had signed the paperwork, he had overheard the cat, one of the organization officers, plan what she would do, when the claim cleared, and that included that once everything was settled she would move to another location, which Gibon failed to hear.

However, from what little Gibon could hear, he let the cat know that no one would use him.

The cat looked at him in silence with certain uneasiness generated by the surprise, and a week later, an Australian officer named Jennifer, who arrived from Los Angeles to take charge of the Harlem organization, with certain "pain" gave Gibon a letter from Flag, in whose content was expressed his dismissal, through that letter, he was being separated from the organization, those foxes had forged a conspiracy with the full intention of stripping Gibon.

As you can see, Scientology had its melody.

Two years later when the time was coming closer to release the money, when Gibon was not in the organization, they wanted to force him to return, but God had already informed Gibon about the pretensions of those, and for nothing that one wanted to turn back, occult sect, wanted to turn back, occult sect, wanted to justify the fraud with the presence of Gibon, but for more efforts and conspiracies it was impossible to make him return, and Gibon had lost trust in them, then they began a series of evil actions and bribes to people who had some kind of proximity to him, in order to discredit him, and resorted to actresses, and policewomen offering sexual encounters, even criminals to follow him to sabotage his car, or people who beat him and if he responded, they would accuse him of violence, among other actions loaded with malice.

The evil try of those was combined between the malice of the occult sect and the organization of evil, who wanted to bring Gibon down at any cost, yet they made Gibon's acquaintances and relatives believe that they were simple tests before they decorated him, and in that way, they had kept Gibon's acquaintances and those who pretended to know him manipulated for a long time, because Gibon became a temptation whom everyone wanted to sell to the highest bidder.

On occasions, before Gibon knew the profile of the occult sect intension, they assigned him to a lady of company, who that night would accompany him, she was an Argentinean pianist, they called her Ana, she offered to take him to some place where he had to attend that night, after the instruction of the organization was finished, at that time Gibon had sold the car and it seemed easier for him to move, Ana drove him to 190th and St Nicholas, where at that time he lived, but the goal was to know more about him, where and with whom he lived? For once they handled the information to be able to lead him to the levels where they had planned, the case is that

Ana realized very well where was the apartment where Gibon lived, and from that moment the pianist had sought the way to relate to Elvira, Gibon's friend, who that night had invited him to the exhibition of her boyfriend's paintings, they kept inviting Gibon to numerous activities, but Gibon never went, but neither did he imagine the plans of occult sect and the organization of evil.

They believed that Gibon was a common man to whom anyone could weave a story, and get away with theirs, however, they were wrong, because they would give rise to the story that Gibon would write, but where the villains would be them.

The real objective was to take him away from his habitat to another place, where their plans would be easier to justify, a few days later.

The organization of evil, in two or three weeks would be bribing and convincing the landlord to ask Gibon for the room, the one that he had rented with a collection made by the parishioners of the church Words of Life, because they had realized that on a trip that Gibon had made to the Dominican Republic after the death of his mother in 2014, where the conspiracy had been forged and upon his return without owing rent, they had closed the apartment as a way to corner him, but he went to sleep in a van that was his property and had left in the care of a church member, who he had never known to be a homosexual, and who insisted on accompanying him to the court house to try to zip down his zipper during a recess, whereupon Gibon asked him "if he was crazy" and was forced to report him to the church, because his lack of control induced him to a second attempt at indecency, Gibon had to leave, because the tentacles of the organization of evil, disrespecting the hunger of the hungry, appeared, bribing sectors of command, inside the house of God, with the intention of making my father's house a den of perversion, as it had happened in the Jesus time. At the same time they were trying to make it difficult for Gibon, whom they were chasing under the pretext of testing him, because they needed to know if Gibon was a man or an angel, and they gathered false prophets, macaques, and cockatrices, and other ticks, to see what would be the level of Gibon's resistance, whose strength surpassed the condition that the human of the tradition expected.

After the apartment was closed Gibon moved the van, and parked like a spring on the hill of fort George and Dyckman, in Washington heights, occult sect and the organization of evil, who ignored the whereabouts of the one who had moved without a trace, used an emissary known to Gibon, to specify which was the residence of his pursued, and the emissary betraying Gibon for money, because money had always been a temptation since before the time of Judas, indicated the place where the van was parked, the first thing they did was to damage the transmission so that Gibon could not go to work in it, and then, they put surveillance with vehicles with Massachusetts plates, and when he could not move the van, they took the opportunity to steal the computer and documents, which would allow them to forge the fraud against Gibon and to do misdeeds that looked like he had done them, so that they would always have him under the soles of their shoes.

So it was that at the time Gibon slept in the Van, the parishioners of the Words of Life Church, had taken up a collection by giving him an offering of $500, and although Gibon never knew if Pastor Peace was aware of those five hundred, but he, he did rent a room at 190th and St. Nicholas, but a santero who lived there after Ana's exploratory visit, the pianist who accompanied Gibon on the night of the painting exhibition, under the pretext that the santero was bringing his wife from the Dominican Republic and that they needed the space, asked him for the room, while referring him to an agency previously contacted by them, who had gotten him another room at 177th and St Nicholas, but after the person rented it and took the money, he backed out, because the occult sect needed to get him away from the area where he operated, until the agency asked him if he would move in any area, and Gibon explained that if there was no other option, he would have to accept the place that was available.

As long as it was a place where drugs were neither sold nor used, there would be no opposition.

So the agency sent him to a family of two, and with him they would be three, of course, each in their own habitat, there was Mrs. Soco, a 68 year old lady, and her son Gary, a special 42 year old, since Gibon moved in, Mrs. Soco warned him not to even say hello to Gary, because he would not answer him, since she had raised him as a special child, that is, a child with special needs that could range from medicine, therapy or additional help that other children did not require, or specific learning disabilities, Gary was already 42 years old, and had returned to his mother, after Valentina, his concubine, had abandoned him so he resorted to living under Mrs. Soco's protection.

Time had passed and it had been three years since Gibon had arrived at that address, and in apparent coincidence, when Gibon had left the industrial laundry, the next day, the IRS guard had swooped down from helicopters on that place, taking over computers, Gibon had been fired for no reason, but it was all under the disposition of the occult sect and the organization of evil, who had already hatched their plan, ignoring that "the donkey thinks one thing and the one who is riding it thinks another", ignoring that Gibon would uncover their plan.

When Gibon became unemployed, he was forced to apply for unemployment insurance, but the weekly allowance was not enough for him to eat and pay the rent, however, one of the Department of Labor counselors at the time had told him that since he was attending Scientology, they had passed his case on to them, Gibon did not understand what he was talking about, and without saying anything he followed the unemployment application process, Scientology didn't say anything either, and they gave him a pink slip to keep Gibon away from them, so they could freely forge what they intended to do.

Although two years later, they began to offer him positions in other facilities like Michigan, with the intention of getting him out of New York state, so that Gibon would not find out about the conspiratorial actions, when he refused, they began to provoke him and taunt him over the phone, rejoicing at the wrongdoings that affected Gibon and his family, and referring to Elly, who being a boxer and karate fighter outraged at what had been done to Gibon, had taken down more than one abuser, and then he had been taken and locked up for his "disorderly conduct" because some poor people when they feel that they have violated the rights of their relatives and believe that the system won't do justice for the good they tend to resort to rebellion, and the system ends up killing them or driving them crazy, something similar had happened with Elly, the first of Gibon's children who affected by the events, resided in the facilities of the behavioral center in the Bronx, and in a mocking song the unconscious "scientologist" provoking Gibon said to him:

"Gibon has a crazy son, Gibon has a crazy son."

All because Gibon had refused to move to Michigan, where they wanted him cloistered in such a way that they could justify the fraud; from that moment on, Gibon became aware of the inclemency of those who neither minded nor cared about human pain.

Anyway, Gibon kept silent, and continued to wait, but he already knew that the city, in its eagerness to justify its baseness, had resorted to those, seeking to disarticulate him.

Later, when the time came, Gary through Soco, his mother, had suggested:

"You have your vehicle you can make delivery," stated Soco.

Such suggestion came up when Gibon asked her for a $25 reduction in rent, and Mrs. Soco neither wanted to nor could, because the $150 a week Gibon paid her was in addition to the amount of rent she was paying.

And Gibon thought:

"There is no escaping what has to be, she refused to give me the rebate, and such action has now led me to be my own boss."

And that is how Gibon started in the Bulley's deliveries, where the pack, that micro business group, stood out.

CHAPTER 26

COEXISTENCE

Although Gibon and Gary, lived in the same apartment, in three years these had never addressed a word, since Gary and Soco slept in the living room, and Gibon in the master bedroom and he only saw them when he left to go to work and when he returned to sleep, until one day he spoke to him for the first time, when Gibon took one of his brothers who as he had arrived from the Dominican Republic, wanted to show him how he lived, sharing with strangers, with whom you didn't know if you could leave a gallon of water in the fridge in case by whim or by order they induced them to poison it if they had been forced to accept a bribe; the case was, that Gibon tried to show him why he could not receive him where he lived, having to rent him a space for a month, in another place, so that he would understand what was the reality of the immigrant in New York City.

Well, when Ferdinand visited him, Gary the dwarf was alarmed, to the extent that he made him run, which outraged Gibon, who was not used to going through that kind of recklessness.

But Gibon who understood that man values what he sees, according to his level of consciousness, made it clear to him, that he was showing his brother who had come from the

Republic, the place where he resided, but Gary because of his special condition, refused to understand, and told him:

"Cousin, you can't bring people here."

Gibon let it go, because a lot of those specials were more shameless than crazy, and because of Gary's defining condition, he wouldn't listen to him.

The second time he went to Gibon, when he tried to sell him some tennis shoes, he didn't buy them, but gave him $20.

He never told the pack that Gibon and he lived in the same apartment, but one night when Gibon was returning home, the organization of evil had sent three people to follow him, to enter the building, they acted like they were residents of the building, and the oldest of those who followed them, pretended to be the father of the young people who were a female and a male, who obviously, were noticing what apartment number Gibon would enter, who always took precautions, but that night, he did not care.

The next day when Gibon went to work, other emissaries of the organization of evil came to bribe Mrs. Soco and Gary to provoke Gibon to see his reaction.

Occult sect and organization of evil, they did not stop conspiring.

Since Gibon, saw the attitude of Mrs. Soco and Gary, he already knew that those had been marked, he was among Zombies and had to take his measures and be careful, he did not leave anything uncovered in the refrigerator in case they were to poison him or ultimately add some sleeping pills to make him fall asleep while driving.

From the meeting of the occult sect with them, the tests of Mrs. Soco and Gary were generated, it began with that she began to take attributions that Gibon had not given her, and Gary had begun to raise his voice, both were combined to find a pretext to generate a provocation, and for this they resorted to any slander, as a reason to throw in his face, such as that he had entered the bathroom and had left it dirty, and much more.

But because Gibon knew what it was all about, he made him believe that they were right, that as they said it was, and he went along with what they said, as they expected, with the utmost courtesy, until Gary, like a rampaging dwarf wanted to disrespect him , and Gibon intentionally told him in front of Mrs. Soco, that if he hit him he would hit him back, and Gary tried to do it, but Gibon blocked him and slapped him, at that moment Mrs. Soco got in between the two of them, and insulted Gary, mainly when Gary told Gibon.

"This is not your house."

Gibon replied, "This may not be your house because you live for free, but this is my house because I pay half the rent, so respect me, dwarf."

Mrs. Soco, corroborating with what she said interrupted, told Gibon to stay calm and he obeyed her, then she clarified to her little mammal.

"Yes, this is his house, he pays rent, the only one who doesn't pay rent here is you," expressed Mrs. Soco.

Gary was somewhat bewildered, for the first time in his life, he had felt abandoned.

At that instant Gibon started to move to his room, but before he entered he looked at Gary and stuck his tongue out at him, that's when Gary like a grumpy baby, got irritated.

"Look, he's sticking his tongue out at me, I'd better clean up that dirty room," he said.

Gibon left him talking to himself, but Mrs. Soco, not expecting such a little joke to get out of hand, began to scold him and tell him:

"You, if you're a bully, how come you're throwing yourself at him? You were going to break my glasses" said him.

Gary was silent and like a big baby, he lay down, face down, and began to look at the screen of his cell phone, and dazzled by the brightness of the device, a little later he fell asleep.

A few days later Gibon forgot a razor in the bathroom, and he knocked on the bedroom door three times, Gibon wasn't going to open it but thought better of it, he opened it and when he did, there was Gary handing the razor to Gibon, like a repentant baby, Gibon, took it silently expressed his gratitude and closed his door again.

The second week of May began on a Friday 13th where the dogs barked and the wolves howled, Gibon always thought that the nature of the evil one was always cowardice, people were very sensitive about the scourge of the corona virus or COVID-19, plus the forced quarantine, where most needed to "stay home", so many were exasperated, manhandled by violence, insensitivity, and arrogance, that day had to resort three patrolmen of the 50th precinct, required to impose order, this time they were not there because someone tried to steal, but by the condition of intolerance of some.

It turned out that in one of the sections there was one last packet of disinfectant left and one of the club members grabbed it before another who had also seen it and who had thought of grabbing it, the second one claimed that the disinfectant belonged to him, therefore it had to be given to him, as Miquelon, Don Crispin's son, one of the members of the pack, who worked as employees of the club Bulley saw what happened, trying to make a fair judgment, told the second of the buyers:

"Friend, 'the fish doesn't belong to the one who sees it first, but to the one who catches it', he caught it before you".

The second of the men who had seen the product without having time to grab it, in seconds, took out a knife and put it to Miquelon's neck, at the same time that he said to him:

"What's wrong with you, "jabado[9]", because he is white like you, and I am black you're giving the reason to him, do you want to die now?"

At that moment everything stopped, many witnesses saw what was happening and called the police, who were soon in the building basement where Bulley operated, several spoke to him at the same time, they told him that if he had a family he should think of them, that everything would pass, and that he better remove the knife from the neck of the employee, and so the man reflected and removed the knife, just at the time that the police approached.

---

[9] Light-skinned person

Since there were many witnesses, Bulley's manager explained what happened to the police, but since Miquelon did not want to be charged, he was handcuffed and taken to the 50th Precinct where he was sent to the Bronx Behavioral Center for a psychiatric evaluation.

Miquelon, being white, turned green, he had just survived the corona virus, he had infected his father, and the father infected Moraima, his mother, the late Crispin's wife, and it could be said that because of him, Crispin, his father, had ended up in the hospital, and indirectly also Moraima, his mother, since all three had been hospitalized.

Mother and son had survived, but Crispin, his father, had succumbed, and Miquelon had just returned from the leave of absence that Bulley had issued to him for the COVID-19, to face another trial of that nature at work.

It had already been told, that the pack was kept in quarantine, which had given motive to occult sect to send a remnant of Garget's to watch closely, provoke and manipulate Gibon, who was the only one of those operating in Bulley, who remained serving, but Garget's who had been sent to operate as a pressure group, finding Gibon alone, wanted to impose on him, give him the passengers they wanted to see if they would impose, instead Gibon told them:

"You can't come from Garget to damage our business, we here, we don't charge prices as high as the ones you charge, besides, you can't pretend to draw a line to me either, neither you are my friends, nor I am your friend, so if you made a pact with occult sect to pretend that you control me, you are wrong, only God controls me."

At that moment a passenger was coming out and Rony who was on his way back, and saw that Cholinfe had asked for a quantity that scared the customer away, said to be heard, as usual:

"When you leave, we are going to have to reformulate the prices, that you have come to damage."

Rony's expressions angered Cholinfe and Anjo, who took the lawsuit personally and began to argue, and Gibon who was talking on the phone had not noticed that Anjo who was from Garget, went first, the Arab interrupted him to let him know, Gibon nodded that it was okay, but Anjo, began again to throw hints and Gibon answered him:

"Don't talk to me, I don't talk to rats."

Although Anjo, kept grumbling, Gibon ignored him, anyway, the discussion was dissolved by the appearance of Mark the deputy administrator, who demanded silence.

In fact, in terms of survival, a theory had been generated that said: "Loosen so that your neighbor grabs, but if you loosen and your neighbor doesn't grab, then you grab for yourself".

The permanence of Gibon in that place was due to God's disposition, who was always looking for a way for him to stay, because there had been so many oppositions, that if Gibon had not had the support of the Holy Spirit, all those incarnated demons would have done with him what they wanted, but no, they had no power or strength to overcome him, God was with Gibon.

Since Gibon's arrival at that place, it was a war that seemed like it would not stop, the first one to slander him was a brown man named Williams, it was about seven o'clock at night, and supposedly a woman had talked to him to ride her home, and he went to get some boxes, and the woman was outside and without Gibon knowing that she had talked to Williams. She dealt with Gibon, and as his price was more attractive than Williams', Gibon was putting the purchase in the car when Williams arrived. He tried to take it out but Gibon did not allow it because the woman changed her mind and did not want to go with him, he wanted to rebel and Gibon confronted him and with affection he touched Williams' shoulders with his open hands telling him:

"Calm down, Williams, leave it."

This was enough for Williams who called the police and told them that Gibon was choking him, that was a lie, a week after that they put Gibon in court, Williams went to the airport to ride a passenger and at Kennedy Airport, they discovered that he was driving with a suspended license, they took his car and put him to pay an amount of money that he did not have saved up, and in that way he ended up paying for the mistake of slandering Gibon.

Williams was later forced to drop Gibon's charges so that Gibon would drop his, because under pressure from the police, Gibon charged that Williams tried to attack him with a knife, and the police found the knife on him.

A little later Arnulfo appeared, with two proposals, either they would buy a Jeepeta he was selling or they would let him work at Bulley.

Gibon bought him the Jeepeta, Burdock tried to steal a horn, but Arnulfo denounced him and Gibon took it from him.

After some time Arnulfo returned to be allowed to work, he had gone with a car rented by the distributor, and insisted, and insisted until he was allowed to work, but then later, at the request of the organization of evil, Burdock indisposed them against Gibon, and he had also stopped talking to him.

One day Williams arrived with an outburst of alcohol and drugs, Arnulfo argued with him, and he introduced a key in his forehead, and Arnulfo chased him with the police and Williams fled to North Carolina and never returned.

All this led to Gibon distancing himself from the members of the pack, and he only spoke to Jochelo, Fredesvindo and sometimes Rocko. The bribes from the organization of evil so that they would make fun of Gibon distanced them, and he had limited himself to only answering those who spoke to him.

Most of the members of the pack were bipolar, but the craziest were Cholinfe and Burdock, they thought very little when they spoke, everything they said was voiced, and they barked to terrify, but deep down, they were more cowardly than lynxes, they were like the dwarf Gary, who was always shouting for attention.

Gary the dwarf, was like the Pack's pet, he always visited, when he left Stoping, a supermarket where he went to pack the purchase in exchange for tips ranging from a dollar, or more, that was an every day mission, then one day Alonzo the Boxer proposed to take him to the Tavern, to help him keep watch. The tavern was a place where they drank drinks and Alonzo the Boxer ran a game of dominoes, decks of cards, and dice, for each hand Alonzo charged 25 cents, and the players placed their bets underneath.

One Sunday afternoon, the diners gathered, Alonzo the Boxer invited Burdock to participate, and the dwarf Gary diligent and skilled, was mounted on the counter where he would watch better and like a doctor Watson used a pair of binoculars with which he delighted in contemplating in the distance, the movements of those involved.

The evening looked like it was going to be wonderful, but a little recklessness on Burdock's part spoiled it, as it turned out, they set up a hand of poker and when they were in the middle of the game, Gary the dwarf noticed through his binoculars that Burdock was drawing cards up his sleeve, and with all the splendor of excitement cupping his hand as if it were a loud speaker he called out:

"Burdock is cheating; he's got another set of cards up his sleeve."

Everyone looked silently towards the counter where Gary the dwarf stood, and Mazan bula, a fat man who competed with the maps, for the tattoos he had, suddenly turned the table, and instantly there was a rush, rush, where the bottles whistled through the air, and one of them came close to hitting Gary the dwarf who, turning his head to one side, avoided it, became desperate, felt so uneasy, that he discovered that the counter was too high to jump, he shouted at the top of his lungs:

"Let me down from here, let me down from here, 'shiiiiit' I 'knooooooow me," he said, in a voice deeper than a baritone, so the bartender, who at the beginning of the fight was serving a beer, suddenly found himself in the middle of the room, and ran to the counter, grabbing Gary, and lowering him instantly, but when he tried to put him on the floor, he received a bottle in the arm, making his wrist tremble, feeling an unpleasant pain that induced him to release the dwarf in the air, who was still floating holding on to the bartender's arm without putting his feet on the floor, he fell turning around while protecting himself to the inner shadow of a table, it was a fight of all against all, while others were rolling on the floor, Mazambula was strangling Burdock, who with his tongue half out cried out for Alonzo, and said: "I'm not going to let go of the dwarf, I'm going to let go of the dwarf!"

"Oh Alonzo, Oh Alonzo."

Alonzo, who heard him, came to his aid, and threw a few punches in the ribs at Mazambula, who was like a mass, but that had no effect, because Mazambula was not only tall and fat, but had a body like an elephant. Rupertico, one of those who were losing at the card game, and who felt resentful, came up behind Alonzo and gave him a whistling blow that drove him to kiss the floor.

Yayo the bartender, seeing that everything had gotten out of control, called 911, which immediately departed from the 34th precinct, so it did not take long to appear between Neagle and Thayer streets, five patrol cars had arrived, and two fire ambulances.

The players, hearing the ambulance sirens and the noise of the police, tried to escape out the back door, including

But those who did not know the escape mechanism were caught and the wounded were taken to the hospital, while Gary the dwarf was not detected because he slipped into the garbage bin under the counter. That night something serious had happened, the tavern had been marked for suffering, a gas leak generated a dangerous fire that in the shortest time, reduced to ashes the historic joint, whose expanded flames approached the edge of the adjoining building where a laundry operated, causing damage that for a while disabled the laundry service.

The neighborhood was in a fuss, and many religious people commented that this was the work of the devil, who was always beating with his tail all those who made a pact with him, giving him a time of happiness, and the rest of the way generating tragedy and evil.

A few days later, there stood Alonzo at Bulley's door, waiting for someone to come out to transport him, it was his turn, and in all the splendor of color, he was shining in the sunshine.

He was dark with bluish skin, he was dazzled by white women, because he believed that a beautiful woman would always motivate even chimpanzees, and that belief had been clinging to his psyche since he was a child, when he went to the zoo and saw a white girl, and discovered that that presence induced him to jump up and down with excitement. Since then, he had grown up convinced that the presence of a white woman would always induce the grace of monkeys when visited at the zoo, and would easily befriend them, so he had resorted to such a strategy, in order to attract the attention of white women, seeking to move where they walked, so he had formed a cord of obsession, and when he saw Beatrice or Mary Ann, approaching the front door where one entered or left Bulley, his pupils would dilate, as he tasted, as if something sweet had been in the groove of his palate, he would close his eyes, as if praying for the grant's favor, that his sight might enjoy the presence of such beauties, but Burdock, being reckless, was always on the watch.

"Open your eyes, Alonzo and stop hypocrisy, you are not a Christian to pretend to be praying, besides, these women will not pay attention to you even in a dream, wake up, do not humiliate your race, from the moment you see a white woman you start to dream," Burdock specified.

"Burdock, don't be impertinent, here no one has a moment to rest even to admire the natural creation," said Alonzo, and those who heard him laughed.

On the other hand, Donko, who although the trials of life had hardened him, listened in silence, but the subject, induced him to give his opinion showing his human sensitivity:

"Listen to me, there is no one here who knows more than me, Alonzo is right, the woman is a flower, whose perfume is inhaled with emotion, so let her receive therapy in the heart, it is the sign that he is still alive, feeling such a vibration."

"Wow, he's even a poet" Petro said, while the others laughed.

In reality, the carnivalesque culture of the system induced

people to make a trumpet out of a whistle, occult sect and the organization of evil, they knew it, and they were always looking for ways to keep those who could think distracted.

In any circumstance the technology had advanced and it was easy to detect artifacts, or all kinds of components containing explosives, leaving the bathrooms at the mercy of the users because it was forbidden to install camera inside them to preserve the privacy of users, had created the detector of explosive slingshots, which consisted of a simple device similar to the smoke detector, and the ozone detector, with the difference that this one, at the same time was a kind of drone that when passing in front of any explosive matter, it would immediately send a signal to a central, that would indicate the direction of where any explosive content was being handled, passing the alert to the anti-explosive unit of the nearest precinct, being achieved in this way to give a strong blow to terrorism, whose mechanism prevented it from acting freely, as they did before.

CHAPTER 27

TALENT

In this sense, the expression that "there will always be people greater and smaller than others" was enhanced, obeying the function of limitation imposed by ignorance, because knowledge saves and elevates the overcome souls.

But while the others suffered, Gibon pitied and sang:

"Espaminonda Eleodoro, kept in her house a treasure, everyone thought it was gold, Espaminonda Eleodoro, had an ideal treasure the carnival queen, everyone in town loved her, and she looked at none, Espaminonda was the hard, who had it every day, all aspired to it, and she was like a star, her light radiated at night, and the sun by day had it, she was called Star, light her nature, was a Goddess incarnate, of tender and pleasant nobility.

She was radiant and exalted, her condition was light, and everyone who saw her loved her youth.

Eleodoro kept her, like a treasure in scale, her condition of tenderness, broke the ties, and Eleodoro knew that she was grace and harmony.

That's why the people honored her, as their philosophy, because in every direction, it was the light they wanted, only the titan Eleodorus, was the one who presume her."

At the end they applauded him and some members of the club approached him to congratulate him and to comment that they did not know that he was the bearer of that talent, while the uneducated ones were filled with envy and did not even approach him, because they saw how others admired him and they lent themselves to sharpen their resentments.

Winter had still burnt the tops of the trees, spring was not yet sprung, and the sun peeped out with certain timidity.

A new day in the monotonous melody, and the Pack in list, waiting their turn, Rony arriving and open-mouthed expressed:

"The only friend I have here is the pastor, the others are treacherous," he said referring to Gibon.

He bowed to him without saying anything, and the others, feigned a smile. And Gibon hummed:

"The American females would like to kiss them, with their stars and stripes, that look well adorned, and in the expression of love, the definition remains, of a rainbow of races that inspire me from home.

All yearn for his justice, all cry out for his love, they merited forgiveness, showing their self- denial, their breasts seen from afar, they brought you comfort.

How beautiful she is, the woman of any race, she is sweetness to wake up, she is tender to dance!

Leaving an example in her action, of favorite forgiveness, the woman of any race, is tender in her sensation, is a pleasing sign of love".

Skillful as his expression, they were so admired that Gibon

forgave them, and for the sake of forgiveness, new proofs were hoisted on every note of love.

On the other hand, Estrace insisted on maintaining communication with Gibon, because the Cat paid very well for her services and to avoid losing such coins, Estrace would call Gibon and then close the phone and when Gibon returned the call, then she would act confused, and like a madwoman she would answer:

"Hi, you're Carlo's nephew?" And since Gibon knew she was trying to annoy him, he intentionally answered her:

"Sorry, wrong number" And he would close the phone.

Everything was because the Cat had Gibon's phone intervened, and whenever she needed to know his location, she would make someone call him, and if he answered the phone, she immediately had the coordinates to locate him and follow his steps, in the hope that Gibon would make a mistake, to justify himself and bring him down, but the power of that one, overcame her evilness, however, God was and remained with Gibon.

Occult sect and the organization of evil, as we know, used to distribute the tasks and sometimes, they acted at the same time after some target.

However, everything was set, as the organization of evil infiltrated the governments of the planet, forcing the puppet rulers to plunder the public treasury at the sacrifice of the people, in order to pay a fee to them, in the refined style of sacrifice, for the sake of corruption.

While the people "whispered":

"A nation that tolerates and induces corruption is an impression without ethics, without reason and without honor, which by not sowing the example, leads the people to oppression."

And Gibon, worried about the lack of love, which the population was losing, expressed his intention:

"Pain, that entity that shows itself through my bones and my skin, often tells me here I am, and although its presence bothers me, I have been forced to tolerate it, because behind every action of harassment, I mourn the pain, it never makes me cry, I am stronger than that," said Estrace after her attempts to make believe that Gibon was the definition of her cat management, lasted several months without communicating with him, implying that she had received a slice of the resources dating back to 91, then after a few months she went to Bulley like the sphinx of an apparition, made believe that all was well, and instead of looking for Gibon she avoided him, she suddenly appeared with a certain amount of sass, and as if nothing had happened leaving a message for Gibon, to pick her up, that she needed to talk to him, when Gibon went for her, she asked him to accompany her to a catholic church in Yonkers, she gave her a lost address and after making him ride around a few times, Gibon stopped to ask someone on the way, and she without knowing the people who were asked for the address of the church started to talk to them about her personal matters, and to ask them for phone numbers, which in the moment were denied to her, while Gibon out of politeness, not to leave her with the word in her mouth waited for her to make a pause, and told her:

"Estrace, don't be crazy, how can you give your personal information to people you don't know"

She kept silent and Gibon accelerated, when they arrived at the church, because there was no parking lot he stayed outside waiting for her to return and when she came back, she appeared tearful and depressed.

She kissed Gibon on the cheeks, and then laid her head on his shoulders, who, surprised, withdrew it diplomatically when she commented:

"I'm going to marry you."

"What?... you are going to marry me? And why is that? What are you up to?" asked him. She kept silent, then she took him by the hand and led him to a stone located behind the church, there she told him about Tody, about a supposed boyfriend she had who ignored her, etc.

Gibon listened to her in silence, then they went into a mini market where they bought sodas and coffee, which they enjoyed on the way back.

The next day mysteriously the roof of the room where Gibon was sleeping collapsed, and a day later, a pickup truck as tall as a truck smashed the back of his transportation.

The organization was acting, insisted on making it difficult for Gibon, while Estrace tried to get him out of his habitat, then, she invited him to the beach, Gibon tried to please her, she searched the wrong address in the GPS, and they got lost on the way, Gibon was moving in a circle and she reiterated it to him, and said angry words, and blamed him that they were three hours on the road without being able to find the route to the beach, and they stopped to ask, but people did not know how to explain, and she went into crisis behaving in an uncontrolled manner and insulting Gibon, who admonished her in the following way:

"You are a woman with a high level of lack of control, who often lives lying, trying to take people out of context in a malicious way, you tell me that we are going alone to the beach, and now in your anger you tell me that your mom is waiting for you there, and besides your mom, there is a group believing that by being near me, you will be able to justify belongings that have been withheld from me with the intention of appropriating them, you are a dangerous and crazy woman, who only likes to use people for your benefit, but you are wrong with me, and anyone who tries to take one dollar of what belongs to me will go to jail," he said.

"No, because you've got me hanging around the same place for three hours," she replied.

Gibon laughed as he told her:

"It's not my fault, you searched for the address wrong. God has us like Moses, walking in a circle, because it is not convenient for me to go where you are trying to take me."

Estrace was increasingly losing control, she began to hit the windows, and Gibon watched her with a high degree of patience, while she became irritated and everyone she asked wanted to make her believe that Gibon had been driving her for three hours and had lost their way intentionally. She saw a green taxi and stopped him, and asked him for how much he could ride her to Cony Island, he said $30, and she hurriedly grabbed her belongings from the back of the car and got into the green taxi as she said to him, "I'm going to take her to Coney Island," she said:

"Don't call me anymore."

Gibon patiently replied: "The one who calls me is you," as he watched the taxi speed away from the place.

Three hours later, Estrace called him with the biggest nerve of her existence, to tell him to pick her up in Manhattan but, Gibon who knew she was going through a high emotional deficiency answered ok, but left her waiting and never contacted her again.

Then again on another occasion Estrace called him and tenderly asked:

"Dear, where do you live?"

And Gibon replied her:

"On the street, and I sleep in the car."

Estrace smiled, and kept silent, she knew that Gibon didn't trust her, because she was only looking to benefit from him.

However, she was unaware that the pack had called her "the cat woman", because whenever she saw a cat she was so sensitive that tears came to her eyes and she made it clear that a cat was worth more to her than a human.

A few days later, he saw her pass in front of Bulley, she was distracted and Gibon calling her by her name greeted her, she turned her head, she did not recognize him because Gibon was wearing a mask that covered his face, but when she recognized him she smiled without saying anything, and once again she turned to see him, smiled again and went on her way.

CHAPTER 28

DISTRUST

The organization of evil did not cease in their evil deeds, and once again, trying to break Gibon's health to disable him, they crashed him from behind, while he was waiting for the light to change, the thing was that they wanted to win time, they did not want to release the money, and had begun to pressure Robert Wolff, Gibon's lawyer, so that he would delay the process, they wanted to confuse Gibon.

However, Gibon continued the fight and also put pressure on Robert Wolff and told him:

"You are my lawyer, not the opposing party's one, so it is your duty to keep me informed of what they are up to and what they are offering you because they will have no peace until they return what belongs to me."

"Yes, I'm working on it, I'm waiting for confirmation of the date for the litigation."

"You have three cases with me, so start solving the 1991 case, that money is already out, and you have to take it from whoever has it, they have been conspiring against me, in a fragrant condition of discrimination and racism, and it is not good to break the law by conspiring against me, besides I have noticed that you are buying time for a purpose that I ignore, I want no excuses, about that case, I will not allow anyone to mock me any more than they have mocked me so far, the police mistook me for someone else and illegally sent me to jail, and now it is time for justice, and I will fight with everyone, and against anyone who pretends to take me for pious and lazy."

"Don't worry Gibon, I'm working to find a solution," he said.

"It's ok Robert, I hope for a solution, it's time, it's been 29 years and now it's God's time to do justice, and the demons have no power or faculty to stop the will of the divine."

"Okay Gibon, I'll call you in two weeks."

"Well Robert, I hope so, see you soon."

They said goodbye, and Gibon was a little calmer, they needed time to make up the fraud and pass it off as evidence, to Gibon, to justify himself before justice and public opinion, they knew that Gibon articulated the pamphlets and that he could easily denounce his crimes, whose subject matter could induce the Justice Department to an investigation.

Obviously, as the occult sect and the organization of evil, had had for long in their hands Gibon's compensation funds, and had not given it to him, so to justify their condition without exposing their corruption, being Gibon insured with the state farm insurance company, the emissaries of the occult sect and the organization of evil, had reached an agreement with it, to justify the distribution of those funds, to generate some accidents and pass part of the funds to Gibon, claiming that 29 years had passed since the case that led to the compensation was generated, and that by the time they were at that time, much time had passed, and therefore the politicians of the city were not interested in spreading their negligence in terms of racism and discrimination against minorities.

That's how the state farm insurance company got involved in Gibon's affairs, since he had been insured with them for many years, which not only charged him for car insurance but also, for a long time, charged him for insurance on a house that Gibon didn't have.

After the October 17th, 2016 accident, which they had tried to use to cover up the 1991 case, they acted to provoke a series of accidents involving Gibon, claiming that it was a way to recover the settlement funds from him, since he had been the subject of an alleged fraud.

When Gibon discovered such thing, he thought that even for his own benefit he would not lend himself to such an act of corruption.

Then when Gibon realized what they were doing and not being able to continue with the cover-up of the 1991 compensation using the 2016 case, they opted to provoke the accident on July 1st, 2021, and the state farm insurance company referred him to the Par Chester clinic in the Bronx, where since he appeared on that stage, they assumed a manipulative posture telling him: "These exams are for compensatory purposes" At the same time they applied radiation with the intention of photographing his heart, while he asked that what did his heart have to do with the blows from his accident?

However, the real intention was to make him sick in order to disable him, and thus not pay the compensatory funds.

Then the clinic administrator told him:

"You need to take emergency insulin."

Gibon looked at him as if he were scrutinizing him, and answered:

"I'm not going to take insulin, I'm not afraid of death."

Then another member of the medical staff pleaded: "Oh, he's resisting. .... He's refusing," he said.

"I will not allow you to make me sick, nor leave me invalid," said Gibon, as he left.

A few days later he moved to another clinic, took on another family doctor, and began to examinate himself with Alex Berstein, while on his own he started to cleanse his body with natural root and leaf teas.

The radiation had affected his circulation and the pain in the affected parts had become sharp, then they tried to operate on his shoulders and legs, he received many calls and proposals to be disabled, but he did not listen and said:

"I will only retire when I reach the years I am due to retire, nor will I accept any late offers of employment," he said, as he assumed to continue to do delivery at Bulley, until the time merited.Gibon was strong and resilient, God had strengthened him, and by his example he sought to set the precedent that no human being anywhere on the planet would allow himself to be silently vilified without breaking the bonds of torment by removing the foot of the oppressor from his neck.

Gibon had learned that in New York, you couldn't even trust the fingers on your hands, because if by mistake you pulled out a finger, and the pulled out finger was the wrong one, if the eyewitness was violent, they might take the position of hitting you, and it was that most of the inhabitants of that context had no friends, they had interests, everyone was exploring the Achilles heel of the other, in order to verify if they could get something from the person involved, even if it was to sell it.

Ana P met Gibon in the community, she was very outgoing and Gibon found out that she once worked with a lawyer in New York, he asked her to introduce him to one, that's where Robert Wolff came from, "she begged him, to help Gibon", however, Gibon had given her four cases for Robert to work, Ana P was a notary and notarized, however, Gibon trusted Ana P, but it seemed that the other four cases had been sold behind Gibon's back, and it had been almost eight years before Gibon had realized what had happened, so Robert was dragging his feet, waiting to see what happened again.

Because the case that the shick was handling had been passed on to Robert Wolff, after that one had a year and a few months, he convinced Gibon to sell it for 35,000 dollars and swore to him that despite the attempt to camouflage that case for another one, it was an "all transit" insurance case that had nothing to do with the state's farm insurance company, and he asked Gibon to bring the documents, Gibon agreed even though he knew that the Maxi Gómez case was still pending, which was the 91 case where Gibon had been confused with the 91 case, and that by resorting to various tricks they were trying to delay the compensation until the time came for Gibon to retire, since they had not been able to disable him, nor send him to cause accidents.

All that was easy to understand because in the systems where the mafia operated and was infiltrated in the governmental strata, all kinds of corruption were raised, so Gibon kept studying the Robert Wolff's attitude, since he was not sure if Robert had received some kind of glorious greeting behind his back, since the occult sect and the organization of evil, did not let one pass, and were always ready to bribe even the cats in order to achieve their purpose.

Robert Wolff, despite being a skilled advocate in accident cases, suddenly and unintentionally found himself manipulated in such a way that when he tried to say something to Gibon, an undercover secretary would say to him:

"Don't tell him anything, we still don't know what the organization will determine," she said, and Robert was forced to obey.

But Gibon didn't understand how it was possible that if Robert knew that the undercover secretary was dictating the rules to be followed, why was he offering information that he couldn't back up?

All this comes to reference because one day when Gibon and he were having a telephone conversation, he informed Gibon that he had gotten him an offer of 60.000 dollars and that he was going to try to get him 10,000 dollars more, but apparently, his counselors admonished him and then the next day he called him and changed his mind telling him that he had made a mistake, that the offer was 35,000 dollars, of which he and the Shick would take 33% and Gibon would get the rest. Gibon accepted it without stopping to think that behind that change was the manipulation of the organization of evil and occult sect, for the same reason, when a president or a governor refused to do what they wanted, they sent a beautiful woman to flirt with him, and "as the flesh is weak", prepared the environment for such a reaction, they reciprocated the flirtation, and some time later, they denounced the act with a scandal of public opinion so great that many times those involved had to resign from office giving space to the corrupters.

It was necessary to eradicate the culture of dishonesty, on earth, for a renewal of the spirit, where other conduct patterns for a better balance of the planet, and a better understanding of who we are and what our origins are, and the reason for the existential trial, Gibon used to say....

"In New York, although the governor had signed the tax reform laws, the protests continued and it seemed to be, not to state it radically, that the police power would be reduced, and that the minority sectors would begin to have the upper hand, but in fact, it was not so, because once these reforms were in place, crime skyrocketed, and chaos was the daily Hail Mary.

All these problems were spreading all over the planet, the monotony was already populating the conscience of the peoples that looked stagnant, many did not know what to do, and others lived in the glory of the past, and living in the glory of the past crystallized the human being, because nothing had to remain static. Therefore, it was not necessary to cling to anything to let flow what was to come, it was necessary to let go to self-release, what was experienced was already lived, it was not necessary for events to be repeated, because what was yesterday, would not be today, and even if things were similar, they would always be different..

Everything changes as time goes by, even if you love the old, the new will always come.

That was one of the truths that Jesus Christ spoke, but very few understood it, because "many are called and just a few are chosen!"

In reality the forgiveness of men is generated at the moment of awakening, at that time when life has already been understood, because the being experiences all that they chose to experience, that is why it is often said that one should not say "of this water I will not drink" because when thirst is felt, all water must be drunk.

While everything was going on, the troubadours were singing:

"Some said they were thieves, others said they were proofs, those voices, who were they referring to?

They have lost their goodness, they have no more mercy, they have become evil, they have become evil.

Where will we turn to, the good guys have got confused, now we have to test him with saliva and hair.

No one knows where you're going, and as you pass a corner, you're provoked by evil.

The youth no longer think, they will live like zombies, and if God does not appear, they will herd him with the whip.

It is time to wake up, stop living online, for the earth is approaching the time of what they will say, and many greater tests, not too late will come.

Certainly, we all bring a selection, or an assignment, which at the time of revealing itself, it is in vain to resist, because without your being able to control it, it walks towards that which you flee, and all that you despised approaches you to embrace you.

Many times there are opportunities disguised as mistakes, and what you thought was evil, becomes goodness."

That is why Kinkin Joseph Valentine, disconsolate and without clergy, pronounced what he lived, and to those who treated him, with gentleness he told:

"Before you saw me I was a man of power, after I lost my position, none of you want to see me."

This is how Kinkin Jose Valentin expressed himself, Cariñito's cousin, fighter and party animal, sold garbage by the kilo, and intoxicated the nation, but he did not choose wealth, and acted in free will, and one day he was talking in the streets drowned in alcohol, America subtracted him for a better life, his wife abandoned him, the fortune took from him, saying that the heritage that he showed in New York, were spoils of inheritance that he never reported.

The government took him, gave the wife's her part, and he

who fought for it, the government forgot about it, exchanged his freedom for only half, and the other half that remained, the wife took the money and when he wanted to investigate, not even a penny was found, this upset him so much that even Ruperto Rene Cariño suffered from his discomfort. He took a chance in Bulley, seeking God's mercy, but his faith gave way and he saw his cousin Kinkin, who drowned in alcohol, this grieved Cariño. Kinkin José Valentin, was a fighter without honor, whom his people forgot.

While Cariño René in Bulley, concentrated on making a new life, while his cousin Kinkin, felt discriminated against as if he was a relax, until he gave himself up to drink.

In New York he suffered, and Vianela deceived him, the matter of the money he took from the people, and doing honor to his cause, he gave it back to the people, and Kinkin, who gave it away, left him in the street.

This grieved Cariño, Kinkin, if he was a champion of the sale of sawdust, he impressed Vianela, with money and without love, that's why she sold him, when the DEA made a deal with her, even Cariño trembled. He gambled the girdle, he was an expert on finances, and Vianela sold him, when the DEA bought him, in those years of prison, Kinkin regenerated, and in his eagerness to be better even the floor mopped, something already transformed, he contacted his cousin, and Cariño accepted him, showing his sympathy in Bulley every day.

The pack vainglory him, Plutarco Rene Cariño, lives making his chants.

While Cariño consolidated, Kinkin lost everything, the money that he reached, Vianela spent it, she agreed with the DEA, and the money gave her, when Kinkin had fulfilled the years that the judge dictated, he thought he had money, but Vianela spent it, and THE DEA snatched the largest amount, it was so much his disappointment that he became drunk, it was as he took to the streets and even the neighborhood amused.

CHAPTER 29

CONSPIRACY

The punch bowl had been repaired, that was the name that the pack had attached to the vehicle in which Burdock worked, now the bodywork looked better, and as Gibon and that one, did not have good communication, Gibon asked Jochelo to find out the address of where Burdock's repairs were made, to take his cars to repair some sabotages generated by the organization of evil and the occult sect, which did not cease to vandalize his transportation, as a way to prevent him from working and to subordinate himself to their offers.

For this reason Gibon had lost trust to visit the mechanics he frequented because having the emissaries of the organization of evil behind him, they would come forward to offer him bribes in exchange for fixing what he needed and damaging what he didn't need fixing.

In the trial period Gibon had gone through an Odyssey, because he was followed by the delegates of the occult sect, and the organization of evil, and where they saw Gibon parked, they sent a mechanic to his home to damage his car, the next day when he intended to leave for work, he used to lose long hours stranded, waiting for a mechanic to show up to repair it,

The organization of evil used to resort to these techniques of domestic terrorism, to get Gibon out of circulation, so that he would cease to make delivery in Bulley, so that they would receive the city's budget to create a position for him, so there were many who were after the purpose of being Gibon's boss.

The organization of evil, and occult sect sometimes pretended that Gibon did not speak English, so they justified their long wait, however Gibon could read and write English fluently, but because of the racist stance, they thought they could re-violate his rights, again they were wrong, because Gibon would leave them alone, and sometimes, even made them believe that they would get away with it, but in a retroactive conditioning, they did not, Gibon thought that they had not and would not get away with it.

They were wizards of evilness, but the universe defined the cadence of the true, and none of those who were called to get involved would have loopholes to escape, because even Gibon's esteemed niece was used for an experiment, thinking they could bring him down, claiming to her that what they were doing was a way to clarify that he had never been involved in any degenerative act such as drug dealing or any kind of addiction.

Zuly, convinced of their good faith, agreed, but as she had told them, the organization of evil had been after Gibon for over 29 years without him realizing it, and on the morning of that day they had contacted Zuly, they had noticed that Gibon was going to the Department of

Motor Vehicles in Yonkers, and they were following him, to the extent that when he returned, after turning in his license plates, they had placed a clear plastic bag filled with cocaine, marijuana (cannabis sastabis) and other drugs with the intention that when he saw it he would bend over and touch it so they could photograph him and make a case that would disqualify him from compensation.

Because Gibon kicked the bag and kept walking, they turned to Zuly, to call him and offer him a typical meal from his home country.

So that the prediction would be fulfilled that in the apocalyptic age "there would be no son for a father, no father for a son, no brother for a brother, no nephew for an uncle", Zuly showed up in a car driven by a stranger to bring him a sancocho[10,] something he found odd, but since she had her personal address at Gibon's apartment while staying at her boyfriend's house in Yonkers, Gibon, unaware of the purpose, accepted the food.

The man who accompanied her did not show his face and had the front of the car facing north, ready to return. Gibon asked her who her companion was; she replied that he was her boyfriend's friend, whom he had asked to take her to drop off the food ration.

Gibon had not yet realized what was happening, but on his way back from the border of Yonkers and New York City, between Broadway and 261st, there was a bus of the route 9 of the city, waiting for him to board it, there was no other passenger than him, it seemed that before there was another bus that had more passengers, because that one,

____

[10] Traditional Latin American soup

was prepared to be boarded in such a way that as expected happened and he boarded it , but something strange was happening, and in the front seats, where he was supposed to sit, appeared several bags of marijuana, creating a supposed atmosphere of temptation, but since Gibon saw it he told the driver:

"Hey what's going on with you men? Clean this seat, I don't smoke," he said.

"Oh, what happened?," answered the driver, pretending to be surprised, being aware of what was happening.

"You know, and you are seeing what is happening, this marijuana is not mine, and they put it in the area where I am sitting, with some intention, but, I'm not going to fall, pick up your filth," Gibon ordered him, with determination.

The driver got up and picked up three bags that had been distributed on the first three seats.

After that Gibon compared what had happened on his return from the Department of Motor Vehicles, and what had just happened.

He then complained to her sister about Zuly's actions, seeking to embarrass him.

His sister Lency, retorted, kicked and defended her daughter, and whenever Gibon tried to refer something about her, she changed the subject, one day when he was walking on 191st and Saint Nicholas, he saw Zuly looking at him and tried to avoid him, then he called her:

"Aye, what's wrong with you, what did you do against me, that now you're running away from me?" Gibon questioned.

Zuly, feeling uncovered, responded:

"I haven't done anything, but since you're angry, I wouldn't want to have any confrontations with you."

"It's not that I'm angry, but it makes me sad that my own family is selling me out for nothing."

"Stop that paranoia, no one is selling you out."

"That's right Zuly, 'do not do to your neighbor what you do not want them to do to you', because each one receives what they sow." Gibon replied.

"Okay, I can't talk to you anymore, I have to go."

"Go with God, and I hope you get what you deserve."

Zuly didn't answer and was seen walking away, into the distance until she was lost after entering the reception area of a building.

A few months later, occult sect, in payment for her dubious behavior and servile actions, removed her from New York, moving her to Los Angeles, California, where she would pursue a career in acting and modeling for her daughter Jais.

CHAPTER 30

PROCESSING

Cervantes said that "the people were always ready to brand the wise as mad and the ignorant as wise" for humanity everything they did not understand was madness, and what looked different from its condition, was an aberration.

That pack was made up of dogs that barked but didn't always bite, although their greatest discomfort was in their economy, so they were always ready to sell their aunts, their mothers and their closest relatives, and even those they didn't know.

In Burdock's case, before he developed his evilness, his naivety outweighed, his restlessness, and as he was a provincial from the savannah of the sea, the first time he travelled to the capital, he had gone in the bed of a truck, and on dismounting he met a man crushing ice, and sprinkling raspberry on it, and he was so impressed that he was dumbfounded, so without asking, he went back to his village, and when he was asked about the capital city, he replied:

"Well Gertrudis, I'm not going back to that capital."

"And why?" Gertrudis said.

"Oh God, woman, in that capital they know so much, they're even going to manufacture people, you know the last thing I saw was a man selling crushed ice, with cow's blood" he said, referring to crushed ice with raspberry.

And it all happened when, passing from ignorance to evilness, he tended to confuse magnesia with gymnastics.

Since then, it had been a long time before he had embarked on a clandestine odyssey, but he had been marked by destiny all the same.

And at that time, he showed the greatest pride towards Gibon, his envy towards Gibon was so great that it became admiration, since the last time he wanted to hit Gibon, and the spirit knocked him down, since that moment he had assimilated the expression that "no one messes with the children of God".

Well, a few days later Gibon visualized Burdock greeting him with courtesy and respect, and so it was, even Gibon was surprised how Burdock had understood that he should never bother him, it was good to respect him, and so it happened.

On the other hand, the organization of evil, as we had mentioned, was looking for ways to plunder the compensation that had been generated in Gibon's favor for human rights violations, for which a series of undercover agents and members of the organization's harassment section were after him. They had resorted to a series of fraudulent actions ranging from theft of documents, to use his identity, because they had claimed in his name without letting him know, but making believe in the claim that Gibon authorized them to claim it, and then keeping the money, or claiming more and paying

Gibon less.

And as we mentioned before, the organization of evil and occult sect, had resorted to bribing all those who were close to Gibon to act as clowns in the set up circus, and as the city had offered Gibon a job many years had passed and had not given him anything, after those 28 years, at the 29th anniversary, they began the process of an apparent justice, with such an intimidating charge, that even the secretary of Homeland Security, had seized or tapped Gibon's email.

The organization of evil pretended to use Gibon, ignoring that God was talking to him, and when they tried to formalize the looting, God informed Gibon, who began to investigate on his own, but one day the organization of evil, thinking that they would get away with it, planned to cause an accident and after such action they involved a Russian to go through Gibon and hit him, but as God was watching over Gibon, the spirit accelerated the vehicle so that instead of Gibon hitting the Russian, it was the opposite, and it was the Russian who hit Gibon, and so it happened, but then the clinic where Gibon took the therapy had assigned him a lawyer of dubious reputation who the neighborhood called "SHIKH", who was tempted and accepted the conspirators' bribe to delay the case of the accident generated by the Russian Ilka, in 2016, to disguise the compensation of Gibon's human rights violation, in order to justify the embezzlement, but since Gibon was aware of what had happened, and he thought that if the conspirators and the organization of evil continued to act like a mafia, it could be that in the United States Justice system they would be imprisoned for prevarication, fraud and theft, having to spend more to get out, than what he would get from the repartition, since such actions, were typical of criminals vested with power.

Those who were still not sure of what was going to happen, were still waiting for the procedure, however, they could not do anything, because Gibon had the evidence at hand, and if they continued to resort to baseness, he was going to make a public denunciation, where the press would appear and the conspirators of the organization of evil would be in evidence.

When Gibon became aware of the SHIKH move, he removed it from the 2016 crash case, and handed it over to Mister Wolf, who also could not evade the bribery and manipulation of the organization of evil.

Mr. Wolf, also, was buying time to see how he could present his defense, without muddying the conspirators, and who, being aware of Gibon's human rights violation compensation case, was afraid just to bring up a past of pain and betrayal, because somehow no one was free of guilt to throw the first stone, all wanting to cover the sun with a finger, and as "between firefighters should not step on the hose", they sought to protect each other, pretending that all conspiracies generated were framed at the levels of simple evidence! How much hypocrisy, disguised as tenderness, how many betrayals that brought disappointments.

Those who remained away from such a conspiracy kept silent, while feeling a sense of shame. At that time, the level of humanity's consciousness was closer to stupidity than to justice.

However, Gibon thought that the best strategy when someone was fighting against two powerful groups where one represented the government and the other represented the criminals was to appear independent to the government and independent to the criminals, so that neither of the two adversaries could show power over the one they had chosen to persecute.

Gibon did not always get along well with the members of the pack, sporadically, he would talk to two or three, such as Fredesvindo, whom the pack called the soft one because supposedly when someone was careless he would skip his turn and ride the passenger, and with Jochelo, that obviously would answer those who greeted him or spoke to him.

Some members of the pack were bipolar, but the craziest one was Burdock, who was always bothering the others, or throwing hints.

After President Donald Trump, had defined the public charge package, food consumer business had dwindled and to reach the economic goal of the day, more hours had to be put in, Burdock saw Gibon in the morning, and then saw him again in the evening, and started throwing hints at him and said:

"Those without families don't take a break, I have a family and I take my break, rest and eat at home, but there are others around here, who just sleep in the car," he said.

It had been a few days since Burdock had been provoking him, but Gibon paid no attention to him, however, that day he forced to answer him:

"There are people who want to control others, but lack the ability to control themselves, in your blindness you think you can go around insulting and dropping hints to others, but what you just said, is only applied to you," Gibon said.

Burdock kept silent, not daring to answer him, many of them thought Gibon was unpredictable, and if they got violent, he could easily give them a portion of their own medicine.

Then a passenger came out, it was Yoryi's turn, who very seldom expressed himself in a loud voice, although when he joined the Pack, he kept muttering under his breath, and because of Burdock's influence, he began to keep silent in front of Gibon.

He had only had a problem with an evangelical to whom he had awakened the demons, and asking God's permission, as the pack said "he gave Yoryi, even with the bucket of water".

And it seems that this meeting of an angel and a Demon had brought some results, because before that time, Yoryi identified himself as an atheist, and then he was heard to say that he believed in God, and one of the pack who was called Vilinsky who heard him asked him:

"Oh Yoryi, what happened? Because you said you didn't believe in God," he said.

"Not before, now I do." Yoryi said with full determination.

Everyone who listened to him kept silent, nothing was said,

although others whispered, that he had changed his way of thinking, because the occult sect had granted him a credit to change the car, because after the persecution, the bribes had expanded.

Well, the thing is that after Yoryi left with his passenger, Burdock, who had been talking to him, came out and took refuge in his car, it was Gibon's turn.

"February was a gentleman, a month of love and understanding, the day that dawned was like a melody, and even the sun had unfolded with its rays, and the sweetness of its path.

I had forgotten to tell you that in the pack there was a close friend of Burdock's wife, who rode her, but we don't know if he charged her, her name was Kendra, but besides Kendra, there was an Arab, a Nicaraguan and a Mexican who arrived, and didn't last long, after he left, he didn't return, besides, Kendra was the only female among a group of macho men, and among them, some "faggots".

Kendra didn't show off much among the pack, she was about 60 years old, she worked distributing students in the educational system, and in her free time as the pack said "she was looking for her in Bulley" she also did delivery. Most of her time was spent on the phone, she had studied with nuns and had a very particular style of moving among everyone, she seemed shy although the pack sometimes made fun of her, to which she did not pay attention, she even attributed to her a courtship with little eyes, one that together with Don Franko moved the shopping carts that the members of the club vacated.

Don Franco lived by shouting for all to hear, that "Gibon was rich."

But that day, Gibon arrived and there was Kendra with Alonzo the boxer, who from the very moment he saw him arrive, hugged Kendra and said with all the subtlety of his expression, so that Gibon could hear him:

"Here I am with my woman Kendra, nobody talk to me bullshit!," he said.

"Be careful, don't let Ojitos hear you, so you won't have any problems," said Rony.

When the others heard it as a joke, they started to laugh, at that moment a passenger got out, it was Kendra's turn and she went to take him.

Ojitos was younger than Kendra, he had olive-colored eyes, but that romance ended as it began, and the pack did not cease to mock, and said:

"That relationship was nothing more than a couple of hookups".

Two women came out and it was Gibon's turn, they asked for Kendra, and Gibon explained the conditions, she appreciated his intention, and for the sake of hesitation, they rode with Gibon, when they were half way there, Kendra called out stealthily:

"Hi, what happened that you didn't wait for me?" Kendra asked.

"I had to leave, Sofi is in the hospital and I have to go see her."

"Oh yeah, say hi to her, I'll come with you later, and her

good-for-nothing mom, is she there?" Kendra asked.

"No, that gueva[11] is not here," her friend replied.

"Well, better this way, I'll call you later, I have a client coming out," Kendra said.

"Okay, see you later, we'll be right there."

At that instant Gibon turned left, as if turning back, stopped and proceeded to put down the purchase, she paid him $20, and after thanking him, turned back.

Returning to Bulley, he found some of the Pack, and Rony who saw Kendra arrive, said as a censure in front of those of more of the Pack:

"That woman has no job, she's been here since 11 in the morning, it's already 8:30 at night and she still hasn't left, she doesn't get tired of 'screwing around'," he said.

"You are just like her," Vilinsky said.

"But if that woman works at the school, why is she looking for taking these pennies from us?" Rony added.

"Oh, she thinks she have the right to win extra pennies too" Vilinsky said.

Rony grimaced, and a late night downpour surprised them all.

On another occasion he could no longer hide his bipolar condition, and a client came in to whom Gibon sang the hymn of the pack, as she liked it, she agreed with Gibon that when she left with him she would go, Jochelo was on duty and the boy followed behind, when the girl went out with Gibon she went and got on the car, the guy went and got alarmed, and

---

[11] Someone stupid.

Jochelo complained, he already saw her with Rocko Vulcano, a little far away she stayed, with ten dollars for tip to Jochelo she could calm him down, and the boy was silenced, she gave Gibon who rode her twenty dollars, and he was satisfied.

When Gibon returned, Rony felt envy, and began to slander, and Gibon did not kick him and said desperate and recording.

"Look here, the one who paints his hair with liquid."

And Gibon answered him:

"There's an old man in disagreement who doesn't inspire me with worry, he's bipolar and envious, he's like a rabid dog."

Rony liked to make fun of others but when they made fun of him, he went crazy.

And two women whom he wanted to take when they saw how that one got, chose Gibon, and the Rony sped up, and like a madman he proceeded, and although Gibon moved away the Rony vociferated, and the women said, that one got out of control, and envy and jealousy he felt.

There was in Bulley a group of servants who lived in constant contradiction with their egos, always looking for a reason to get Gibon's attention, on one occasion he had asked Katiana about a disinfectant product that was widely consumed during the pandemic, and she had told him that it hadn't arrived yet, but at the same time he added diverting the conversation:

"What would those who know me say if they saw me here,

as a personnel officer, talking to you?" She said as if trying to make Gibon aware of her position.

To which Gibon replied:

"I do not think they say or think anything, I graduate of high studies, and that does not take away the condition of Human."

She kept silent, she felt bruised in her ego, and from that moment on she began to ignore Gibon, and chose not to speak to him again, and although he greeted her, she did not answer his greeting, then seeing what was happening, Gibon also began to ignore her and stopped greeting her, and it was that the Latino by culture believed that when they occupied a position where they could make decisions, they had to pay obeisance, and that was not the nature of Gibon, instead Rene Cariño, was a magician knocking dust, he maintained a good relationship with Katiana and Mark, because he always like a Chihuahua lived licking the hands of those, that in spite of occupying positions of command in Bulley, they lacked a real leadership that allowed them to be loved and admired, but in spite of everything, the same Plutarco Rene Cariño tried to introduce himself to those by the eyes, for convenience, everything to make believe to the members of the pack, that he was linked with the bosses, looking to win the confidence of those, so that when he needed to manipulate some, that the others corresponded to his requirements.

On another occasion when the probation period for Gibon had begun, where everyone wanted to show off at Gibon's side because the occult sect and the organization of evil were giving bribes and perks.

At that time Mark and Gibon had a friendly approach and he had asked Gibon to rescue some shopping carts that had been abandoned, and wanted a photo as proof that he had recovered it, once Gibon had complied with Mark's request, Gibon was going to leave, but another member of the administrative group who was called Mary Ann, tried to make him leave through the back door, but Gibon refused and told Mark in her presence, that he was going out the same way he came in, and Mark approved, while she was surprised, because they didn't know Gibon and thought he was one of these simple members of the Pack, however Gibon interacted with the Pack, but his actions were independent.

Then Gibon had dreamed with her that in Bulley there was a celebration and that Gibon was one step higher than she was, and that from the bottom step she stretched her arms out to him, and hugged him.

Then she would go upstairs to move the carts that the customers were leaving outside, and Gibon would go up to help her and they would get friendly, but Mark, on the other hand, had started to play the foreman in front of Gibon, giving the impression that he was feeling small and wanted to spread his howls to get attention, and make it seem like he was a beast of honor.

CHAPTER 31

INDIGNATION

The indignant conscience of the people is not placated with arrogance, crime is generated as an indelible stain that never pales, so that justice neither feels nor suffers, it wounds without flinching, with implacable balance of wisdom, although it is branded blind.

For as I had told you, Occult Sect and the organization of evil, like "Alibaba and the forty thieves" had tried to distribute Gibon's compensation money to themselves, but when they were discovered they had to back out, and even some of those who got to spend some of it, and when Nona Shick was replaced from the case they tried to use to cover up the fraud, trying to buy time they agreed with Robert Wolff, the new attorney in the case who replaced Shick to stall the process until they could make up the missing funds.

It is true that "two big noses cannot kiss", but between dogs and hyenas there is little distance, it is not uncommon for them to sporadically "dance and shake hands".

The insurance company State Farm Insurance told Gibon that they needed a year to collect the money because by abrogation a court had assigned it to them for that purpose, the mafias of the system were given to the devil, having plundered money that belonged to the one to whom

God had assigned it.

However what State Farm Insurance had told Gibon happened before the fraud was discovered because in the files they had disappeared the October 17th, 2016 claim number: and left another accident they had caused him on May 31st, 2017, claim number: 32- 0538-D53, disappearing the October 17th, 2016, claim number: unsettled: 32-9H61-685, with that claim number they had tried to camouflage the compensation that dated back to 1991, of a case where the city had deprived Gibon of his freedom by confusing him with another by judging him in the middle of an illegal process, sending him to jail without identifying him, holding him for 9 months even though they had his fingerprints, honoring racism, prejudice and evilness, and knowing all the suffering that Gibon had brought to his life, yet conspiring to tie more burdens to him, and plunder his benefits, programming an intentional fraud loaded with malice, as if Gibon with thirty years residing in the city of New York, was a dog without human rights, this is called a crime against humanity, because he is not guilty, who being innocent is made guilty by those who have the power, but those who having the power allow and get involved in these acts of corruption and racism, these are the criminals invested with power, who have not developed the conscience to understand that power is to serve, not to be served by it. That was how, without identifying him they imprisoned him and as time passed without giving him the agreed work that they never gave him and whose payment funds accumulated, by then 29 years had passed, it was the year 2020 and instead they had another accident that they had sent to provoke on behalf of Gibon from the state of New York to the state of Atlanta, God did not allow his fraud to prosper and much less, that those who were not called to do so, benefited.

A great part of the pack was totally lacking in advanced instruction, so that it was not uncommon for one of them to come out at any moment with a bullying attitude, and the serene ones had to reprimand in silence and pray for the ungodly, in order to suggest the pride of such spirits, so that they would not provoke.

Jochelo was one of the most moderate, and one day stress induced him to assault one who is called Juan, and then be forced to cover his medicines, or to pay him for the wounds he had caused, with money, because in order that Juan, a war veteran did not install a plan of violence that would induce him to lose his life or go to jail, he negotiated what in a fit of rage he caused, because Juan had tried perhaps without any malicious intent, to jump over Jochelo's turn, taking the passenger that was in his turn, Juan bled to death and had to rush to the hospital, then, a day later, when Jochelo wasn't expecting him, on the hill at 238th and Fort Independent, he intercepted him in the middle of the street, three blocks from Bulley, ready to retaliate, but at the moment of proceeding, Rene appeared, who in the intention of avoiding a misfortune offered to guarantee that he was responsible for Jochelo would contribute five thousand dollars for hospital expenses, and Jochelo, to avoid something worse, accepted.

From then on he realized that violence was expensive, and that "it was not a good thing, since it kills the soul and poisons it."

And he knew what it was to act out of control, because he had experienced it in a past of bitterness and disaffection, because before doing delivery in Bulley, he had gone through a bitter moment that induced him to leave the profession of taxi driver, and was that the taxi commission and Limousine had fed him so much that one day, an inspector of the commission of Taxis & Limousine sat him in the back seat of the car he was driving and in a fit of stress, Jochelo, accelerated at a deadly speed, and while the inspector asked him to stop, he told him:

"I'm not going to stop until I see you jump out the front window."

"Hey, don't be crazy, I just wanted to know if you were in order, and I see that you are, why don't you stop and we'll settle this another way," he said.

"How do you think we are going to fix this? If you are abusers!" replied Jochelo while dialing 911 and said "Hello, my name is Jochelo Eleazar, a Taxi & Limousine inspector just kidnapped me, he is driving desperately and there is no way to stop concluded"

"Bullshit, it's the opposite, he is the one who is kidnapping me," the inspector replied, but when he said it 911 didn't hear him, but indicated him:

"Try to calm down, they can't do anything to you, everything will work out" the operator told him.

As the race started at 95th and Broadway, the 911 operator let him know that when he passed by the corner of 135th Street, to take his hand out that they were going to see two police officers waiting for him, then when Jochelo got the information he took a detour to Amsterdam Avenue and the inspector tried again to deny it.

"He is the one who is trying to kidnap me," he said, but when he said it, Jochelo had already closed his cell phone.

At that moment the inspector moved forward and moved the lever of the car that was next to Jochelo's leg and left it in neutral, and in the attempt the inspector's identity plate was left under the carpet of the car, and some agents of the commission who were aware of what was happening through the radio transmitter had it located arrived to reinforce it and made Jochelo get out of the car, looked for the plate under the carpet, seized the keys, gave him a ticket for 1500 dollars, and took the car from him.

When they went to the court of T&LC, Jochelo destroyed the license at the feet of the judge, and since then he stopped being a taxi driver, it was not worth to make him an offer, he did not accept any, and he never thought of getting involved with that commission again, since then he decided to start doing his own business in Bulley...

He waited in silence for that uneasiness that was inside to dissipate, without being a torment, to then bring it out with a roar, to lay the foundations of how he eradicated that discouragement, to cheer up the sorrows of a generation of free condition in its actions, conscious of the duty of justice, before freedom, which would bring peace.

After that, the pack let their guard down, and they stopped picking on each other. Many times, to confuse the boredom, they used to joke with the followers of the five S:

He said: soft, sensible, simple, and without sweating, people were always inclined to his beliefs and tastes, and said that don Miguel had managed to preserve a mane of two locks of varied features, one was white gray, and the other was black bear, but don Miguel loved to pamper his two lovers, and the one who liked black hair, he let her caress his hair, until the black hair disappeared, the same thing happened with the one who liked white hair, he also allowed her to play with the white lock, and he never felt it, in that jocular way Don Miguel remained bald, It is an appreciated way of seeing what can be, people are always ready to find an answer, and when nothing costs them, they easily make a party, leading those who are more, to suffer calamities, satisfying their egos, through a bad game.

But Jochelus Eleodorus, who believed that joking now and then was a healthy way of escaping from tensions, did not cease to meditate on the wickedness of men, and seeking to give Gibon comfort, he remembered certain malicious actions of a shameless salesman.

It was the month of March, and approaching the major week, Christian souls tended to become sensitized beyond their condition, and so, in honor of the major week, some of those who thought they could get away with it, got caught in their own web, and the false prophets, as was to be expected, often decided to try it on their fellow man. It happened that while Jochelo was resting, there was one of those peddlers who came knocking at the door of his house, to offer him the pleasant opportunity to acquire the Word of God at a very good price; the abusive man showed him a luxury bible, and immediately made a condition, and as the bible had a crucifix in the center, and the pages and edges were carved in gold, and Jochelo, just by contemplating that condition of golden expression, allowed himself to understand the attraction of love.

And in an accelerated reflection, he saw the opportunity of pleasant elevation, to enjoy the words of the Lord, for him it would be a joy of redemption.

Jochelo was in love with such a sweet design, and for such condition thought to assimilate that reading better, because that offer of such nature had moved him to a purchase without resentment, and without loss of time, he was already ready to sign the acquisition, not without before receiving the impression of the salesman, who had appeared with more bad intention than love, for what without preamble he told him that that Bible was a precious garment that was only obtained in the Vatican at a price of 5000 dollars, but that for reason of the major week, the papal council had decided to make it arrive to the parishioners for a minimum sum of 80 dollars, the interest in him was increasing, and he did not delay in seeing the offer as an opportunity, and taking out of his pocket four 20 dollar bills, that he extended with desperation to pay with love, he tried to close the deal with honor, but the cunning salesman, seeing the interest of the buyer, stopped him in the ceremonial, and with premeditation he explained it to him better:

"Brother, I'm really sorry, we don't accept cash, we only accept checks made out to the Passion of Forgiveness Church."

And Jochelo, even more motivated, went to pay without hesitation, and in doing so received as a war trophy a beautiful pen to lubricate in the checkbook and filled with that pen that seemed more like magic, a check for 80 dollars, excuse me, I meant 80 dollars.

Jochelo swore that in many years he had not done a business of that caliber and kindness of that involving the clergy.

He returned the pen, like an honest scribe, and the seller, caught it with love, and more when Jochelo offered him a cup of coffee.

Thought Jochelo, and added,

"Don't leave me without having a cup of coffee," he said as he poured a black stream of red wine from a porcelain coffee pot into a little well of little flowers, arranged for that purpose.

"Oh, how generous he has turned out to be!," said the vendor to himself, in a theatrical soliloquy, as he raised his voice and said, "I am delighted," he expressed, as he caught, held, and brought, without further ado, the cup to his lips; he took a sip to taste and savor it, and after he became confident, he gulp it in one sitting.

Lucky the vendor, the coffee wasn't so hot anymore, it was lukewarm, smooth, and with a hint of nutmeg.

Some days had passed, before Jochelo noticed some anomaly, and that those moments of joy turned into disappointment, he had sent his brother-in-law Cyril to cash a check for 120 dollars from the same account where he had made the payment for the bible, and in the attempt the check bounced, at the same time he found out what happened, he told Jochelo who with some disappointment said:

"It can't be that that check bounced, I deposited 5000 dollars the day before yesterday, how is it possible, if only 80 dollars were paid from it."

It didn't take Jochelo long to go to the bank, where he explained what had happened, and even the intervention of the FBI was noticeable, and when they checked the bank documents in their possession, they saw that everything was correct, because the document showed Jochelo's handwritten signature.

The Federal Bureau of Investigation explained to him what had happened and made it clear to him that since that was his original signature, which at no time was different from the one he had written, there was not enough evidence to proceed with the case.

Jochelo truly understood that the world was full of evildoers, and that even if one chose the life of pain or joy before incarnating on this planet, it was disappointing to discover that even those who seemed honest in certain aspects of free will were still phonies.

What had happened was that the vendor and his gang of thugs had given him a beautiful pen with removable ink and in the space where they wrote the eighty dollars, they had erased it and replaced it with 4,900, leaving the account with one hundred dollars, and since the check that Jochelo sent to change was for 120.00, it bounced because they had only left one hundred in the account, to prevent the bank from getting suspicious.

Jochelo's frustration had taught him "not to believe in those people who, when mentioning God, tended to change their tone of voice",

And many times he used to soliloquize in the hectic course of his daily life:

"Gentlemen we have to open our eyes, when New York doesn't sleep, the gangsters are awake."

And Gibon who heard his expression hummed a song to him, to the love he was waiting for but never came:

"In silence I wake up, to see the light flowing, the light that shines on the road, where you walk.

Today I love you and in silence, I perceive you and say nothing, because you are my love of essence, and I require your presence.

In silence I only think, and today I'm thinking of you, because only your presence makes me feel happy.

Silently I love you, and you still don't know about me, but I await your presence, in order to make you happy, silently I wait for you, because you are my sincere love.

And a tender brunette who heard him, almost dazzled, stealthily approached him in silence, contemplated him, the sphinx of Gibon decoded.

And he, who was looking at her sideways, thought:

"What does this black woman want?"

The brunette, she was a skilled, expert in prieto[12,] but Gibon

______

[12] Dark-skinned person

was brown, and it generated admiration in him. So much so that she kept looking at him with an angel's smile, but since he was silent, didn't ask or tell her anything, she decided to talk to him and affirmed:

"You are good and beautiful, continue as you go, do not change horses or deviate from the path," she told him and kept walking, while his silhouette disappeared when she reached the corner of the block.

In the following days surprising things began to happen, he stayed away from the pack, while they were shocked he took his turn in silence, he chanted the mantra of I am, while the power of God was invading him, everything that had been difficult, was becoming easy, some friends and family who had deserted his side, under any pretext, returned, the door of mercy focused on him, and the violet flame enveloped him, and was projected as light in the darkness, love and hope was reborn, belongings that seemed lost appeared, communication was reinstated and the peace of the world was shown.

CHAPTER 32

UNCERTAINTY

The pack acted according to what was given to them, at that time they acted as a mob of ignorant people who mercilessly hindered those whom the organization of evil assigned for that purpose.

Sadism was their illusion and wickedness their perversion, they always attracted someone to tell them their problems and then make fun of them, it was Burdock's favorite style, and some of his cliques.

It was in this way that Ruki Jetse, having suffered a sad disappointment, she approached Gibon, telling him that his only daughter and the charm of his yearnings, had enrolled her in the Saint Theresa School since she was a very young girl, where the nuns had set her the guidelines to follow, so that she would not become addicted in the convent, and although she had a shocking name for a little nun's pupil, when the mother superior agreed to enroll her in the hope that the name would not influence her devotions, much less her ambitions, because Matilde Clips was not a name for a novice and much less for a possible future nun, and at first she showed herself to be a devoted saint, but in the last two years of high school, she began to stand out from the line, until she met a Bulgarian who spoke Spanish and made up a makeshift school to teach Bulgarian; so they put up a sign that said Bulgarian could be taught for twenty dollars, Petro, a Mexican Dominican who saw the sign paid him the required amount, but when Matilde Clips came in she sent him to sit down, Petro sat down and waited for Matilde to give him the introduction, so she didn't wait for him to start:

"Welcome, I am glad to have a fellow citizen interested in broadening his cultural level."

Petro, who still didn't understand what was happening, became dumbfounded until Matilde Clips added to him:

"Well, let's start with the letter: 'A'"

Petro in an irritating attitude interrupted her:

"Aye baby, stop there, what the hell are you talking about, you told me you were going to teach me Bulgarian, what's your story now?" Petro questioned.

"Precisely, that's what I'm doing."

"No, no, give me back my twenty dollars, why would I be interested in another language, let alone Bulgarian."

"Oh, yeah, and what did you think, depraved??

"The same thing you're thinking I'm thinking" Petro said.

"Oh! Get out of here! If you don't want me to call the police on you, you depraved."

"It's okay lady, it's not that big of a deal, take the twenty dollars," he said as he walked out grumbling, and as he walked Petro thought out loud and said:

"That fucking chapeadora[13], she knocked down my twenty

---

[13] Mujer cuya prioridad es el dinero o bienes
materiales de sus parejas o amantes.

dollars, I thought I would see her clandestine clinic-made artificial ass, oh, and what happened, twenty tulips she knocked me down, and left me snoring."

When Petro told it, the whole pack barked:

The prophet wandered from path to path and complained in the expression of the self, who ignored the destiny he brought on his path, and spoke like Job:

"Already, I cannot perceive what I have been doing, that from my mother's womb God has loved me, and after he has illusioned me he has released me to walk alone in this turbulence of indecency, where at every corner imprudence awaits you, cheerful giver, gracious lord, splendor of essence and light, maker of honor and understanding, since I have known you he has seen me as your son, and after he has deluded me he has let me loose on the road and I walk like a lost man, in the midst of crocodiles, of the wicked and daring," he said, and after listening to him, God answered him:

"My son, I am always where you can see me, but you do not see me, You always give good expression, you are a pillar of liberation, you were chosen by the Lord to grant liberation, the struggle is deep and very high honor, because at all times, God chooses a liberator, to attract liberation."

Then the technology had advanced to blast wave detectors, and in the intention to confuse Gibon, they all used to unify, and occult sect and their gang of criminals and lawyers, had planned to undermine the assigned legacy, and they fought not to hand it over and made Gibon believe that there was a fraud, but Gibon's silence worried them more and more, because they understood that Gibon would not accept their abuses any longer, they understood that Gibon would somehow resist them, so those undercover in the tactics of the organization of evil, they tried to prolong the time of the delivery, and as it was better to be honest than a lawyer, Robert Wolff forced by occult sect did not cease to lie to him, to win time and prolong the solution, but Gibon who knew the contextual cynicism, and every day they resorted to an evasive seeking to justify themselves to cover up their misdeeds, accommodating the parameters to make it look like evidence for a spoiled child, who would not allow himself to be spanked by his guardians, and showed the intention of a punishment to Gibon, which would never be seen as an action inspired by the spirit of the thief.

Thus, he continued to turn around New York, ignoring that the evil they were doing to Gibon, they were doing it to themselves, because of that "everyone's evil, the fool's consolation".

Gibon, with the utmost serenity, waited while he made Robert Wolff believe that he was swallowing his justifications.

Some of those who believed that Gibon had received some of what the gang of conspirators made it appear that they had delivered to him were constantly approaching him with business propositions intended to deceive him, or to make him lose the money which they supposed Gibon had in his hands.

They were unaware that God had vaccinated Gibon against evil, so that none of the evil they directed at him could affect him, and some emissaries who knew that in a medical appointment they had injected him with radiation to make him sick and disable him, approached him to ask him:

"How are you?"

"I am well and will be better" Gibon said, and they were confused.

For Gibon the world was beginning to be different, but those of more, lived in the midst of a society in chaos, where politicians had been corrupted, and where by necessity had to choose the least rotten.

He thought that consciousness should flourish, to balance the world's senses, he wanted to rescue a lost world, which should be directed to the path of understanding, where love would be redefined.

The world was confused, peace was clamoring to be established, violence was striking in the face, abuses were overwhelming, it was necessary to tolerate so that justice could come.

The sacrificers, unaware that the day would come when they would receive the consequences of their actions.

And Gibon sang for freedom and the honor of God, and said:

"I am that which I am, I am health, I am attraction, which generates love, I am youth, I am opulence, which generates light, I am virtue, I am eternity which generates peace.

I am the healer, I am the one who I am, I am the attraction, who builds in God, the flame of love, I am the opulence, who gives the world peace and awareness, I am the brilliance, the flame of love, I generate the sunshine and understanding,

I am the one who I am, I am grace and honor, I am the one who heals, I am the healer, I am the one who builds in God the best.

I am opulent, and the brilliance is in me.

I am that I am, I am God the creator, I am flame of love that generates the sun, I am eternity that attracts goodness, I am love, I am understanding, I am grace and honor.

I am goodness, happiness, wisdom and youth, I am health.

In me there is no cross, because now I am light, I am transmutation, what was once dark, shines like the sun, I am who I am, I am health and love, finances and goodness move with me, I am the way, I am the destination."

Then there was a moment when the pack was silent and Gibon was pulling in an empty cart that a customer had left, and looking over to where he was, Vilinsky commented to Burdock:

"What does Gibon gain by being away from us?"

He thought he would not be heard but Gibon who heard him answered him:

"Believe it or not, I win everything and nothing, nothing, because there are few things in common between us, since some of you only talk about gossip and anal burps, mocking even the cat, without contributing in your attitudes, nothing that contributes to a positive change, also you are only aware of two things, the passengers who go out there, and to see who leaves the car open to steal from a sweater, the car jack or a misplaced horn.

And I win everything, because seeing your condition, without becoming a victim of your pretensions, I approach where you are, and I thank God, for putting me a step ahead of you, because in this way, I find myself overcoming the narrow context where you move, while facilitating me to reach the degree of consciousness that I possess to recognize that I am different, to be able to express in the mastery of Christ: "Forgive them father, because they do not know what they do" Gibon said, with all the splendor of his honor.

The pack assumed a snarling attitude, looked at each other, as they expanded their jaws, showed their teeth with the intention of barking.

What bark? Let's say with the intention of biting him, but when he growled they ran out of saliva and an appetite seized them all, and in a suffocating consternation, they fled to the drinking fountain, abandoned the transportation service, while they began to line up in front of Bulley's cooler, which was next to the toilets.

"How strange, the transporters are not in their place," commented someone that was leaving, and explored with the sight.

"Oh, what's it happening?," commented someone of those who responded without being asked:

"It was that a car of taxis and limousines was driving around, and some people had an urge to defecate, and others to drink water."

"That's right," replied another one who came out with nothing in her hands, as she continued walking.

Inside the grocery store, the club members were selecting

what they and their families would eat together, braving the winter storm that was raging outside, leaving the sidewalks white, like gray-haired old women.

After drinking water to satiate their animalistic courage, they began to leave, one by one to the first floor, but they didn't take the passengers out through the front, they took them up to level two, and took them out through the parking lot, through the back, to avoid being bothered by the T&LC harassers.

In reality, the pack was not snarling, it was simply growling, and since Gibon knew this, he was looking for a way to change the conditions by avoiding violence, and he kept on singing:

"I am that I am, I am health, I am affluence, I am youth, I am love, I am salvation, I am attraction and definition".

Something strange was happening, Gibon was getting younger every day, and as he said it was, he was transforming, all those who once attacked him, had begun to keep silent in front of him.

For humans the non-traditional was madness, but as they grew old, Gibon grew younger, and richer, as the Pack barked through their mouths, the doom of their hearts, as they cursed, Gibon flourished, cried elevation, created blessing:

"I am the opulence of God in my hands, and I use it today, I am the presence acting everywhere, I am the active presence bringing money into my hands, and I use it instantly, I am the presence of perfect health, as the breath of God, acting, I am the presence of forgiveness in the mind and heart of each of God's children, I am the pure mind of God, transmuting resistance for sight and hearing to manifest, to heal every condition of disease, therefore I am my perfect sight and ears.

I am that I am, the unlimited presence of God, and therefore I am the only intelligence acting, I am the omnipresent and unlimited opulence of the father for my use.

I am the victorious presence in whatever I desire, I am the presence in every command I give fulfilling it, filling it, and I am commanding that I am light, power and illumination.

I am the one presence, intelligence acting within these individuals, transmuting their limitation, to evoke that I am the active presence of all channels of distribution of all things acting for the good of myself and those who self-decree the essence of the attraction of good, therefore I reiterate that I am the riches of God flowing into my hands and use which nothing can withhold, for all is governed in the presence I am, which governs every channel existing in manifestation, and governing all I absorb into my mind and body the power of the explosion of light, to say and say that I am light, health, opulence and youth, which recycles every action every action of obstruction with the determination to cleanse the planet, my home and my environment, and I am the presence here and from now and forever, which keeps immaculate all that surrounds me or approaches my presence.

I command here and now that health will not leave me, nor

anything that will benefit my eternity, because I am who I am, and I am the definition that I know is acting with all power, to dissolve the negative suggestions that anyone will invoke, with the intention of affecting my environment.

I am the presence overriding all wrong desires, so that none can affect me, my home, or my world for I am the presence that makes all conspiratorial action cease, now and forever, and I am the presence in my mind, in my home, in my world.

I am the conquering presence, I command this presence I am to perfectly rule my mind my home my affairs and my world.

I am the presence thinking through this mind and body, I am the only presence there, here and now.

And so, I am the only presence and activity on guard and acting.

I am the powerful presence governing everyone's activity, and through my presence I am, I give you the courage to control your adversities, for that which seems adverse, is not right, it eliminates the speech that grows, for I am invincibly protected, against all management, imperfect, so I accept the full activity of my powerful presence I am, commanding the time necessary to achieve the purpose.

I am the powerful presence commanding the time, as much time as I need for the realization and application of this powerful truth.

I am the only intelligence, presence, light and power, acting." Gibon concluded.

Suddenly something happened, Burdock wanted to go violently on Gibon, but when he tried to do so, he fell without being able to get up.

"Riiiiiiiig catalepa," Burdock sketched, in his trance.

Alonzo the Boxer, who had brown skin, turned purple, gritted his teeth, clenched his fists, and, possessed by a common anger, also wanted to go at him, but Gibon, who had noticed the reaction, said:

"I am the dissolving presence of that condition of violence and oppression, therefore I decree that its attitudes and conditions be governed harmoniously. Do not forget that I am the powerful presence that rules my world and my life, I am the peace, harmony and self-sustaining courage that carries me serenely through all that may confront me."

At the time of the events that I have just exposed, only the most violent and perverse of the pack were at the main entrance and exit door, and they joined like robots and locked themselves in their respective vehicles that were in front of the exit door, the rain had already diminished, small drops fell that extinguished the fire generated by the ex-three, and Rony appeared, who was called the sorcerer, who heard and saw what happened.

"Pastor, my blessing," he said to Gibon.

"By the grace of the Lord, may you have peace and much love," Gibon replied.

Rony went to the window of Burdock's bus, which at that time was called the punch bowl, not because it kept punch, but because the pack thought it was like a place to pee, because of the many bumps and patches it had; but I wouldn't want you to think I'm a mumbler, let's see how they started the conversation:

"What happened, that now you are hiding?" asked Rony, to Burdock, who lowering the glass answered him:

"No, it's just that this guy is crazy, and to avoid problems it's better this way," he answered referring to Gibon.

"Ah, but if so, I'm his friend, let me talk to him," he said, but when he moved Burdock stopped him:

"Wait a moment, don't do it now, so that he doesn't believe that I told you something," claimed Burdock.

"Don't worry, he's not going to think that, I know him, he's different," Rony affirmed, and as if he had gone to bring, a case of redemption, he approached Gibon:

"Pastor, and what was it that you did that your friends are hiding?" Rony asked.

"Rony, I have only shown the truth of the father, but as they do not understand it, they are seeing me as an aberration, what happens is that the traditional human wants to give violence to the unknown, I simply pronounced the mantra of liberation, but as they are tied to the flesh, all that irritates them," said Gibon.

"And how is that pastor?" Rony asked with feigned innocence.

"I only expressed to them what must be, and let them know that I am the governing presence of all that I use for my highest expression and use, I am the great law of divine justice and protection at work in the minds and hearts of all the world.

I am the law, I am justice, I am the judge, I am the jury, I am the almighty, only divine justice can be done here.

I am the supreme intelligent activity of my mind and heart.

I am the presence that commands the inexhaustible energy, the divine wisdom making my desire fulfilled.

I am the inexhaustible and intelligent energy sustaining me, I am the substance being used, and now I bring my desire into visible manifestation for my use."

At that moment a client of Bulley's was coming out, and he went to Gibon asking for help to organize a purchase that she was bringing in a cart, Gibon, interrupting his exposition approached the lady and assisted her as she required, and when concluding, the lady gave him fifty dollars as a tip, Rony the sorcerer surprised by what he had just seen said where the others could hear:

"It's true, the pastor has something, that woman who helped him, just gave him fifty dollars without moving from here, something is happening, for an act of that nature the most they give is five," he said.

The others had envious expressions, and Gibon transmuted again:

"I am the acting power, I am the substance that is being used, and now I bring it into manifestation for my use.

I am God's wealth and in action now manifested in my life and my world.

I am the divine love that fills minds and hearts everywhere, I am the power of God, almighty, the presence I am clothes me in my transcendently protective garb of eternal light.

I am the perfect poise in me speaking and acting at all times, for I am the presence."

"Pastor, I congratulate you, that's a new way of preaching," Rony said, interrupting Gibon, while the rain that had dissipated before, reappeared in the context as a torrential storm, those who were in their cars, stayed inside, and those who were outside entered Bulley, in the list was on duty Ricardo who before the rain restarted, mounted a purchase in his bone white vehicle.

In reality, the pack was given to the dog, Ricardo Calvo, an infiltrated by the organization of evil, and because Gibon refused to obey the lines drawn they had begun to pressure Ricardo, to start a provocation cycle against Gibon as Burdock used to do, that repentant had stopped doing dirty work, against Gibon.

Now Ricardo was looking for a way to call attention to Gibon's name, to see if it would generate violence, and followed him by honking his horn so that Gibon would move quickly and in order that Gibon would run the red light, to find some reason that would induce the occult sect and the organization of evil to make it more difficult for Gibon, in short, they were adding a spark to a new lesson of harassment.

Then one night, Gibon was trying to find a parking space, but he had not noticed that Ricardo was behind him, so looking to speed him up, he honked at him, but as Gibon did not take pressure from anyone, he went ahead, stood parallel to him, and told him:

"You could have passed the light, and because you were slow you didn't," he said.

Gibon, somewhat surprised that at that hour of the night Ricardo was behind him, replied:

"What are you doing following me? Are you not even in the street to leave me in peace? You're a nuisance in Bulley, you're a nuisance outside Bulley, stop harassing."

"Who are you for me to be after you?" Ricardo replied.

"I am that I am," Gibon added.

"Ah, you're crazy."

"The one who is crazy is you, and those who are paying you to do what you are doing."

Gibon pointed out to him, staring at him.

Richard, who couldn't hold his gaze, sped up and left, mumbling.

In that condition was the pack, ready to give everything for everything, in their intention to discredit Gibon, and the problem was that they were in the service of evil, and Gibon in the service of good.

God was at Gibon's side, but they did not see Him, because the blindness caused by ignorance and ambition did not allow them to see Him.

Ricardo seemed a good person, but the bad company perverted him, he was a hard mouth person, and he didn't always know how to behave, or he didn't always let himself be understood, due to his little schooling, he couldn't always understand the values of the others, and above all of Gibon, with high education, in the middle of the pile, and although Gibon looked for the way to make himself understood, the pack, refused to understand him and obeying the parameters of the organization of evil, they provoked him in some way calling him crazy, which was the way to demoralize those whom they had as a stone in their shoe, and as Gibon did not allow himself to do what they wanted, they were always studying the way to make him feel bad.

Gibon served with love, and some would intentionally haggle over the price, to test his heart, however, when they were rejected by others, and Gibon would ride them for their bidding, when they got to where they were going some would pay double or more than what they had bid.

"To give this to those who don't think about service but only of getting the highest amount that one can pay, I better give this to you, who cares more about serving, and who always ride people for what we can afford," hey said.

Gibon nodded and thanked for the disposition in his favor expressed by those who received his service, while still expressing to God his satisfaction, and rendering honor to the God of his being he said:

"Thank you sir for health, thank you sir for youth, thank you sir for opulence, thank you sir for science. In this way he maintained his style of survival, to impose himself on the monotony."

However, some minority sectors were owners of a limited and very impoverished mentality, they believed that if they paid the cost of the service, they would lose but it was not like that, but those who sustained their faith in limitation, often remained in their condition of poverty, and manifested it in their actions because of that "by your deeds you will be known, they ignored that it was better to give, than to receive".

It happened that the pack, after the Garget's men arrival, had lost face and had begun to experience shame, and when they opposed Gibon, God opposed them.

The Garteans had come with a purpose, to impose themselves to do the will of the organization of evil, to provoke Gibon who was the center of attention, and to try to take control.

The indications of those were defined when Cholinfe was waiting for someone, Gibon was on the list behind him, and Donko behind Gibon, and a passenger came out that Cholinfe was not going to take, and thinking Gibon that Cholinfe had left, he programmed himself to take the departing client, and Cholinfe who was outside the hall where the clients were expected to exit the elevator, seeking to get Gibon out of his emotional condition, shouted:

"How is it possible that if I am the one going, the pastor comes in my turn, to give price, when I am the one called to do it," he said.

"The first thing is that you have to lower your noise by two levels, because of what José Angel Buesa said in desiderata: "Avoid noisy and aggressive people, as they are a nuisance to the spirit" and for another new reason that the dog does not always bite as it barks, so calm down, serene brunette, you have to control yourself, you are very nervous."

"My wish is to stay third, and let you ride her," he said buying time because he was waiting for someone else, but at that moment another customer came out and it was Gibon's turn, so he answered:

"No need, I already have mine," he said.

At that moment a person approached someone called Anjo, and being Don's turn, he passed it to Anjo, for which the pack later went around protesting, and Ricardo was heard to say:

"We have to be alert, they are planning to divide the passengers between them, therefore, we have to arrive early, so that they get tired and leave," Ricardo said to two or three of the pack.

The levels of justice were lost in ignorance, and it was true that many times they had come disguised as errors, and among the Gargeans had come the fat Mazambula, a silent character who had gone to Bulley to fish in troubled waters, so that some members of the pack did not see that presence with good eyes, and claimed to Rene affection that appeared before the pack as the mediator, to find a way for the intruders to return to their places.

When Rene affection claimed to fat Mazambula, to return to Garget, he justified himself, claiming that if his nephew Anjo, who was also from Garget, was taking passengers there, he also had the right to do so, a discussion of words and sayings arose, which induced Arnulfo who was listening, put his spoon and said:

"Hey, blessed Mazambula, if you're not from here, you don't have to argue."

Fat Mazambula found such expressions foolishness, so he replied:

"I don't like people like you, that one moment you are with one, and then because of your unstable condition, like a chameleon you go and change your mind," said him.

"The problem is, we can't have tecato[14] here, and you're a pothead," Arnulfo added.

"Barbarian, the time has come where the birds shoot the hunters, what are you talking about? Actually you're a lard mopper, you inject it into your veins and now you're on methadone."

"Do you want to fight?"

"Come, follow me," Arnulfo said as he walked to the corner where he was going to the parking lot, followed by fat Mazambula.

Once away from the door through which the passengers were leaving, they fought, and between their faces and bellies, they tumbled until other members of the pack approached and separated them.

The presence of the Gargeans was creating tension among the members of the pack, and when Gibon claimed that "the sun was rising for everyone", they retorted:

"Lies of the devil, pastor, you know that this is not even enough for us, so that those guys have come to invade us, to endanger our food," said the pack, practically in chorus, as if they had rehearsed the chorus.

"God will provide," Gibon said.

___

[14] Drug addict

"Well, if that's the case, you give him his turn, but I'm not going to give anyone a turn."

Rony said, a little irritated.

"Anyway, we must be patient, and thank God, the corona virus has taken many who could not take anything, and we are still alive," Gibon added.

At that moment, Cholinfe arrived, looked at Gibon, and for annoying him said:

"I write it down pastor?

"Man, I've been here for a while, I'm the one who has to write you down," Gibon replied, while Fredesvindo distracted them, humming a chorus.

"Offer brother for the glory of the Lord, offer brother for the pastor to buy an engine."

Everyone left in laughter, and the tension dropped.

CHAPTER 33

CONTROL AND MANIPULATION

There was a design of hope along the way,

Everyone was looking for what they had lost,

But they did not know what the destination would be.

Gibon said in his eagerness to counteract the condition of the proud:

"If I am that I am, it is not necessary for me to believe everything I am told, which most of the time, suits the convenience of the one who says it!"

Regularly politicians and some pastors, at that time, were vehicles of influence and transformation, according to the interests they supported.

God, the father, was always the matrix that generated all the channels, which in the evolutionary processes of the limited planets, would show their individuality, appearing as Gods of worship, granting blessings.

The word would come to be the manifest thought, and the free will, was the justification, depending on what was chosen before birth, and what you wanted to do after growing up, which was not always related to what had been chosen, so it generated the struggle of the opposite, which spread the confusion.

Then the radical experiences were called sins, it was a control regulation of the incarnated entity on earth, who was judged according to his actions "By your deeds, you will know each other", and it was that if he interacted overcoming the pre-established social standards tilting the balance towards evil, society would not accept that sinful act, and would seek the way that such action was punished, however if he did it generating an edifying good, such action would induce to grant a reward.

Many times the parishioners of the congregations did not always obey the dictates of the pastors, and conflicts were generated in the congregations, which induced some pastors to express themselves in terms of radicalism, threatening to remove from the congregation the parishioners who did not obey him, and it was because not everyone understood that life was either chosen or assigned and that when someone had karma accumulated from another life that had to be resolved in this one, they chose to be born either as brothers, or as children, or as pastors, or as parishioners, so that whoever brought karma debt, could solve it by receiving the "whips of the collectors" in order that if in another life someone had killed the "collector", in this one, the collector would kill him in that one. "Who kills with iron, dies with iron", and for balance of what justice should be, Jesus said: "Do not do to your neighbor, what you do not want them to do to you". Reason for which each one would receive what he would give.

That was the game for planet earth in the wheel of reincarnation.

Many chose to be poor because the suffering would give merit that on his return would elevate them, but being on earth with the burden that generated that selection to be stripped of real power, the spirit felt strangled by suffering, but that suffering was what generated the greatness on his return, because any life of the nature that was, was a degree more for the elevation to the higher planes of light.

It was for this reason that Jesus pronounced that his kingdom was not of this world, and even at the moment of crucifixion he, detached from the rancor of the passion said: "Forgive them father, for they know not what they do".

All that would come to be a demonstration, that ignorance would always be the mother of all evils, and that from.

"There is everything in the Lord's vineyard".

The nature was pleasant and surprising, the beings were born, and understood that they lived, but the pack even wanting to think, did not define, what the reason for his philosophy was.

Gibon, however, expressed himself with the intention of redemption, and said:

"I never exasperate or despair, what corresponds to me reaches my path, because God is the light, the virtue, the knowledge that is you, we must always move forward where the silhouette of the light is reflected, let us always move where God indicated that you live, let us continue walking in the flow of the rebirth of each being, because light is hope and virtue, we will walk in the reflection that is you, because nothing is to be lost by trying, nothing is to be lost by obtaining it, because the Lord nourished us with the voice, nothing is lost if we walk with honor, towards the path of redemption.

Hallelujah, glory to God, Hallelujah I sing, the Lord has redeemed me, now I come and I sing. Hallelujah glory God, grace for redemption, that in heaven and on earth, the Lord is my Shepherd." Gibon concluded.

But the pack, more intolerable than their condition as dogs, was becoming discomposed, exasperated, and suddenly Burdock took the floor.

"Pussy, if we don't get that guy out you're going to drive us crazy" Burdock said.

But Gibon, who heard him, even though he knew that he was provoking him, in order to shut him up, answered him:

"You and how many others will try or will be able to get me out of here?" Gibon asked him.

Burdock was silent, for he spoke like a loud speaker, assuming that he would not be heard, but sometimes he was silent, and made like the one who was talking about someone else.

The pack was made up of Hispanics from Mexico, Central and South America and the Caribbean, Arabs, Dominicans, etc. by the very nature of the mixture, some tolerated each other but did not always understand each other, and very rarely was there harmony, because when they started to gossip, only God escaped, and the others had to be careful!

Among them there were some islanders who in their evolutionary nature inherited the evilness of the Spanish, and the naivety of the indigenous, many were submissive kiss-ass, always wanted to put the spoon where they were not invited, so it was easy to put in the middle of their countrymen without reflection or measure consequence, they were xenophiles, and almost always felt love for the foreigner, who came to be for them as an amulet to exhibit and show off in front of the others, they used to confuse evilness with wisdom, and they brought in their blood the ancestral inclination to "exchange gold for mirrors".

They were ambitious and ignorance induced them to be accomplices of plundering, that marked as a target the public treasury, and through politics, they were ready to mock the people and to boo their rulers, who in turn, by ambition assumed commitments ignoring the results, they were a kind of ammunition of blind faith, that for a quarter of the treasure belonging to the people, for them and their families, they gave to the highest bidder the third part of the treasure of the population, without any remorse all for the intention of swelling the bank accounts of their closest relatives, that is to say, for ambition of particularized possessions, they sold the empowering people.

They used to do a favor with a second intention, if they were businessmen and gave a job to an elegant woman, they thought that gave them the right to harass her by asking for sexual favors.

By idiosyncrasy, these freaks were macho, amorous, jealous and talkative.

"Everything passes and nothing remains, the tasks of suffering, which harass your feelings, are also carried away by the wind, the words that transcribe are signs that you once expressed what is, but if you don't preserve them, you can also lose them. All expression is of a certainty, like sand in time, it is the sphinx of a concert, and if love is torment, it is also carried away by the wind."

CHAPTER 34

CURIOSITIES

In the way that, the pack in its murmurings approached any subject that was exposed to it, often with logic and balance, and at other times as nonsensical conceptions.

In that moment of exchange, they were taking turns waiting for the buyers of the club to leave with their purchases, but meanwhile they were having a racial discussion, generated because an Albanian woman named Albita was asking for Gibon, and as he was riding someone with when he told her that he was not there, she turned her back and left, they contemplating the beauty of that human sculpture, they embarked on a commentary on the matter where Jochelo, taking control of the word, said:

"There is no doubt that he is a mujeron[15] but those European women have an approach, a beauty and a condition, that even a sanctimonious call attention, and if you do not believe me, ask Gibon, who has experiences with Europeans, a friend one day sent him a Spanish to meet him and when the Spanish saw him, gave him a flower, and at the same moment a passionate kiss of more than two minutes, and Albanian and Spanish look alike."

"What do you know about it, Jochelo?" questioned Petro.

---

[15] Spanish word that Hispanics use to refer to a voluptuous woman.

"Albania is a country located in the Mediterranean, south of Europe, near Greece, bordered by Montenegro, Kosovo, and Macedonia, Albanian and two other languages are spoken, in addition, is the main producer of marijuana in Europe, i.e. Albania has embalm and relief," said Jochelo, presuming to be a professor.

"I imagine that the racket is marijuana and the outlet is women, Oh, yes! How beautiful they are! That ivory whiteness makes it look pinky," Petro replied.

"Ah, hang on there, there are more whites than blacks in Albania, because when an Albanian girl was growing up the first thing she was taught was that the black was originally from the earth, and Darwin's theory that man was descended from the monkey was based on them, and if she came of age and chose to mix or mate with one, she was told, you're going to mate with an animal? .... Don't forget that they are descended from the monkey," He said. But as he spoke, he didn't realize that Alonzo the boxer, who was as black as a jet, was listening to him:

"What the fuck? you do talk nonsense, don't go around falsifying reality, we blacks are more, and we are everywhere, where the hell at this stage of the game can you think of discriminating against us, when in reality, we are like erotic fantasies for every white woman," Alonzo said.

"Stay out of this, Alonzo, I'm not talking to you," Jochelo told him.

"How he is not talking to me, you are talking about the blacks, and I am black, and so are you even though your skin looks lighter, that's why they say that the Dominican is the only black that despises himself," Alonzo the Boxer said.

"If you say it for you, I believe you, because I heard you calling your cousin Palomino, who is black like you, a Haitian of the devil, and I am not black, my grandfather was of Spanish descent."

"The Dominican has shit in his head, he's a black, slick, muzzled nigger, and he wants to be a blue blood," Alonzo said.

"Of course, it's just that you are looking for a partner to justify yourself, but the Dominican is white, brown, coppery, crossed, and serene."

"There's the problem, you have no identity," Alonzo said.

"The one that doesn't have it's you, you look like a Haitian," Jochelo replied.

"Stop that," Rodo interrupted, a chubby man who looked like a jar, but who was more conciliatory than a priest.

At that moment Wing, the Bulley manager, came out to ask him that he needed them to help by bringing in the empty shopping carts that the customers had left on the sidewalks, and so they kept quiet and began to bring in the empty carts where the customers were moving their purchases.

Jochelo was always on the lookout if he had to show his teeth, and he always remembered those years of his broadcasting life, when he would talk on the radio and please the listeners with his favorite music.

Rony was something of a workaholic, he would be seen going to and from a supermarket called Stoping, which was next to the Bulley club, and he would pick up passengers at the supermarket, and he would pick up passengers at Bulley, and he kept up such a pressure of life, that the others, when they saw him appear at the club, would just say nothing else without him listening:

"Look, here comes agony," Vilinsky said.

Rony loved to make fun, and the center of his relaxations was Jochelo, with whom he had annoyed for no reason, it could be that this dispute was brought from another life, because Rony enjoyed making Jochelo suffer, who was already old and affected by diabetes, many times he let himself be abused by him.

Sometimes Gibon when he was alone with Rony would come up to him and say:

"Rony, don't be a bully, don't make fun of Jochelo, he is a man who has a health condition, and it is not good for him to be agitated, don't go and provoke him to be angry and regret it, look what happened with Juan, so don't keep bothering him."

Rony was overflowing with laughter and unfounded justification, until one day, he agitated Jochelo so much that he brought him to the brink of despair and Jochelo was about to grab a rod to put him in his place, but Gibon, and the members of the pack, intervened and prevented a fatal outcome, then Jochelo said somewhat angrily:

"If he keeps bothering me I'm going to file a report with the administrator, so that they know if something is going on, and then I'm going to file a report with the police, because he has had enough of me, what he wants is to make my life miserable," Jochelo said.

Then all those who were present, including Gibon, approached him one by one, and told him not to continue bothering Jochelo, or he would be responsible for what happened, after a moment of reflection he promised not to bother him anymore, and so it was, although he suffered from a condition of bipolarity, because there were days that he was calm, and another day, he came ready to make it difficult for others.

Anyway, as time went by, there was a moment in which a change was generated and the disagreements between them disappeared, it was said that for that purpose it was necessary Rosalba's intervention, Rony's wife, whom Jochelo had known since she was a child.

CHAPTER 35

ELEVATION

Gibon was born in a world in turmoil, where confusion and little love made the land taste pain, God would free them and entrust them to a deliverer.

Like a lamb among wild beasts he let him loose, and he tasted sorrow and pain, expressing in time the lack of love, showing the experiences of the heart, God expressed to him with much love:

Today I grant you a body smeared with health, like the essence that you show, by the power of your rebirth, which emanates from the essence of my being, creator of consciousness that is transmitted, to erase your suffering, with a life of joy, in full understanding of your philosophy!

A new existence has come to you, in a beautiful renewed body, now begins to be loved, by the woman you had always hoped for.

God gave you the essence of his glory, saving at every step your memory, he sent you to free the oppressed, his word guards your path.

You have always been a light, a shining ray, and although they wanted to change your destiny, you are the splendor of a living God, and the father at every step, guards your path.

With the passage of time there is no torment, power, health, and justice, you carry it within you, and for every attempt to cause you pain, or for every new conspiracy, that they hatch against you, for those who attempt it there will be threefold suffering.

When the voice of God spoke to him, he felt a mighty lightning touch him, his body was lifted up, and a prodigious power came over him. By the power and might of God, those who were sick he healed, and the oppressed he delivered, the earth with him was transformed.

And what was violence was eradicated, all that was peace was restored, and in a world of love, humanity was transformed.

The promised paradise had arisen, on a plane of light and neatness. A new blossom, with a new orchard, let another generation be born.

They were all ignorant of what war was, they only knew what love was, and by love, they felt peace.

God beheld, so pleasing a splendor, and increased his love, as he rejoiced his heart. And in the midst of the turbulence, grouped voices repeated:

"Look how good God's people look, look how beautiful God's people look, now we are having fun and not suffering, we are having fun and not suffering, the glory and peace is given by Jehovah, Hallelujah glory and peace, everywhere I walk I see happiness, everywhere I turn I breathe peace, everything is glory and happiness, Hallelujah glory and peace, Hallelujah glory and peace, Hallelujah glory and peace."

And Gibon awoke from his revelation, and at eleven o'clock in the morning he went to Bulley, and in that November afternoon it happened that Gibon was passing by on his way to the bathroom, and a parrot that was on his owner's shoulder, with the intention of attracting Gibon's attention, expressed himself in a loud voice:

"Behold, now a son of God is passing by, serene and haughty," Gibon kept walking and ignored him, as if he didn't hear him.

"For God's sake, Cleto, stop looking for trouble!," the owner warned him.

The kite without giving up, whispered to his owner, very close to his ear:

"You'd better not try to move from where we are, because then you're going to get in trouble, I have a prophetic word for that man," said the parrot, which was more like a cross between a parrot and a parakeet.

"Now you're going to waste my time," replied the owner.

"It is better that you stay, because if by disobeying God, you make me lose my plumage, imagine what will happen to you."

"It had better be from God, and it had better not be your invention."

"You stop being like Thomas, have faith, ah, look there he is back:

Hello man, says our Lord, don't be like Esau, who out of desperation, for a bowl of soup, exchanged his blessing."

Gibon did not flinch at the parrot's voice, although he wanted to be surprised, but he knew that when God had a purpose, he used to use everything that men thought inappropriate, he gestured and even opened his pupils, but the parrot rushed him to it and added:

"Don't play dumb, you know what I'm talking about."

"Amen, divine species, thank you, may the Lord bless you."

"It's good that you bless me. That's the guarantee for me to keep my plumage, keep walking and go with it!"

Gibon bowed to him, and as the parrot asked him to, he walked on.

The owner looked at the parrot as if asking for an explanation and the parrot replied to his request:

"Hey, what's wrong with you? I'm doing my job, besides, I was better today, and I didn't ask for any offering money," he said, and laughed.

The owner, who was a park preacher, kept walking down the aisle of the line, and those who overheard the parrot talking to Gibon were amazed, so amazed that a grandmother of the club's membership, letting out a whistle through the box of teeth, said:

"Fuck, it's true that we are in the end times, a bird talking to a man!"

Suddenly, Romualdo intervened, a brazen and wild man who listened to her with concentrated attention:

"Please don't discriminate against us, madam! We are human too," he said, with the fuss of an irritated girl.

"The devil is coming this way Do not get involved that is not with you, I'm talking about natural birds, not artificial birds," he said.

Those who had noticed what had happened, laughed out loud.

The homosexual, made a cartoonish grimace, ready to reply, but was interrupted by Nicole, one of the cleaners, in Bulley, who at that moment was backing up with the mechanical cleaner, with the intention of drying a detergent that had spilled in the aisle, while the buyers dispersed between the lines that led to where the products were, while in the moment they left the space free for him to pass.

November brought cold and madness, people did not reflect, and stress built them dwellings, and all the pressures, induced them to rehearse madness, but everything obeyed a cause, which was not always love, nor hope.

Now it was Bulley's security watching on camera, an action of lovelessness.

One thin woman, puffed up like fat and another skinny like her was probing her:

"Tell me, what you did to get fat in such a short time? You came in so thin, and now you want to retire like a fat girl," said the thin girl to the skinny girl.

The woman, knowing that she had been discovered, tried to drop everything, but it was too late, they had already observed by the cameras that she had introduced a purchase between her coat, so she was caught and stripped of what she was carrying, she was also warned not to dare to return to the store.

An officer from the 50th Precinct security detail led her to be fingerprinted and taken to court.

It had not yet been discovered whether the man stole for evil, or for illness, however they were things that even if they could be avoided, those who had assumed that life, exercised it without shame, as something natural.

All the hustle and bustle of daily life was generated in the work of survival.

CHAPTER 36

CONTEXTUAL EVILS

"It is that the kiss of your mouth drives me mad, and induces me to give you roses, those that your heart invokes."

Gibon thought that when the time came, the spirit would reveal to him who and where were the authors of so much evil, and thus, without the intention of revenge, in time, they would also taste a spoonful of their own medicine, and even many of them, like Judas, would be inclined to suicide, because the evil in the free will, induce repentance.

And the organization of evil and occult sect, which had been formed as groups of unconscious people, moved like a horde of madmen, who had just come out of the psychiatric center.

Gibon kept thinking: "The organization of evil now has impunity, controlling governments, the world no longer has peace, and the coercion is so great that the ethics of love has now become pain.

They are facing all, confused in understanding, that hope awaited, the coming of the Lord, who would do honorable justice, and to all those who suffer, will bring deliverance".

Who is wicked by nature, though they pretend to be good, can regularly deceive no one; they can never prevent evilness from bursting out of their skin, for, as the spirit shows the saint, so it denounces the wicked.

It turned out that the organization of evil had used the services of Burdock and Gobi, both of whom were more fond of money than women.

That pair, as fanatical as they were abusers, came one day after accepting the bribe to shamelessly provoke Gibon by taking away his clients when it was his turn, or by putting him in foolish conversations that were not of Gibon's interest, seeking to make him angry, supervised by an indescribable witch, because you could't tell if they were a pagan, a Christian or a Scientologist, they were always trying to make Gibon dizzy in order to weaken him so that Burdock and Gobi could control or dominate him.

On May 26th the day cleared suddenly, with the typical swiftness of a tropical summer without aurora or twilight, but with scattered clouds that looked like cakes sprinkled with grayish foam, and the splendor of the sun bouncing off the colorful spring flowers.

Everything had been serene until those two ruffians had decided how the rest of the day would be for Gibon, and after waiting until it was his turn, Gobi tried to take it from him, but Gibon opposed him, he hadn't even realized that when Gobi pulled the cart, he had cut himself and then Gibon kicked him and was cornered on one side with the pressure of the witch who had paid the bribe that afternoon, and in an oversight the Gobi and Burdock combined so that Burdock when Gobi threw Gibon to open to see if he could hit him and when Gibon returned with his fists he blocked with his body of resentful chimpanzee, so that afternoon they were for Gibon and in an oversight Gibon was with some tennis nails, Gobi gave him a top and Gibon was stuck to the wall and at that moment with the participation of Burdock, Gibon hit the floor, then in another rematch Gibon made him understand that he had not hit Gobi more, because of Burdock's participation, then Gobi wanted to challenge him again but Gibon mocked him and left to take his passenger and the others prevented them from facing each other again, then automatically the police appeared, when they saw the blood on Gobi's hands, they thought that Gibon had hurt him, he thought that Gibon had hurt him, but Gibon who did not know what had happened explained that Gobi threw him and he scratched himself with his glasses, then Gobi did not press charges and the police left, on another occasion Burdock confronted Gibon, they threw some punches but Burdock like a clown asked him for a truce, and for a few months there was no more misunderstanding, until they renewed the bribe.

When they returned to conspire against Gibon, they had sent a taxi driver who moved around Garget, when Gibon was serene before he arrived not the slightest noise was perceived outside Bulley, suddenly the Elder appeared, he was a young man, When Gibon saw him, he discovered his phantasmagoric expression, a ruthless enemy, of imperishable hatred, he arrived rolling up his sleeves in a provocative action that induced him to fight.

Gibon, with the utmost serenity, faced him and without knowing how, grabbed him by the neck and asked him:

"Did you come here looking for trouble?"

The elder had been silent, but when he answered "No" it was too late because he was already flying through the air.

Induced by Gobi and Burdock who resented what happened, they made a police report, when Gibon arrived, in a desperate way Gobi called him on the phone and told him:

"Hey you, come on, the man is here, if you fall asleep it's going to take time to do something to him."

And they were at it, until one day the police came and found him there before the three days were up, and Gibon was unworthily arrested in a new fabricated case, where the villains of occult sect and the organization of evil were falsifying what had happened, elder took a picture of him at a time when he was following Gibon, and he gave him the front, and then the villains who intended to intimidate Gibon told the judge handling the case, that Gibon had argued with his wife, and they gathered like thirsty hyenas, lawyers, paralegals, assistant prosecutors conspiring to steal Gibon's compensation, and then disguise it as a car accident.

It had been nine months before they told the judge that it had not been a fight with his wife that it had been with another man, they had given Gibon a pro bono lawyer of Arab descent, who they called "Odin".

When told the truth about it, the judge conditioned a vote on the case if Gibon didn't go to jail, or if there was no further fighting.

Two days before the case was to be dismissed, three gang

members were sent to follow him wherever he went.

Then there was a moment where he stopped at a traffic light, where they took the opportunity to hit him from behind, when Gibon came out to see what was happening one of the three gang members, hit him in the face, first he punched him, waiting for Gibon to react, violently, then seeing that he did nothing, he gave him the second, but Gibon was still serene, when he gave him the third, then the other two had to take him holding his elbow, he had a broken hand.

One of the three gang members told Gibon:

"Go away, go away."

Gibon remained serene; the plans of the wicked did not prosper.

Those ruffians expected Gibon to respond with violence, to prevent them from dismissing the case and building him another one, however, God was still in control, because the gang member was not hitting Gibon, he was hitting the holy spirit, Gibon did not feel any of the blows delivered because at that moment, he was in the covering of the holy spirit.

The elder gave Gibon an order of protection, and was never to be seen of him again.

And although Gibon didn't know him, he had been sent to find trouble in Bulley, to see if they could remove him from his place of work, because as he had told them, the occult sect and the organization of evil had managed to get a restraining order against Gibon, they wanted to damage Gibon's reputation, making the victimizer a victim.

In addition, they had enlisted a Bronx defense practitioner, who on that occasion would verify Gibon's immigration status, Rosa needed to have the clearest information about him, but later, when Gibon wanted to contact her, she did not call him back because they had already set up the fraudulent actions they had planned to make an innocent person look guilty, for whatever purpose.

Everything that had happened had been forged by the occult sect, and the organization of evil, through Elder, Burdock and Gobi, who, being fonder of money than women, had accepted bribes.

With the intention of harm Gibon.

A few months later, the organization of evil sent another emissary to bribe Burdock and Gobi to try again to get Gibon out of his boxes, the drama on that occasion was that when Gibon arrived and signed up for the turn, Jesusito, a newcomer to the Pack and servant of the organization of evil, erased him claiming that he had arrived first and had not signed up, Gibon knew what they were up to, so he made it clear to him that everyone who arrived should sign up to avoid confusion, and he made him understand that they could disrespect each other but not disrespect him, who was like a sacred cow.

Gobi, who intended to send Gibon told him that there was no sacred cow there, and Gibon clarified that he was like a sacred cow, because he did not depend on the will of any of them, at that moment Gobi came very close to Gibon threatening him, letting him know that he was going to burst him, when Gibon saw him approaching him, he took the key of the car in his right hand, Gobi who noticed the action asked him if he was going to use the key, Gibon kept silent and the Gobi withdrew a few meters from him, to which Gibon told him in his face that the problem that he had had with elder, had been promoted by him, the Gobi told him that he was crazy, and Gibon let him know, that the crazy one was him, and asked him:

"Do you have a revolver?"

Gobi, somewhat surprised, answered him:

"Revolver?" Then Gibon, who realized that he had been surprised, added:

"Because if you have a revolver, I have a machine gun, so be careful."

As soon as Gobi heard that expression, he turned away from Gibon and entered Bulley's waiting room, followed by Burdock who asked him:

"What happened?"

Then Gibon, who sensed it, realized that they were combined, had received a new bribe.

A light-skinned woman of small stature, who served as an emissary of the occult sect and the organization of evil that was waiting for someone to pick her up went to Gibon:

"Stop sir, you are making it worse, if people see you in that attitude, they are not going to ride with you."

"Thank you for your suggestion, what is assigned to me, no one removes it, lady, and I know my history, this is a repetitive action with the intention of taking me out of focus, but they will not succeed, I will resist, whoever falls" Gibon pointed out.

The woman was silent, and at that moment, a customer came out and asked to be transported by Gibon.

Gobi and Burdock, this pair of sinister characters, had made a pact with the organization of evil, with the aim of making it difficult for Gibon, but as Gibon stood between reason and prudence, and knowing that such provocations, obeyed the plans of the occult sect and the organization of evil, they were looking for a way to make him react with violence to arrest him and deliver him to psychiatry, He, on the other hand, like a Christ, tolerated in silence, hoping that the laws of nature would one day give the wicked a taste of their own medicine, so that they would understand that who kills with iron, dies with iron, as the law of talion asserted.

Actually, they had committed so many errors and evils against Gibon, that they feared that he would reach a position of power, which would induce him to take revenge, however, they ignored that nothing depended on what Gibon thought in free will, but on the commitment that he had assumed before God, because men had no power over Gibon, therefore they could not do more to him than what God allowed him according to the life that Gibon had assumed before he was born.

On May 27th, when Gibon had already retired from the activities in Bulley, he received a surprise call, Rodo, who a few days before had hit him for not waiting for him to finish parking, was calling him to apologize, and to improve their friendships because Garget's people were invading his work area, and were undermining his income.

Gibon told him that they would find a way to solve that,

and that he had no problem with him since he had never disrespected him, regardless of the misunderstanding over the accident where Mr. Pascualo had made an insurance claim.

That day, Gibon also questioned Pascualo about the key number he had copied from the car he was driving, because there was always a sabotage that only someone who had a copy of the door could generate, and Gibon thought that Pascualo was somehow involved with such actions, he believed that the organization of evil had given enough money to him to facilitate the sabotage with the intention of damaging Gibon's nerves, but they did not know that Gibon had the strength of tolerance that God's envoys brought.

Gibon used to tell him that those who were behind such mischief would come to repentance, and that many of them would end up committing suicide. The latest stunt generated by them had been to sabotage the air conditioning system so that it would throw the water upwards so that the car would remain full of water when the air was on, so that the carpet would rot and smell, so that the customers Gibon transported would protest and not ride with him.

For this reason, when Rodo called him at night time, he thought that he did it under the orders of an occult sect with the purpose of locating him and once located, to resort to his evil deeds.

Gibon was so surprised that he thought that if in three years he had never been approached by him on the phone or in any other way, why at that moment?

Then he didn't doubt that he was certainly being used trying to track where Gibon was at that hour.

The next day when Gibon went to Bulley and discussed what had happened the night before, Burdock barked all at once:

"That was drunk he was," Burdock said.

Gibon was silent, but Jochelo intervened and corroborated with Burdock:

"The thing is, Rodo knows he can't call anyone here to pick him up in his drunkenness, and he's already looking for others to bother."

"Well, he knows that's not going to happen with me, we can greet each other here and collaborate, but for me to go out and look for someone outside of here in those conditions, I don't think it's possible," Gibon said, and they all looked at each other, keeping silent.

CHAPTER 37

FOLKLORE IDIOSYNCRASY

Jochelo hummed the refrain of a song:

"The animals smoke in the corrals, generate discomforts, which hurt their larynxes and the smoke builds them pedestals, blocking their genitals, hitting their health and building their cross."

"And what do you care, I do with my life what I want," replied a man who was in front of him inhaling a cigarette and smoking like a chimney.

"No, you're wrong, this is a restricted area for smoking, we don't have to swallow the smoke generated by others, if you want to die, die alone, don't be selfish," replied Jochelo.

"Don't be selfish you, you don't know why I'm smoking, it's the way to not go crazy, they increased my rent and I still have the same salary, it's thinking how to solve the responsibilities assumed in this city, and now I can't even apply for coupons because I'm asking my brother."

"Get in there, you don't want to be giving your opinion and dropping hints," replied Rony, listening, with more evilness than solution.

The man who smoked, seeing that he could generate a conflict, inhaled the last drag of the cigarette and throwing the butt on the sidewalk, entered Bulley, leaving two pugilists facing each other.

The laconic expressions of that wounded beast were like an inducement to violence, but Gibon, knowing what was in those provocations, stepped forward and said to Jochelo:

"Don't listen to him, remember that he just wants to annoy you."

Rony, with the facade of an agitator, never missed an opportunity to try to get Jochelo out of his senses, often arriving unexpectedly, throwing hints at him in a way that leaned more towards perversity than joking, all with the intention of making him angry for no reason.

Sometimes he would arrive with colored waters with scents to pretend they were magic potions that attracted customers more easily, and he would provocatively sprinkle those waters looking for Jochelo to be splashed to see him angry, and when he knew he had achieved his purpose he would laugh, sadistically, enjoying having made him angry.

In a summer afternoon, he approached Bulley carrying with him, flowery water, and red and yellow and green paint, depriving in witch he spilled them on the sidewalks, Jochelo who realized what happened, was ready to inform the administrator, but Wing had already seen it by the cameras, and forbade Rony to approach the club's facilities.

The rest of the pack, who were not far behind, then went around saying that Rony had to go to the office to "make his first communion", which consisted of getting down on his knees and begging to be forgiven and to be allowed to return to do the delivery in front of the door where the purchase went out.

"the monkey even dressed in silk, stays monkey".

Who is evil by nature, no matter how they pretend to be good, can deceive no one, because evilness sprouts from their skin, as the spirit shows the saint, so shows the evil one, it is the way the spirit denounces, and people who perceive the conditions speak of certain people as having "good or bad vibrations".

All the actions performed by the organization of evil, obeyed to leave Gibon in an economic imbalance, because they thought they could control all men who moved on this planet, but with Gibon was different because the more evil they did to him, the stronger he became and he only waited for God to indicate the answer he should offer to the villains, in reality, Gibon would have liked to give him a drink of his own medicine, but as God was in control, he could not and should not do anything if God did not allow him to do so.

A little later Burdock appeared, he was showing off the repairs they had done to the "punch bowl," Gibon told Jochelo in Bulley's parking lot that he would like to get the address to take one of the cars he had parked at Bulley's for repair, and Jochelo promised to inquire about it later, Gibon had lost confidence in the garages he visited because the organization of evil used to follow him and go ahead of him with the objective of overcharging him, or damaging some of the parts he had good, so that he would have to pay again to repair it, because there was no other interest than to ruin Gibon.

Burdock had seen Gibon in the morning hours, and saw

him again in the evening, at once began to throw hints and said that there were people who did not take rest, because they had no families or apartment, so he had no choice but to sleep in the car.

Since Gibon knew that these hints were directed at him, he answered him:

"The problem is that there are other people who pretend to control others and lack the ability to control themselves."

At that moment there were only Yoryi, Gibon and Burdock, who, not finding a way to refute Gibon, kept silent.

The next morning the Arab who had joined in obstructing Gibon with Rene's support had arrived, because many Dominicans were xenophiles, and tended to love the foreigner more than their own people, and since the Arab knew that Gibon was a pastor, and pastors in America had good relations with Jews, the very thought of it made him irritated, and he kept pulling at Gibon looking for a way to drive him into a space where he could slip and fall.

They erased Gibon from the duty roster, so that they could leave first, and when he realized that they had erased him so that they would stop practicing what Gibon considered an abuse, he took and tore the roster, This upset the Arab who had become a good friend of Rene's and he appeared to think that Gibon could fit in his mouth, he was alarmed and took advantage of Burdock, who didn't let one pass to get into the discussion, and as Gibon didn't have good communication with him, he felt that he had lost respect for him again, he asked him :

"Do you want me to kill you?"

And there, a brawl began to form, the pack growled and wanted to bark all at the same time, with the intention of biting Gibon, who was on duty.

The Arab came out and took a passenger who was leaving, saying that he was his client, and as the client confirmed it, Gibon let him ride him.

Instantly a lady came out and accepted Gibon to ride her, but when Gibon was mounting the purchase appeared combined Burdock and Arnulfo, while Arnulfo recorded, with a cellphone, Burdock provoking began to throw punches and there was a moment in which Gibon accommodated, when Burdock threw a punch at him, he blocked him, he studied the movement and gave him a kick in the right leg, where he made him stagger, then he introduced a Jack through the chest and Burdock, fell from Bruce, hitting his buttocks, someone passing by shouted to Gibon:

"Wow, you are a strong young man, you should be hit with a pipe," he said. But Gibon paid no attention to him.

Burdock and Arnulfo wanted to interrupt their deliberation, but they did not dare, as Gibon had already begun to lead

The client told Gibon that even if he was provoked he should not fight, and gave him her phone number, in case he had to serve as a witness.

When they returned they were all calmer, they had gone to gossip with Wing, the manager of Bulley.

The Arab who felt much supported said:

"There are 20 of us here and none of us want you."

"It doesn't matter, they didn't want Jesus Christ either, and today He is the king of the world."

"It is that we are many against one," The Arab added.

"That still doesn't matter, the tree that bears fruit, they throw stones at it, besides, the Gods are many and Jehovah is one," he said.

He left to drop off another passenger, and on his return he went to a place where he used to have lunch, that day they were scheduled to reserve a difficult time for him, for lunch they used to charge him an amount, that day they tried to charge him double, but someone intervened and clarified that the order cost half the amount they were charging him:

"There's a mistake, that order is not worth twenty-five, it's an order of ten," said the one who was acting as supervisor, while Gibon sang happily:

"Thank God, thank God, thank God, thank God, that there was a voice, that defended me".

In reality, all that conditioning and testing was due to the disposition of the occult sect and the organization of evil in its role as a harassment committee.

And behind the perversities of the harassers, in the American nation, there was the immigration repression, which had been unleashed as a relentless persecutor of undocumented immigrants, notwithstanding those who played and sought ways to survive in the middle of the environmental condition, and some Mexicans who supported such conditions, but who brought oriental features, had begun to learn English from their homes and hardly spoke Spanish in the streets, They were thus posing as Filipinos or Chinese, outwitting the immigration agents, who had racism in their blood, and being mistaken for Filipinos, they were not bothered, however they too were hurt when they began to attack Asians for their oriental features, and many Mexicans were beaten by street activists, being mistaken for them.

But there were so many stories of those times, that if I were to narrate them, I would lack ink and paper to write the lines of the content.

The organization of evil, had elucidated in the most hidden corners, the evolutionary pattern of Gibon, and it was not difficult for Claudy, one of the mothers of Gibon's youngest children, to whom they made the story of confusion and manipulation, the first of her children, who were not Gibon's, were being prepared to be policemen and they were controlling Gibon's children.

They were the youngest, and sporadically they used to use them to keep Gibon away from their activities.

Gibon operated out of the Bulley at 237th and Broadway in the Bronx, and the organization put on shows where they used their children, and on one occasion they pretended that his son May, who was 13 years old, had left the house, they took him to a park in Brooklyn and had Claudy, his mother, call Gibon and make him believe that May had left the house, and Gibon left the Bronx to pick up May in that remote part of Brooklyn.

Occult sect and organization of evil, they wanted to check what kind of father Gibon was, so they set up that kind of test.

Then in early 2020, a month later, Gibon was led to believe that in an alleged fit of rage, May had thrown his school supplies and computer to the ground, so they were forced to take him to a children's mental hospital for psychological care for children who had acted as May had allegedly done.

They left him for observation for a couple of weeks, and during that time, Gibon did not leave the hospital to take care of his son, however he always believed that it was a set-up of the occult sect and the organization of evil, in complicity with Claudy, to make it difficult for him, because they were exploring Gibon's Achilles heel, in order to try to manipulate him.

Gibon loved his family, but since he knew the purpose of the organization of evil, and occult sect, he would not let them get away with it.

Claudy, obeyed the apocalyptic precept of "neither son for father, nor father for son", and at that time, who lacked conscience and money, if they offered them something, they would sell even his aunt, because surviving was the way to justification.

CHAPTER 38

NATURAL TESTS

The XXI century had brought earthquakes in different parts of the world, and in those times a disease had emerged that had depleted the population of the planet, governments were cornered, and even the godless thanked God for being atheists, the corona virus (COVID-19,) which was the name of the disease, was wreaking havoc in the scenarios of the world, and panic had seized humanity.

Schools had been closed and students had been induced to continue studies through social networks and their emails, virtual classes.

The coronavirus, referred to a family of viruses, discovered in the twentieth century in the 1960s, however the origins had still been unknown, until in the twenty-first century, by the year 2020, had been highlighted as an epidemic called as severe acute respiratory syndrome SARS-Cov2, or Coronavirus Disease (COVID-19), was killing humanity, and the life of the inhabitants of the planet had received a radical change in existence.

Especially because that generation had never experienced anything like it, however many thought that the virus was a conspiracy announced to which no attention was paid, because it had already announced something similar in a text by author Dean Koontz, entitled: The Eyes of Darkness and on page 333, said textually: "They call the stuff Wuhan-400' because it was developed at their RDNA labs outside of the city of Wuhan, and it was the four-hundredth viable strain of man-made microorganisms created at the research center" but in addition, on page 312 it was commented that by the year 2020, a disease as serious as pneumonia would appear, which would spread throughout the world, attacking the lungs and bronchi, and resisting all known treatments.

And many were confused, because the disease itself would disappear as quickly as it had come, and then it would reappear and strike ten years later, it would be like by the year 2030, where after striking mankind again, the disease would disappear completely.

Then, the corona virus was the pandemic of 2020, which was cracking the planet in the different lines of existence, because the economies were collapsing in the great empires, as well as in the minority nations.

Th e World Health Organization had declared the disease as a pandemic, many smiles were erased, and many of those who had been "crowned with the summit, saw at their feet the abyss."

However, public opinion at the time rumored and insisted that the corona virus had been manufactured in laboratories with the intention of eliminating the aging population of the planet, mainly in China where draconian family planning laws and the one-child policy, eliminated in 2019, had induced the Chinese population to age quickly. It was expected that by 2030 China would be the country with the largest elderly population, with more than 40 million people over 60 years old, and had warned that the growing ranks of the elderly in the region would become a major problem for all of Asia, because the cost of health care for the elderly by 2030 would accumulate a figure of 20 trillion dollars.

Play it for the attention of the pack, he said of China's aging population:

The wise Confucius used to say, promoting his ideas of filial piety: "take care of your parents and take good care of them when they are old" but, after the first world war a Chinese emperor had arranged that all the old people at 85 years old, were abandoned in a mountain, and that was a sad practice that was resorted to every year, but it turned out that a soldier of the Chinese imperial army, had to abandon his mother when he turned 85, and while they went to the place arranged for such a destination, his mother was cutting twigs all the way, and the soldier told his mother:

"But mom, why are you doing that, if you are not coming back"

The mother looking him in the eyes replied: "Son, I am not doing this for me, I am doing it for you, so that when you come back you won't get lost on the way."

The soldier for the first time looked unarmed and without hesitation embraced and kissed his mother, took her by the arm and went back with her, straight to the emperor, once in front of him he said:

"Your excellency, dispose of me as you wish, because I have lacked the courage to fulfill your condition, I could not leave my mother on the mountain of the damned, because I believe that she does not deserve that I pay her with ingratitude, she brought me into the world so that I serve the country, and you. That is why I am a soldier, she took care of me and educated me, and with such action she served the motherland, because she gave me to the motherland, for the same reason I aspire to return to the kindness of such sacrifice a little of what she has given to me and to the motherland, I want to take care of her until the force of nature claims her."

The emperor, moved by the bravery of that soldier, stood up, approached the one who had dared to speak to him in such terms, and made him a general for having awakened him to the vision of ruling.

The mountain of the damned became the mausoleum of error, and the old people who still remained in that place had been transferred to the village of love, where they began to live with the corresponding relatives. The draconian planning laws that allowed each family to have only one child remained, but due to the growing wave of old people, it was abolished in 2019, and the decision that families could now have more than one child was established.

The Pack, who listened to him attentively, kept silent, but it was the turn of a deliberation, and when he turned his back, the first to show his cynical features was Burdock:

"Hey Rony, I think you're going to have to give Jochelo some water, so he won't be 'Talkative'."

"Hey Burdock, we can't throw dirt on everything, but the reality is that the corona virus is here, and from China it came here."

The Pack that was in contact with the people to whom they transported the purchases, got tired of that sterile condition, and did not cease to have their concern, so they had begun to disinfect with alcohol, and some of those who managed to get masks added it to their faces, and followed the protocol of not talking so much with the customers, unless it was necessary.

But something had happened, Crispin Rupert absence had moved to the mumblings of his friend, Plutarco Rene Cariño because he had not appeared in Bulley for several days, had called to his house and his wife Moraima had reported that Crispin was hospitalized, due to a prostate problem, but by the poisonous mouth of the pack, paraded the occurrence of commenting that he had acquired the corona virus.

Gibon thought that "those demons" would always be ready to refer to the worst, and began to spread the word that Crispin Rupert had been affected by COVID-19, the corona virus.

"Let's see now if he will continue to deprive in babe," Burdock said, with all the splendor of his wickedness.

Crispin Rupert was 74 years old, but he did not honor that condition, and used to jump like a goat to attract attention, and often said that his intrinsic energy was due to red peppers, and the consumption of tomatoes, and some of his acquaintances considered him to be an old man of the universe, more fox than conscious, a seeker of opportunities, without them knowing that he was opportunistic, while Gibon who was his admiration and his disappointment, contemplated him in silence without issuing an opinion.

Crispin Rupert, originally from Nicaragua, a fellow countryman of Nicanor, was a sugar chemist at the service of the Sandinists, always ready to satisfy the most dubious services, which is why he was qualified as one of those willing to deliver whatever was required of him without any hesitation.

He was assigned by exchange to the sugar industry in Cuba, where some time later, he had met Moraima, a Cuban woman from Santa Clara, enrolled in the Baptist Church.

Moraima would come to legalize her status as a resident of Cuba, and later an opportunity arose where the Baptist church, had a conference in the United States, where Moraima would be one of the speakers, as they still had no children, the Castro government, allowed Moraima newly pregnant to leave Cuba, Crispin asked for permission pretending that he was going to Nicaragua to resolve personal matters, and as a married couple the church had obtained a joint visa to New York, and leaving Havana, they had decided to take refuge in New York, where they would finally manage their residence as political refugees.

Once breathing American air, satisfied with his accomplishments, he said:

"If God has led me to freedom, it is because I will undoubtedly meet the deliverer face to face."

In reality, unstable minds often lived in disequilibrium, and the pack, in its survival, would change its mind from one moment to the next and one day appear conflicted, and another day calmer.

It was difficult to talk about vultures grown in crows' nests, but after all, whenever someone wanted to become violent, Gibon prayed silently and said:

"With three I measure you, with three I scare you, the blood I drink you, the heart I break you, stop your fierce animal, for before your birth, the son of God was born, and before him I was born, and the cheerful giver, vindicator, owner of gold and silver is my lord."

And when Gibon prayed the Pack was pacified, because, in reality he did not tolerate evil, because he knew that evil was due to the ignorance that was a product of the evil that emanated from the entity they called the devil, and to whom some members of the occult sect and of the organization of evil, worshipped.

Then before the decadence of humanity, Gibon, looking up to heaven, cried out:

"Oh, father, I want strength of spirit, with full reconstruction of body, so that health, bliss and youth, intrinsically, may be manifested to me abundantly, in the course of my actions," he said.

And automatically his body was transformed, and became so young that people who had not seen him for a long time, no longer knew it was him, only the children, the assigned wife and some of his closest relatives who had noticed what had happened, could recognize him.

By then Gibon had already left the Pack.

I wanted to talk to you about Gibon in an advanced theme, because while he remained close to the pack, things happened:

However, nothing more insightful than the trajectory of the hallucinated Arnulfo Requema Fernandez, born from the womb of a woman unbreakable as the fantasy of a barbarism, since his father had abandoned him from conception in the womb, as a faithful delegate of providence.

By then Gibon had already left the Pack.

I wanted to talk to you about Gibon in an advanced theme, because while he remained close to the pack, things happened:

However, nothing more insightful than the trajectory of the hallucinated Arnulfo Requema Fernandez, born from the womb of a woman unbreakable as the fantasy of a barbarism, since his father had abandoned him from conception in the womb, as a faithful delegate of providence.

But he would be a man devoted to the work of laconism, and although he once censured the condition of adoration, Vargas Vila said that "religion and servility formed a single hymn to despotism and vice," because for him, "the fanatics and the ignorant were the best wood to make lackeys". Arnulfo was conditioning to be, what he had to be, an adept of the cause par excellence and firstborn of his mother, Eustaquia Fernandez, Blessed of the Sacred Heart, who had consecrated her son, in the service of the clergy, as a pledge of preservation, had a husband, a heart-throb and a career drunkard, so that such reasons induced him to succumb on the way, leaving her under the favors of the Seraphine nuns of Calvary, who cared for her and her offspring throughout the pregnancy, and then until he was nine years old, It was difficult for them to keep him in the convent, and then they chose to confine him in the seminary, where at the age of ten, he was an altar boy, so that the struggle between the human and the divine could be generated, making history between fulgurations, so that later he would be a somber apostate, to be buried under skirts of glory.

But without further ado, let me tell it to you simply:

At the age of ten, Arnulfo interacted with Father Ambrose, who elevated him to his position and made him his personal assistant, alternating his time as a consecrated Blessed and as an assigned masseur, to the extent that he found himself defined by interacting along the way, until he developed an inadequate habit.

As time went on, Arnulfo grew like an orangutan, and at the age of 22, his size surpassed that of Goliath, so that some priests were intimidated and there were those who were wary of not being assisted on a certain day, because Father Ambrose had him as the amulet of his personal possession, until Judith, went to disturb the peace of his consecration.

Arnulfo had already overcome the condition of altar boy, and exercised his position as Ambrosio's assistant, to the extent that many times he was allowed to begin the mass, everything was so well, that Father Ambrosio and he, continued massaging each other's backs, until the appearance of the Italian, a beauty as if she had fallen from heaven and sometimes seemed like a virgin, and a little later as if she had been an angel, and Arnulfo looked at her on the horizon of history, as the consecration of an apparition, or as the wing of his freedom.

Her name was Judith, Judith Bracamonte, the beautiful prettiness of those that where they pointed, they landed.

And she stood in the front row, with a tight blouse up to where there was flesh, and her breasts seemed that when seen from the front of the pulpit, they looked like two dynamite firecrackers that were out of control Arnulfo's celibacy, who was looking at her with deep desires, while she pretended not to see, but underneath she perceived his expression, which could not help tasting, as if it was impregnated by the taste of a strawberry of sweet condition to the palate.

She, on the other hand, insisted in her provocations, showing herself with the intention of making him succumb, and so in her task of conquest, many times she arrived dressed in a little shirt so tight that the button almost burst, and Arnulfo perceived her breasts, like two freshly cut pears, turning from striking to provocative, while Arnulfo's eyes shone happier than those of a hummingbird, and admired in silence, he crossed himself and pronounced:

"Oh, most holy, it is true what they say that women are as tasty as they are dangerous, that they are half of humanity, and the mothers of the other half, that they educate us to obey them, that they are the strong sex, and we are the weak, forgive me Lord, do not put me to the test with that temptation, because if this were to continue, it would easily make me lose my modesty and reason, and it is dangerous, because I cannot contain myself from inhaling it in my imagination, and just tasting it, induces me to sin."

As he thought he closed his eyes, and the parishioners thought he was praying, and when he opened his eyes, he found himself facing Judith with that mischievous smile that made him tremble.

But that intentional presence of Judith, that made his heart restless, had sown the condition of his definition, for two months the Italian had concentrated on attracting his attention, to the levels that he already felt disgust, and did not want to massage the backs of Father Ambrose, so this had generated a dilemma and a great internal conflict, in the extension of that clerical locality, because Father Ambrose did something he should never have done? He fell in love with his assistant, and he, with Judith, but Ambrosio did not resign himself, he excommunicated Judith, and continued harassing Arnulfo, by that time Judith was 25 years old, and Arnulfo 23, and he, by the force of the spirit, had to confess to her. She belonged to an expanding sect called "Atlantis Redentora", which had the intention of stealing the parishioners of the Catholic Church and other sects that competed with it; she did not miss an opportunity to impose herself.

They were beautiful girls, and trained to lead the men, who once, in the hands of them, who did not work on the outside, devoted themselves to housework and obeyed their wives as their mistresses.

Arnulfo was taken out of religion, they tattooed his body with more vignettes than a map, when they damaged his life inducing him to vice, Judith remained in control and while he was with her she never allowed him to consume crack, however, a few years later when the organization assigned Judith to another victim, Arnulfo wanted to die, Judith left him without any money and in the street.

Arnulfo fell so low that, forgetting his priestly formation, he wanted to play the pimp with Fifi, a poor woman who helped him, but to better understand what happened, let's see how disappointed Fifi murmurs to Adela over the phone:

"Hi Fifi, tell me about yourself," Adela said.

"Oh daughter, and what can I tell you, Arnulfo has me worried, I found out he is being unfaithful to me, now he pretends to be with a Dominican."

"Fifi, don't be so insecure, they are just friends," Adela said.

"Friends? The mouse is friends with the cheese, and he still eat it, almost all Latinos are womanizers, and Dominican women, they squeeze and don't let go," Fifi replied.

"I can see that she is taking you away from Paulina, who is saying that Haitian and Dominican women have something that makes men go after them, but there is no need to be alarmed, Arnulfo has a clerical background, no woman is going to get to him," Adela added.

"Yes, so clerical that before me, he had Judith, one who left him in ruin, and taught him all the evilness, and even, I knew that he massaged a priest who was called Ambrose," emphasized Fifi.

"It's all in the past, he thinks that by staying with you, he has regenerated," Adela said.

"I'll have to tell you everything so you understand me, Arnulfo is not the saint we thought he was, now he's with Margot, she's Dominican, and they say that when it comes to mating, Dominican women don't consider anyone, I don't want him to spend the money that dad left me, so I'm going to transfer that money to another account, just in case," Fifi said.

"Now I understand, you don't love him anymore, if you did, you wouldn't do that, time will tell."

"Adela, it's not a matter of time, I have to do something with that man, he has been making fun of me, the last thing he has done now in his delirium of humiliating me, is that grabbing twenty dollars, he stands in front of the mirror and tells me: 'You see these twenty dollars, these are mine and the ones in the mirror are yours, and I want chicken.' Did you hear that Adela?" Fifi said to Adela who was listening to her astonished on the other side of the phone.

"Yes, I'm listening, but how daring, that man has become, well, being so, undress, stand in front of the mirror and do the same to him," Adela told Fifi, as a good advisor, so it was that one day, following the advice of her trainer, she undressed, provoked him, and when he got excited she stood in front of the mirror and told him:

"You hear Arnulfo, don't you dare touch me, because the silhouette of my sphinx that you see in the mirror is yours, and the original one, which is me, belongs to the chicken farmer" expressed Fifi.

From that day on, Arnulfo was so traumatized that he dedicated himself to work without mercy, and to get drunk to get rid of that pain.

It was when he found some friends, because he left something bad to get into something worse, yes, he had found some friends who had involved him in the sale of pills in nightclubs, there he had already met Valentina, Valentina was a beautiful woman, with a face of disinterestedness, although deep down, she loved money.

A year had passed since Fifi's abandonment, when Arnulfo found Valentina, he continued doing business downstairs, he kept selling his little pills, but as always, there was a friend who loved to throw the other in the middle and told him that he would do something better, he would do a business with a pool table inside, to him it seemed divine, so being the pool in the floor below he made his game, when his friend Alexis Bracamonte was attending the bodega, he was in the pool table and vice versa.

That was how he saw that silent beauty who went to buy everyday consumer products, and obviously, she also saw the presence of Arnulfo, in front of the store, and believing that he was the owner, he facilitated her access until they both win each other trust, she had an elegant boyfriend but no money, she had to manage much of the profits of daily consumption, and in addition, she was looking to help her boyfriend, needing capital for an investment, she opened the heart of her existence and Arnulfo found her beautiful and in an act of desperation, he used the pool table as a bed and met her.

That encounter made Arnulfo fall in love, so later, Valentina, as she was called, resorting to her charms, spoke to him for a loan, she ask him for seven hundred dollars, claiming that she would use it for rent, but in fact, she gave it to Rudy, her boyfriend, who used the money to buy narcotics which he distributed in detail until he became a major drug dealer, one day it was his turn to make a delivery, he was betrayed and killed, as Valentina was still related to Arnulfo she took refuge in him, but it turned out that one night in one of the nightclubs where he distributed his narcotics, the money she had access to from Arnulfo's savings ran out, and during that time, Valentina had fallen into economic disgrace and not knowing who to turn to, she saw Gary as the possibility of survival, because although Mrs. Soco had raised him as special, he had his savings, and in his condition of ugly and stubborn, finding a woman of the physical condition and tolerance as Valentina, was like a blessing, then the dwarf conscious of the savings that supported her, taking advantage of the condition of that one said to himself:

"To this mami, yes, I am capable of bringing down the stars from the sky," he said.

Valentina was a quiet woman and liked to be safe, so they rented a space in upper Manhattan before the Jews returned to Washington Hights and set up a cafeteria where they sold smoothies, sandwiches, sodas and a fish soup they called "seven powers".

Then Arnulfo's friends who had won trust, ate and drank,

and did not want to pay, and she told Gary what was happening, he was so small, what he did was to think and bring an innovative idea, which although it seemed ridiculous to Valentina, they chose to put it into practice, not without her warning:

"But my love, you're so small, do you think they're going to listen to you?"

"My love, you are bigger than them, and you listened to me, so leave that on me," Gary replied, and as they agreed, they did.

Making it clear that the circumstances of free will often placed men in places where they did not belong, either as karmic lessons or as worldly trials, Gary the dwarf, not even in his wildest dreams, could have imagined that he would interact with a woman of Valentina's caliber, however, there she was, as a trophy girlfriend, his 'mujeron', as he attested, so he entered the antechamber of the shop and when the confident ones consumed something and said they were not going to pay, Gary from the inner room would answer them, inflating his voice, which resonated more powerfully:

"Aye, what did I hear? I have to go out?," Gary said on backstage.

While consumers responded: "No, no, don't go out, we're going to pay."

Everything was working wonders, until Arnulfo came out of jail and approached Valentina, he had already found out that she was accompanied, but out of curiosity he went and made a consumption and when it was time to pay he told Valentina that he would pay her later because as she knew he had just come out of jail, and he was short of money.

When Gary heard this, he was confused and didn't know how to act as he chose to do as he was accustomed to:

"Aye, what did I hear, I have to go out?" He said, while Arnulfo answered him

"No, no, don't go out, I'm coming in."

He kicked the door in, he had grown up in jail, and he still looked like an orangutan, and when he entered, seeing Gary's stature, he was astonished and asked him

"Where is your daddy?," and Gary, pursed his lips, not knowing what to do, answered him, lowering his voice:

"He escaped through the window"

Arnulfo went out bewildered and asked his friends who was the child he had seen in the antechamber of the cafeteria, and they asked him if Valentina also worked there and took care of children, and they answered that no, that the one he had mistaken for a child was a dwarf who played as Valentina's husband. He was so disappointed that a few days later when he saw Valentina again he told her

"Really Valentina, you women have no mercy, haven't you found someone better to replace me with?".

"Better that than none, I told you to stay away from drugs, that was the one that took away my hunger when you went to jail," she replied.

Arnulfo felt so ashamed, that he went out without saying anything and did not come back that way, because his friends wanted to start making fun of him.

Then it began to decay, in a way that even lard

After a cousin led him to the "methadone" program, he began to get clean again, passed from hand to hand, got a vehicle that he ended up selling to Gibon, met another Dominican woman who took care of him, until he ended up embedded in the pack.

CHAPTER 39

THE DECEPTION

In any circumstance, there wasn't a line of Gibon's life that wasn't explored by that hungry mafia, hungry and thirsty for evil, because they didn't think about what they were doing, and they even touched his health insurance to justify their fraud, they used people who worked at Health first to move his address to make it look like anything involving redemption action was done with Gibon's authorization, and even Gibon's email was controlled by a director of Homeland security they called Elaine Duke, and they sought to justify it all with actions of redemption everything with intimidating actions so that they would benefit and Gibon would be harmed, Gibon understood that whatever they did they had no power over him, he knew they were doing it because God allowed them to, and he was still serene because whether it was proof or evil, he knew that they would not get away with whatever they did, they were looking for Moors where there were no coasts at all, because they would have to go back to where they started and without being able to touch what belonged to Gibon, but besides, they were unaware that Gibon belonged to a line that contributed to the U.S. economy 2. 3 trillion dollars.

The organization of evil, having no new mechanisms to resort, they began to bribe the employees of the post office where Gibon had defined his address, in such a way that when a package arrived to Gibon they would hold it until it was time to return it, to make believe that he did not pick it up on time, and for the same reason it had to be returned, because they would put the notice many times missing a day, and when he found the information slip then they would say that the package was not there, to make the emissary believe that Gibon had changed his address, and when they put the notice on time and Gibon arrived to pick it up there was someone who was last and they called him together so that the one who was behind him would pick up Gibon's package as his, handing it over to the organization of evil, as if Gibon was a puppet without rights whom they could control, all those actions of baseness, were directed to provoke Gibon, because they were still interested in creating bought witnesses to make him look as violent.

On another occasion something similar happened, Gibon received a notification of some books he had ordered, after standing in a long line, one of the postal employees, who was called Pits, asked him for the receipt for the withdrawal of the package, and even though Gibon was in front of him, he asked for the receipt to the one who was behind him. He looked for the package of the one who was last and handed it to him, the one who was last clarified that Gibon was first, but the postal employee replied that he did not see any package there, but Gibon told him to look for it well, because if the voucher was in the box, it was because something had arrived. Pits, the mail clerk replied, that there was nothing, Gibon insisted and at once it appeared, they did not understand that they should not provoke Gibon, however, those insisted on making it difficult for him, because even so, when the clerk delivered the package, he asked him:

"What is that?," questioned Pits.

Gibon answered him: "it is not your business, why should I give you information about my activities? And this that has just happened is going to be included in a magazine," which made the employee look surprised.

But that was the second time it happened, because the first time, it was a female employee, combined with another woman who tied up a mail to Gibon, who for not struggling with her preferred that she took the mail, all for not getting into a dispute, the organization of evil and occult sect were so desperate to justify the fraud, that they did not mind resorting to anything.

On another occasion they sent a package to Gibon that one of the executives of the state farm insurance company did not want it to fall into Gibon's hands, and when it was time to pick it up instead of Pits, they used an employee of Indian origin to do the operation, and on that occasion they made him sign twice to receive a letter where the insurance company said that they were not going to pay, When they took the package, the executive entered his hand and took possession of the package, while Gibon was given a letter that he had already received five weeks earlier, while in a malicious manner, they made him sign for the package that the emissary of the state farm insurance company took with him while he retained an expired letter.

All combined, using the services of the bribed employee.

"How brazen," Gibon thought.

Occult sect and the organization of evil had combined in locating evidence that could counter Gibon's rights, and were resorting to all kinds of traps, provocations, which left no other option but to think that those satraps, with insect-like tendencies, without wings of their own to fly, were for the moment dozing like mud dwellers, showing their pig-like temperaments.

And so they were occult sect and organization of evil, combining low blow actions against Gibon, and many times he used to wonder which of the two crows has incurred more baseness?

However, the more evil they did to him, the more strength God supplied him with, and those vampire villains, with sharp fangs to suck the blood of innocents, not being able to get away with it, had begun to fall into great depression, which had led him to the use of narcotics, and to disappointing suicides, because with "the children of God, no one should bother him".

They felt a natural fear of Gibon, and even considered him dangerous, because he could become someone who would stop their continued oppression and manipulation of the minority sectors, hyenas and wolves unified with three objectives:

To plunder, obstruct and manipulate.

Then Gibon said with all the fortitude of his conscience:

"Many are the unconscious ones invested with power, who have abused it, using it against me and the minority sectors, but when the moment of justice arrives, even if they refuse to recognize it, God will recognize it, and there are those who have conspired against the justice of the divine, even in thought," he affirmed.

At that time, the system fed on blackmail and manipulation, and its henchmen always sought to have on their knees, or under the soles of their shoes, those they considered that sooner or later they would give them water to drink, but Gibon was a natural fighter, he was not born to do the will of men, but the will of God.

In any case, society had generated a critical state of justice, where the defenders had become ruffians, and Gibon was a kind of prey, whom everyone wanted to bite.

Never had the laws in New York reached the levels of brazenness as on that occasion, when the lawful and rotten united to conspire against the minorities, forging to seize the benefits of that sector, manipulating the truth about what they were called to grant without any resistance whatsoever.

Brazenness was greater than good sense, the desire to possess had clouded the conscience of those vultures who had lost the balance of proper reflection, for they would not stop at making Gibon believe in their game of hypocrisy that they would dispossess him.

However, Gibon's faith was above the conscience of such swindlers, who refused to believe that those in their dictatorship of ambition could seize what he had covenanted before God long before he was born, so he conceived such a conspiracy as a criminal association where by free will, the doers of justice, wanted to impose injustice, believing that conscience would not disturb him, But although he refused to stress, he thought that such villainy could not go unpunished, so his soul cried out for justice, because in that place, you could not always be prominent, let's say, and disagree with the procedures of the system, because for them it would have been a pleasure to pursue and destroy their victims if they could, but it suited their plans, play with his head.

The debtors of the system were required to pay, even if they had to resort to pawning their mother, but if it was the system who owed you, at the time of the transaction you had to demand your payment through a lawyer to force them to recognize your rights, and pray to God that the lawyer did not sell out, doing a job out rigged, against you, like the Nona Shick.

Because the democracy of the system allowed some of these lawyers to be sort of gangsters with a license to cheat and manipulate.

But Gibon believed God more than man, because he knew that what he had assumed in front of his father would be fulfilled regardless of what the organization of evil, which had spared no effort to ruin him, thought, and in desperation and with the utmost impudence, he had resorted to the Taxi and Limousine Commission, which also wanted to fish in troubled waters.

They had also resorted to the ticker men, and so many other mechanisms that included, as I had told you, Gibon's medical insurance, they wanted to weaken him, corner him, leave him without air to suffocate him, but they ignored that Gibon moved with the strength of God, that's why not even trying to poison him, they could not get away with it.

When it came to health insurance, Gibon had put in a credit card so that they would deduct his health insurance payment, and they didn't do it so that later Gibon would show up with the insurance suspended, in case he had an emergency, that he would have to pay the full bills, claiming that he had changed his life, when in reality, none of that had happened, it was a racial conspiracy where everyone had combined, with a single purpose, to disappoint Gibon, for them to satisfy their egos, that's why the organization of evil had given Arnulfo a handout, to provoke Gibon. Arnulfo fell into a state of depression, to the extent that he became involved in the consumption of antidepressant, and when he did so, he would arrive out of control, driving his car up the sidewalk of Bulley's street. At the beginning, René Cariño looked for a way for him to leave, but after the group of conspirators against Gibon was integrated, the pastor of the Lord, looked for a way for those who were sickened by envy to provoke Gibon, to generate fights that would justify the Bulley's administration to decree him persona non grata, to provoke Gibon, He was forced to accept the offer of the organization of evil, which intended to manage certain economic resources belonging to Gibon, and that behind his back, through a fraud they had claimed without his knowledge.

But it turned out, that God loved Gibon in a special way, so he warned him of what was happening, motivating Gibon to refuse to accept the evil condition that those had assumed to rehearse with him, so the organization of evil, chose to involve in the persecution, all those who were in the vicinity where Gibon moved, so he paid those of the pack in Bulley, so that they would provoke dishonorable acts against Gibon, so that he would leave the place, and mingle with them.

Because of such actions, that Friday, which was not just any Friday, because the number 13 was shown even on the shirt that Arnulfo was wearing, who having inhaled a marijuana cigarette, felt like a bear, invaded by arrogance and radicalized violence, because Gibon spoke to a customer he was carrying, he had introduced the tip of a key next to Gibon's left eyebrows, minutes before taking a purchase, all because by order of the list where they were enrolled, it was Gibon's turn to be behind him, and having seen Arnulfo inside the establishment, Gibon asked him if he already had a ride, and Arnulfo who saw Gibon talking to him, got upset in an uncontrolled way, and began to insult Gibon, and he asked him not to talk to him, but Arnulfo was still violent, Gibon wanted to joke and smiling he told him approaching him:

"Do you want me to bite you?"

But Arnulfo intensified his violence, and while Gibon was looking for a way to block his punches with his left hand, because with his right hand he grabbed his glasses, not being Gibon's intention to respond with violence to Arnulfo, because he knew that violence generated violence, for a moment Gibon didn't understand. He was careless, when Arnulfo, moving the key from bottom to top, managed to scratch him with the metal, a little above the left eyebrow, causing Gibon to spill blood in gushes, while he was looking for a way to make a tourniquet.

Arnulfo left to take his groceries, but when he returned he was unaware that the police were waiting for him, two police cars and two fire ambulances had arrived.

Arnulfo, even though he knew what he had done, was surprised to meet the police, who, when questioned about what had happened, responded:

"Oh, we exchange a few words, I got upset, and he rose up," he said, though he knew he was carrying out orders from the organization of evil.

As one of the officers approached Gibon, he said:

"Would you like us to arrest him? Because if you decide it we could do it."

Despite the proposal, Gibon saw in the officer's profile little interest in doing justice to see if he responded with violence to grab hold of there, they ignored that Gibon knew everything they intended and would not lend to facilitate the way, although Arnulfo tried to show his artwork, his green and red tattoos, to intimidate and impress, he attacked Gibon but Gibon as if he had been a doll blocked his blows with his left hand and did not respond, he had in his right hand glasses and only prevented Arnulfo from hitting him with his blows and in an oversight he stabbed him with a key between his eyebrows breaking the optic vein that accelerated the blood outlet. Arnulfo thought he had defeated him because he didn't answer him, and he even showed himself before the pack as the Goliath that would make it difficult for David, but Gibon knew that if he answered the villains would get away with it, so apparently he left everything like that, when the police and the ambulance arrived Gibon refused to press charges saying:

"No, I don't want him to go to jail, because he has a family, if he goes to jail, his children will lose their livelihood and his family will suffer," he said.

Hearing these words spoken by Gibon, the agent looked at him with a face of disbelief, but Gibon knew what he was doing.

The officer asked him if he would accept an apology from Arnulfo, and Gibon said yes.

Then the officer approached Arnulfo and suggested that he ask his opponent for an apology, and although he asked for it without much desire as a forced apology, Gibon, with calm patience, accepted it.

Arnulfo had no choice because if he refused in front of the officer, he would be harmed.

He reduced the frequency of his presence at Bulley, he thought Gibon's strategy of not accepting him going to jail may have been a secret condition for some purpose, however Gibon's purpose was no more than a social worker would give to a patient, or a nurse would give to an emotionally disturbed person.

So it was that 15 minutes later the ambulance had decided to leave, but not before that moment Gibon insisted that the paramedic give him a container to pee, or let him go to the bathroom, but his refusal was total, they wanted to see if Gibon would do it in his pants, but Gibon warned him that

that would not be possible, and that if he did not let him use the bathroom, he would do it in the ambulance, one of those that the firefighters used.

As he said he did, Gibon sat up and peed through the crack in the back door. After the ambulance left, the paramedic asked him if he used to pee in his car. To which Gibon replied that it all depended on the circumstances:

"It depends if such an emergency arises, for I have a vessel to do it in, but in this case, you induced me to such an extreme," he said.

The paramedic was silent as the ambulance moved, a few minutes later they arrived at the pavilion emergency at 218th and Broadway.

At that moment they entered the information into the computer, and an intern named Nicol appeared to whom Gibon recited a love poem.

He hummed it with a melody so deep that it induced her to movement, to the rhythm of the melody, as if it had been a cry to the heart, because she lived it with splendor.

After enjoying Gibon's display of humor, he sat down at his computer, and finished entering the data.

The accumulated debt for such aggression including the ambulance and medical assistance amounted to 2.300 dollars, but Gibon did not bill him either, he continued to think that all that was the work of occult sect and the organization of evil, he knew that sooner or later all the villains would pay, regardless of the possessions of material powers that sustain.

A few days had passed, at that time Vilinsky and Rodo were

dumbfounded with Gibon, and taking advantage of the mishap between Arnulfo and him, they insisted that he challenge Gibon, who was the owner of a serenity proper to those assigned from heaven.

The pretext used was that a member of the club made an offer to Arnulfo who was on duty and although he refused it and the others who were still on the waiting list, and Gibon accepted it for a voluntary donation as that one could contribute, when Gibon left everyone started to murmur so that when Gibon returned Arnulfo was at the front door and Gibon passed him by, and Arnulfo addressing him, became somewhat aggressive and told him:

"Keep provoking, you'll see that I'm going to break you again," he said.

"Although it is not my style to confront you, I usually parody Bosch, "who deceives me once, is a scoundrel, who deceives me twice, I am a scoundrel", I don't want you to be confused because that time you induced me to spill a necessary blood, on that occasion I neither attacked you nor defended myself, I only blocked you with my left hand when I could have defended myself with my right, I didn't do it because violence is not a good thing, it kills the soul and poisons it, I could have sent you to jail, and when the police told me that if I wanted them to arrest you, I preferred not to do it, however, although I am not violent, if you attack me again, you will be hurt," he said.

Arnulfo had already squared up to get on top of him and Gibon conditioned to cut him down, but before it happened, Rodo and Vilinski changed their minds and prevented the aggression.

But for God's sake, let me take you back to Arnulfo and Judith's story, which had led him from a nursing clergyman to a desolate orphan, for we might say, that the hero had attacked himself in his rhetoric and lacked words in his expression.

So, then, because Judith had been formed as a cadre of the aforesaid organization that promoted women as Goddesses, and entitled her to have three husbands under one roof, and to put herself in the man's place by doing all that he did to them, a few months later, Judith without wasting time had got an engagement ring from Arnulfo, and she told him:

"My love, now that we are engaged, we must set a date to get married," she said.

"How is that Judith, I am not ready to get married," replied Arnulfo.

"It is precisely because you are not ready that I am proposing to you, do you like to be kissed and loved? So that no one obstructs us, we must get married, I am ready and therefore, so are you. Right?"

"If you say so!," Arnulfo replied with more fear than shame.

They did not speak any more, and two months later, they got married, but that was not intended to stay there, because the excommunication and the harassment, generated reason for Judith to accuse Ambrosio for pedophilia, and the church of cover-up, and for the suffering that all this had caused to her husband, she claimed a compensation to the church, which by antonomasia she was forced to pay, at the same time that she offered him a public apology.

It's been a long time since he's been on pilgrimage, and for all that he's been we thank God, we thank God, we thank God Judith sang, some years after leaving Arnulfo, whose ordeal had left him with some trauma that sporadically induced him to try marijuana, long before he was admitted to the Pack and marked his body with more tattoos than a map.

<h1 style="text-align:center">CHAPTER 40</h1>

<h1 style="text-align:center">JUSTICE AND RESISTANCE</h1>

The quarantine had isolated the citizens of the world and especially in the United States, which exceeded four months and even the states had not opened the closure in its entirety.

And so it happened that a 911 call led to the arrest of a minority man, a survivor of the pigeonholing generated by the corona virus pandemic, after he allegedly tried to use a counterfeit $20 bill to pay at a supermarket called "Antenna".

George Floyd, despite being subdued had been killed by asphyxiation, generating great indignation in the popular masses of the people of the United States, which induced some activists, to take to the streets to make themselves felt, after raising their voice of protest, the death of George Floyd, occurred on May 25, 2020, in the neighborhood of Powderhorn, in the city of Minneapolis, Minnesota (USA), as a result of his arrest by four local police officers, including officer Dereck Chauvin, who was arrested and charged with manslaughter, in the third degree (involuntary) and subsequently charged with manslaughter, and later with second-degree murder (intentional) because despite having subdued the prisoner, he appeared in a video with his knee on

George Floyd's neck, leaving him unconscious, despite the fact that the one who was arrested expressed to be heard: "I cannot breathe"

Also charged as accomplices and instigators in the murder were Thomas Lane, J. A. Kueng and Tou Tho U, who were also arrested and brought to justice.

The people were outraged, they took to the streets, and many police units were burned, those interpreted that the white supremacy continued to put the knee on the neck of the black minority, as a symbolism that the chains would never be broken, and then demonstrated that the conquests achieved, no one would make them go back even with the pretense of death.

The first week of June, something had happened that induced Bulley's corporate management to transfer Wing, so another administrator had arrived, during Wing's administration, during the night hours, a series of robberies were taking place, and many of those involved could not be caught, then Wong of Filipino descent arrived, and a better result was expected.

So, Bulley continued his hectic course.

The organization of evil, composed of apocalyptic demons, boasted of so many evils, and did not cease to keep on trying, and kept on resorting to all the mechanisms within their reach.

In reality, it seemed that the organization of evil and its leaders had gone mad, every day they created mechanisms of attack, and already Gibon was determined to do the impossible so that they would not get away with it, they used money and the power of man to outrage those who would not let them, and Gibon resorted to the power of God to counteract their attempts.

The organization of evil sought out among its membership those with a history of abuse, and Kom Crawn was one of its distinctions, ready to do the dirty work of anyone who merited the honor. Kom Crawn had decorations for skilled service to police brutality; five years earlier, he had broken the head of an activist protesting against the increase in apartment rents in New York State.

Kom Crawn had been requested by the organization of evil to test Gibon, and see his attitude when caught surprised, everything happened on Tuesday, June 2nd, they sent a member of the occult sect went to Bulley with the purpose of supplying food, while he requested Gibon's transportation service, a funeral car parked in the front parking lot, observed the movements of those, to the extent that once noticed the movements were directed to follow them, they left 237th Street, and Broadway and entered, Kings Bridge Avenue, returning to Broadway at 225th Street, then they moved down 10th Avenue until they reached the Harlem Federal Drivers Highway, from where they ran to 8th Avenue and 155th Avenue, before exiting the highway, from the hearse with a New Jersey license plate, the driver was instructing Officer Kom, regarding Gibon's approach, and there was Officer Kom, with the squad car facing the front waiting for Gibon, who was going at a speed of 25 miles an hour, and Officer Kom turned the squad car around and seeing Gibon behind him, he stopped and he with all the splendor of his chutzpah approached and Gibon rolled down the window and asked him:

"What's wrong officer, some mistake? I'm coming in at 25 mph what's wrong?"

"You are coming in 41, give me your driver's license and car registration, sorry for the delay but I have to proceed," Kom said to the passenger.

"Yes, I'm in a hurry," said the passenger.

"I will hurry," Officer Kom said with all his politeness.

"I don't understand, I was coming at 25 miles per hour," commented Gibon.

"Don't pay anything," commented the passenger.

"I have to check to see what proceeds" Gibon replied.

A moment later Kom officer brought a contravention, while recommending.

"If you do not respond to this ticket within 15 days, your license could be suspended," argued.

"All right," Gibon said, as he watched the patrol drive away, making it clear that his mission for the moment was to wait for Gibon and fabricate a contravention.

Gibon felt, that a snake passed under his feet, in reality he did not respect the man who wore the uniform, Gibon respected the uniform, because many of the men who wore that uniform, he believed that they were unworthy to wear it. "Because the man who wore such a dignified insignia, should act with professionalism, courtesy, respect, besides, he should be merciful and proud of his investiture," Gibon thought.

Where ethics still endured, and corruption was not ingrained, those deserving of honor were rewarded, but the unworthy were publicly shamed, that was what the community thought of officers like Kom.

For although Gibon would have liked to confront him and defeat him physically, it was not advisable, because even if Kom the officer was not doing his duty by persecuting and harassing the minority taxpayers, it was necessary that honor be rendered to the power of the uniform, until God dictated otherwise.

And certainly, Officer Kom was not the best, he abused his sister, he abused his wife too, because he was a policeman, with him there was no anger, he was unregenerately violent, he was repressive and abusive too, and his nature was the worst.

In any case, the states and their patience-smeared cities were courageously running through stories of violence, buffaloed by officers who were members of riot squads: Aaron Torglaski and Robert McCabe had pushed a 75 year old man, named Martin Gugino who was participating in a day of protests over George Floyd's death, and who had fallen backwards hitting his head on the concrete that led him to bleed from the ears ,which had generated a dispute between the Governor of the State of New York at the time Andrew Cuomo and President Donald Trump, who had alleged that what happened to the 75 year old "was nothing but a conspiracy theory without foundation."

Many used to wonder why there were not enough violence

prevention organizations, and why existing organizations that sought to prevent violence were ignored.

Although to tell the truth, vice and violence was the charm of those insensitive people who saw benefits in every line, even if those who had to fall fell, for them nothing mattered and they said: "The dead to the hole, and the living to the bun".

For such satraps, humanity was nothing but a number for exploitation or destruction, that is why they used to see as a danger, not to say as their worst enemies, those who created organizations to alleviate the pains of minorities.

"To fight against the prevention of vice and violence" was to fight against the consumption of drugs, cigarettes, and firearms, and against drug trafficking, to allow this fight was like reducing the income of the sectors that feed on human pain, which is why, at that time, there were many obstacles for the foundations dedicated to fight against vice and violence, to reach the funds for such objectives.

Then as Gibon, was a standard-bearer of the cause of non-vice and non-violence, the organization of evil refused to admit his purposes, and was always looking for a motive of provocation that would induce Gibon to rebel, in order to justify themselves, and for that reason, frequently, they renewed the actions of bribing the pack, so that they would shout at him or raise their voices in front of unknown persons, in case Gibon would put some in their place, because they had evidence that he was out of control, or did not have the optional balance to assume any assignment, for them to continue in possession of the resources that by law, corresponded to Gibon, and all this added to racism, the systematic abuse of power, which was leading sectors interested in chaos, to sponsor a rebellion, and it was that tolerance had become fiction, and the masses longed for everything to change, and threw epithets of arduous request: "Everything has to change in society, racism and brutality, have to stop."

It was the reason for those protests, to stop abusive actions and police brutality against minorities.

Officer Kom was a uniformed minority, unaware of his people, paid by the poor to serve the rich, the long time of abuse had made him arrogant, and the arrogance induced him to misunderstanding, and he was so identified with his deeds that he was unaware that death was lurking.

Two weeks after that member of law enforcement who was causing disorder, choked George Floyd, Hardy and Pardy, two members of the international XZ gang, went shopping at Bulley, those beings were acting as a pressure group that had gone to stock up on supplies to supply food to the members of the protests for the death of George Floyd, who were rising on 42nd Street, they had instructions to break windows and sow chaos. They chose Cholinfe to take them, they moved from north to south making a similar route to the one that Gibon had made two weeks before, but this time Cholinfe the driver, had been stabbed with a rod with a silencer, precisely when he began to cross the bridge of 225th and Broadway towards 10th Street, when he was stabbed with a rod with a silencer, he felt a terrible terror when he found himself in front of such a reality:

"What happened? They're going to mug me, I've only made a hundred dollars, look at him there, take him," Cholinfe said with more fear than shame.

"We don't need your money, what we need is your transportation, so if you cooperate with us, nothing is going to happen to you, stop the car, put it in neutral, and you'll be in the back."

Cholinfe had no choice but to obey, he was being held at gunpoint and the gun had a silencer, if they fired, they wouldn't hear the explosion.

"Please don't hurt me, I have a daughter to support," he said, making it clear that the dog doesn't always <bite as he barks>.

"Hurry up and shut your mouth, it's more convenient," said Hardy, as he continued to threaten him with the gun.

When he was in the back of the vehicle they threw him face down, covered his mouth, and tied his hands and feet, Hardy holding the gun while Pardy drove.

When they reached Amsterdam Avenue and 179th Avenue they advanced a few meters and when they approached a triangle that allowed access to the freeway, they took it out of the vehicle and threw it aside, while boarding the vehicle again they advanced southbound on the freeway Harlem drivers, until they reached the 155, while slowing down they were moving, and Kom and Keyla, were patrolling, but as Kom did not let one pass, he turned on his lights while Hardy and Pardy stopped. The patrol car stopped behind them, Keyla was distracted playing Nintendo, Kom was approaching where Hardy and

Pardy were waiting.

"Here come the police, we have to get there before curfew," commented Pardy.

"Let him come closer," replied Hardy.

When Kom was already in front of them, he said without preamble.

"Give me the registration and driver's license," he said.

"Why?" asked Pardy.

"I want to do a verification," added Kom.

Suddenly and unexpectedly, Hardy, pulled out the gun with silencer, and a shot in the forehead granted him, on his knees and with open arms Kom ended, without Keyla knowing what happened.

Of the two, the one who occupied the back seat, shot, and Kom, a mark embedded in his forehead, left him lifeless, no matter how good or bad he did, his return would define him in front of a life of greater expression, where much of the evil in his heart, would become love.

That was the departure of Officer Kom, Keyla didn't even notice, she stayed playing Nintendo.

Then, in the pause of the game Keyla saw that Kom was death, and when she went out and the game interrupted, she took out his regulation weapon and looked everywhere, but nothing else she saw, Hardy and Pardy had vanished, in an instant the night came, and the panorama darkened.

Officer Keyla called dispatch, and by now helicopters, ambulances and patrol cars had populated the area, it was 19:15, the Blues had Harlem surrounded. Helicopter searchlights glided over the treetops, towards the asphalt of the highway, seeking to veil the presence of the murderous souls.

Forty-five minutes later, a taxi driver noticed the lump near the sidewalks of the highway, thought it was a dead man, and called 911, gave them the details, and they went after Cholinfe, both the 33rd and 34th Precinct showed up, Cholinfe was questioned, and he said he was assaulted by two men and they took his vehicle.

The next day, Cholinfe's van appeared, but they kept it as evidence, a little while later he went to Bulley to provoke Gibon, by order of the organization of evil, and he took advantage of the fact that Gibon went to the bathroom and on his return he showed him a drama of heartbreak, as Gibon was ahead of him, he suddenly shouted at him as few crazy people shout at him:

"I'm going to give it to you because I want to, you weren't here and it's my turn."

Gibon with all his calm. Experiencing an act of embarrassment he said to him:

"You lower your voice, the customers might get scared"

Then he intensified his foolishness, in front of the customer, who seemed to be combined with him, to give Gibon a hard time. Gibon asked the woman if she was ready to leave, and she replied:

"No, I'm sorry, I don't want to get in trouble," she said, while calling a Taxi base.

Gibon said to Cholinfe,

"Know you realize what your crazy attitude has provoked?"

Cholinfe raised his voice again, and Gibon warned him that if he continued shouting he would be knocked down, at that moment, Ricardo appeared trying to keep the "blood from reaching the river", and Jochelo let him know that it was a plot trying to manipulate his truth and leave him in a bad position.

At that moment someone came out who went to Gibon for Gibon to ride him, and he went away, and said all fired up, for he told Cholinfe a desiderata prayer: "Avoid noisy and aggressive people, for they are a nuisance to the spirit".

And one who was called Moreno said to Gibon:

"Pastor, there is nothing against you, whoever goes against you, can have problems with me," He said, Gibon looked at him, and left.

It is true that I interrupted, but let me tell you what happened after, after the death of Officer Kom:

The police improvised an intense search, flew over Harlem and Washington Heights, for nothing.

It was never known who killed Officer Kom.

That same night, the organization of evil, and occult sect, had taken Hardy and Pardy out on a private plane to France, they were two international hitmen, recruited for the dirty work, Kom already knew enough, and they decided to kill him.

That facet of occult sect and organization of evil, to simple men, seemed dangerous, they knew they had to watch out, as such organizations made their membership watch out for each other, because occult sect and organization of evil, used to use people, including children until they were being useful to them, but then they looked for ways to drive them insane or murder them, to get rid of them, they thrived on evil, theft and infiltration of world governments, including the police, they would go after a sovereign, they would give money to all sectors to control them and then make them believe, that any gift they would take was as indelible a commitment, as the mark of the beast.

Cholinfe, who had been infiltrated into Bulley to make fun of Gibon, possessed an accelerated, bipolar and disrespectful condition, so his behavior often tended to offend people who felt abused by his unhinged expressions and his attitude of foolishness.

Although Gibon had tried to cut off communication with him, he had sought to get his attention by telling him:

"But how is it possible for you to deal with a young man? for you to deal with me you would have to look for one of your sons," he said, trying to get Gibon out of his box.

Gibon looked at him, smiled, and said:

"Make no mistake with me, you might die in the skit."

"But if you put me to death in the skit, that's not going to be worth anything," said Cholinfe.

"There are so many beings of value in this life, that you are just a reduced ant, without conscience, the worst of the garbage I have ever heard of," said Gibon trying to give him a drink of his own medicine.

"Ah, look at the muscles that I bring, come on, let's have a pulse," He said trying to pretend his shame, he was doing the drama in front of a girl who was observing to see the attitude of Gibon, who had gone through the worst tests and provocations imposed by the occult sect and the organization of evil.

Gibon accepted the challenge, but when they were arm wrestling with their right hands on a parked car, Cholinfe stopped, claiming that he was burning his elbows from the heat generated by the sun on the metal of the vehicle.

Then, not knowing what to do, he kept provoking Gibon, so he told Rony and Fredesvindo, who were there at that moment, that they were witnesses of Gibon's behavior.

Then he said that Gibon did not seem religious, and Gibon told him that he was certainly not religious, that he was a spiritualized being, since religious people were often fanatics who did not admit into their congregations people who did not think like them, and who were the closest to being false prophets like him, who preached being a Christian, and did not control his gossip and emotions.

Then he began to talk to Fredesvindo, with hints of attacks, but Gibon, knowing the purpose, did not pay any attention to him, he told him that Arnulfo had broken him, all with the intention of getting him out of his balance.

Gibon told him that it was okay, that he was a punch taker and that if he could hit him too, he would take his blows.

But to shut him up, there was a moment when Gibon grabbed him by both wrists and squeezed him to such a degree that Cholinfe experienced the pain so that he would understand what was going to happen if he continued to disrespect him, there was a moment when Cholinfe wanted to despair because he was in pain, and Fredesvindo and Rony approached him questioning.

"Is it for real?" asked Rony.

"No, it's playing!" replied Gibon, letting go.

"Don't play with your hands," said Fredesvindo.

"Be careful, you talk too much," said Gibon to Cholinfe, as he let him go.

Cholinfe kept silent, and as it was Gibon's turn, he left, Fredesvindo and Rony stayed with him, advising him not to provoke Gibon, because if he brought out what Gibon had inside him, he might experience a moment of full regret.

Cholinfe was another of those who had arrived from Garget, he was as agitated as a monkey, his extrovert condition induced him to ask a very high price for transportation.

Always aware of what was going on and willing to distort what he heard, he was trusting, he asked customers to give him products that were part of their purchases, he asked for tips, like a child who lacked the logic to understand that such attitudes were not conducive to the service.

On one occasion Gibon gave a protective mask against the COVID-19 to one who was called Chamo, but as there were no more, he did not give it to Cholinfe, who had asked him for one, and he could not keep silent before such a condition, so he confronted Gibon with his behavior:

"Pastor, you know me, and you haven't given me anything, but you don't know Chamo and you gave him a mask."

"Cholinfe, do not behave like a grumpy child, there is more merit in assisting your enemies and strangers, because such action is reflection and motivation of the Lord, there is is no merit when there is a friendship, because if you serve a brother, or a friend, you do it because of the family ties that bind you to them, so when I receive others that will arrive, I will get you one.".

"Thank you pastor, I hope so," he expressed.

"I'll be on it!" replied Gibon.

Rony, on the other hand, who had received one, asked for one for his wife, but Gibon gave it to Jochelo, who had seen the move and claimed his own.

And Rony who was hanging around insisted that Gibon get one for his wife, but Gibon told him:

"Rony, I gave the one I had to Jochelo, give that one to your wife, and wait to see if I get others, so I can get one for you," said Gibon.

"Why did he give anything to Jochelo, he is an envious person who wants everything he sees," expressed Rony with resentment, because at that time Jochelo and he were incommunicado.

Anyway, Gibon smiled and told him:

"Don't worry, I'll check and see if we can get one for your wife."

"It's okay pastor," nodded Rony with a look of agreement, as he walked away to bring in a shopping cart that had been emptied by a customer.

Suddenly, a girl was approaching to join the line that led to the interior of Bulley, they called her "the Vero", she was wearing one of those buns they called "onion", Cholinfe approached her, always ready to give his opinion even if he wasn't invited, and he said:

"I like your onion to make a good stew," he said.

"And I love your face, to give you a cookie[16], to erase your evilness, disguised as a smile," she said, in the spirit of putting him in his place.

"Oh, she came out a poetess, look pastor, with a woman like that, I get rich!," he added, with all the splendor of his impudence.

Gibon pretended not to hear him, and kept silent.

"Well, you're going to stay poor, because I'm allergic to noisy men like you, I don't like you," she expressed like an expert of the task.

"But my love, what did I do to you, why do you treat me like this?," replied Cholinfe.

"I see that you are pathetic, stop with that of my love, because I am not your love, don't be so trusting," reiterated Vero to him.

"It's okay, you're not that pretty, if so, I do not bother you," he said, as he walked away from her.

"Well done, queen, those fresh can't be trusted," said Rocko Vulcan, looking for a way to make the Vero take him into account.

Vero looked at him and smiled, that day they became friends, they exchanged phone numbers, and whenever she went to Bulley, she went with him.

This friendship, between those beings placed face to face by destiny, generated that the pack when she arrived sang a

---

[16] Slap

prefabricated refrain in the restlessness, envy and evilness, which said:

"Rocko swore he was just finishing, Vero thought he was chapeando[17]".

Some weeks had passed when the corona virus was raging, and some needed help, the city through the food banks, distributed rations for those who needed food, Rocko collected some bags and took them to the pack by disposition of the occult sect, the pack that had begun to lower some stripes to the attacks he made to Gibon, insisted that Gibon took some of the bags, on one occasion Rocko offered him a package of food to warm up, Gibon thanked him and told him that he ate it, that he didn't need it, but he insisted that Gibon accept it, out of courtesy he decided to accept it to give it to the homeless, at the moment of catching it a kind of paparazzi of those sent by occult sect photographed him catching the bag, and he accelerated the car and fled so that Gibon wouldn't ask him to tell him why he was taking a picture without his permission, maybe thinking that it wasn't food and it was something else, that's why the malicious one often sees Moors where there is no coast.

To get them off his back he took four bags and took them to some homeless people whose roof was the sidewalks of a dry bridge near Kings Bridge.

Gibon had left New York, on a path of exploration, and during his stay he discovered unusual things, such as he tried to inquire about the prices of apartments to see if he qualified to take a loan to one of the banks of the system, but as the

---

[17] Working

occult sect and the organization of evil followed him wherever he moved, also there, in the country where he was born they sawed his stick and he could not make the operation even having the money for the initial, it was not that he was going to stay, if not, that he was interested in having something to spend the summer, then he remembered Estrace when on one occasion he told him:

"If you get that money now, you dare to disappear and never come back to New York".

Gibon looked at her with some disappointment and replied:

"The first thing is that if I bring an assignment that has caused me pain, it is not prudent that if something belongs to me I should be controlled about what I should do, or what I should eat, or am I a slave to you?"

Estrace smiled and kept silent, and Gibon understood why he was being obstructed from buying property outside the United States.

The pack had entered to obey the new dictates of the occult sect and the organization of evil, and now they had changed the style of addressing Gibon, they had become one and after Rodo asked him to be "friends", the others also looked for a way not to continue clashing with him, however, with all that Gibon had gone through, it would be difficult for them to confuse him, Gibon did not trust even in his shadow, and whenever she coincidentally met Estrace, who at the time she wanted to use Gibon, she would go to Bulley, and if it wasn't with him she wouldn't move, after they had received the cumulative compensation they had withheld from 1991, to 2020, to the harassment committee, she tried to profit from the attractive sum, and it seems they had decided to use Estrace for the withholding, and now she, whenever she went to Bulley, she was looking for a way to go with Vilinski, she was avoiding Gibon, it seems they had a secret that couldn't be revealed, besides, because whenever Gibon saw her, he asked her where her money was, because she once hinted to him that she had something to do with it, so from now on she was hiding from Gibon, and he, as Tody and Mary, had told him that she had a psychiatric record, didn't insist much on her, and he was waiting for the service activities in the city to restart, in order to put pressure on the lawyer Robert Wolff, who was also giving the matter some time for some purpose, although Gibon suspected that he might be involved in the plot, he had decided to wait patiently, since he knew that at any moment he would find out what they were up to, and what was the secret kept by that gang of malicious people.

In truth, in order to manipulate their victims, they would resort to anything and everything, or to find out if they were legally admitted to the country to see what kind of blackmail they would resort to.

Their big mistake was their ignorance, they thought they could play bad guys with Gibon or that they could bully him, they needed to understand, that any human being that inhabited the planet, could be called undocumented, but never illegal, everyone that inhabited this planet, brought the mandate of God, and anyone that in free will, had been affected in any circumstance had the Human right to be compensated as the circumstance warranted.

It is true that the creation had been inspired by joint actions in community socialization.

CHAPTER 41

CHEATERS

They were hoodlums disguised as businessmen, they worked for some corporations that were already known to be cheats, and they sheltered under their umbrella, some small companies with different names, which allowed them to cheat the same people two or three times, some of them had woven a conspiratorial chain against Gibon, and some of them were more malicious than merciful.

Mercy was the grace of God, and the wickedness, the Devil assumed it, so that those marked by the beast, did not reflect when it came to harming their neighbor.

The city had been overrun by shades of violence, and thoughtless crimes.

Many of the people who approached Gibon, went with a marked intention, to stamp their disappointment, however, none had interacted with the brazenness that the deceivers interacted, and so as Gibon's existence in New York progressed, deceivers from different lines appeared, offering them elevating investments, because Gibon wrote pamphlets, and some of them, whom Gibon chose not to call by their names, chose to plunder them shamelessly, taking considerable sums of money, under certain promises, which they did not keep, while others left in broken banks, in order not to pay, ethics not amounting to anything for such ruffians.

Many of them set up businesses of the same nature, to hide behind, and seek to deceive again, victims whom they had already deceived.

Such actions obeyed the dictates of the occult sect and the organization of evil, which had generated a phobia against Gibon, and resorted to all the mechanisms at their disposal to defeat him, despite not having achieved their purposes with him.

Some men believed that within a conglomerate integrated by miscellaneous entities, at the time of a radical action that affected some sectors, they believed that only the victims of their preferred ethnicity should benefit, but they were wrong, because from the beginning of creation, the sun had been conceived to illuminate all.

But due to the condition of racism, sectarianism and ignorance, it had generated the intolerance that induced discrimination and human rights violations, which created the actions of police brutality, due to the misuse of the power of the uniform.

Twenty-nine years withholding the Gibon's benefit o was a clear sign of discrimination, which later they wanted to amend, generating more proof of pain, because those induced to produce indignity, did not know any other mechanism than evil, to satisfy their egocentrism.

An ethnographic discussion between Vilinsky and Jochelo had accelerated the pace, while heating up tempers:

"Shit, I don't know what's going on with the Dominican,

you take it to the boondocks and a lot of times they want to pay you whatever they want, so that you can't even cover the gas, they don't deny that they are of African descent," Vilinsky said.

"The rain is coming to the ranch, you are of African descent, I made it clear before, don't keep repeating the same bullshit to me, because you are also inducing me to repeat mine, my grandparents were blue-eyed Spaniards," replied Jochelo, with all the pride of his origins.

"Oh, now I understand why you have those grey hangman's eyes, says the pastor, don't believe me, but he also says that the Dominican is the only black man who despises himself, they love foreigners more than their countrymen, and the tighter they are, the greater their longing for a white woman" Vilinsky said.

"There are exceptions to the rules, but not all of us are as you say, it is true that we like money, but those of us who live here, we work to get it," said Jochelo.

"What about the ones over there?," Vilinsky asked.

"They also work to survive, except for those who plunder the public treasury, who, being pawns of oppressors, lack conscience, impoverish the nation by taking what belongs to the people, for themselves and their families," affirmed Jochelo.

"Those are other issues, but let's say that yes, it is true that we love money and we look for it wherever it is, and that is not wrong, but it is not appropriate that a Dominican who lives in Washington highs for forty years in an apartment, return it to the owner for an indemnity of twenty thousand dollars and instead of giving an advance for a house, send it to the Republic and then go to swell the list of homeless people in New York City," Vilinsky said.

"In that, I agree with you, you have to invest where you live, and enjoy as much as you can."

The exit of some brunettes interrupted the conversation capturing the attention of those, that instantly became silent, looking for the form to be selected by those that still remained undecided, Gibon began to sing the hymn of the pack that said:

"Car service, told me the lady, and I respond ready to go, if they no came for you, I ready to bring you, if they no came for you, I'm ready to bring you."

That was the Hymn of the Pack, and from there they went on to hum a chorus related to those, and it said:

"Garífuna choechoniga, blacks of struggle and honor, creation inks you for differentiation.

The halo of redemption their work generated, and they were cause and reason of God's inspiration, generated for others wealth that expanded, and to the planet defined in the libertarian guidelines, that there would be no repetition of the cause of oppression."

Then those admiring and rejoicing, they asked Gibon to take them, Jochelo and Vilinsky went into the waiting room, trying to locate any of theirs who were in need of their services.

Suddenly burst into the street Captain Peter Gamboa attracted by the fame of the pack, he was in charge of the fiftieth precinct, and sought ways to maintain good relations with the community, for the same reason many times he appeared in person to attract order on the road, so that anyone who had in a double parking, he sought a way to move before the tickets men wrote it, and such an action generated him the respect of the pack that many times when being surprised infraganti, merited of a chance to not having to pay a ticket of the amount assigned to the double parking, for them it was the blessing and the distinction of the day, and thus they, they took him great appreciation, and he was the great friend who appeared organizing the traffic in the street of Bulley.

On one occasion, Gibon was waiting for someone to leave a parking space to park, and being in a double parking space, he got out of the car and the captain who was talking to Wing, moved to where Gibon was and asked him for his driver's license, Gibon not given to certain styles was distracted and he asked him again, Gibon asked him for a chance, and told him:

"Give me a chance, I'm waiting for him to come out, to take the parking lot," he said referring to Vilinsky who was setting up a purchase to leave.

And the captain said to him: "I have asked you twice for your license, and you have not shown it to me."

Gibon smilingly showed it

"Here it is."

"Hold it up to see it," said the captain.

Gibon obeyed, the captain looked at him and added:

"Gibon Ravelo?," said the captain.

"That's right," then he saw the registration of the car that was in the Mr. Pascualo Alcanforado's name, and went back to where Wing was, and they continued talking.

Gibon thought about what they were planning, since Wing, a few minutes before, had asked Gibon what country he was from.

Gibon, who had been besieged by many, was not always forthcoming with information about himself, so he thought that perhaps they needed to confirm information about him so that any conspiratorial doubts would be cleared up.

It gave the impression that the Bulley club administration had been asked by the occult sect to test Gibon's honesty, and many times while Gibon was in the front room they would bring up carts with groceries and apparently take them out, but leave something to see who would take it and not report it, while the administrators would monitor the cameras to see if Gibon, who was the target of interest or investigation at the time, would report what was found, or hold it for them to keep, and then use that condition as a pretext to discredit him. As can be seen, the "struggle was not against flesh and blood, but against kingdom and powers."

CHAPTER 42

INFILTRATORS

The organization of evil had begun to use the Cholinfe services, who sporadically used to provoke Gibon, although he lacked control, Gibon was looking for a way to keep his temper, but for self-protection and not to please the occult sect and the organization of evil to achieve their purposes, they did not tire and sent a Greek to stand behind him and so it was, while Gibon was driving from Kings Bridge Road eastbound westbound, when he reached 225th and Bailey, he stopped to wait for the light to change, but the Greek man driving a turquoise pickup truck that was approximately eight meters away from Gibon, accelerated and hit him from behind, destroying the entire back of the Jeep, that day Gibon did not go to the hospital but the next day he went to a community clinic, trying to alleviate the pains that had resurfaced, but watching so that they would not inject him to paralyze him, because the impudence of the organization of evil was provoking unnecessary accidents to justify their wave of banditry against Gibon in the city. It was the apocalyptic era where the government of the beast sought to radically change the existential style of everyone, also trying to make humanity believe that God did not exist, and that they were the cause of what was happening, starting with the worldwide implantation of the corona virus, which processed in a laboratory, had gotten out of hand, destroying a large number of the members of humanity, as we had said before.

On that occasion they kept watching him to see if he lifted any heavy boxes in the deliveries he made from Bulley, they would show up at the clinic where he was taking therapy with the intention of impressing him.

A week after the accident, Donko approached him and said, "I'm sorry: You see that accident, it might change your year," he said.

He was not of great stature, however, he was sporadically radical and absolute in his character, and if someone came into conflict that involved physical aggression, he would offer his fist as he touched.

Gibon was silent, as he took a passenger he would carry.

In reality, Gibon did not like the style of play used by the occult sect and the organization of evil, because he saw their actions as a vile act, which went against the logic of their innocence, because every act of the organization of evil was aimed at discrediting the human condition of their victims, showing them as negligent, irresponsible, which led Gibon to think that it was not the innocent who was criminalized by the power, but those who had the power, made the innocent criminal, since such abuses induced rebellion, where the innocent would end up paying because the conspirators and ideologues of evil, often used the ignorant as decoys and at the time of justice, the naive ended up paying for the crimes forged by these, or as Ruperto the priest of the sacred heart said "always pay the righteous for sinners and it is time for the church to take action to induce salvation.

And referring to those camouflaged as Christians, Gibon said:

"You only imitate Jesus Christ in the beard, but in the heart you sow distortion."

And it was that some of those false prophets used to plan evil deeds proper to atheists or impious, and they did everything out of ignorance, because they thought that by executing an action of perversion even if it was harmful and malicious, with such a condition they served the Lord.

But the occult sect and the organization of evil, had a particular style to harass, and the cat sought to please her opinion, and with the strength and brightness emanating from her blue-green eyes had control of the will of several men and used to put them to do their errands, but with Gibon was different, and ended up obsessed, with that one, to his followers of the occult sect said:

"Since he will obey no one, I will feed him from my hands," she said, and the other women laughed.

And so she began to pose as Gibon's wife to certain sectors, and of all that was destined for him, she wanted half, obviously, she retained Gibon's other half until he managed to take it away from her with the law.

Her obsession was so great that, having Gibon tried to escape from the cramped quarters in which he lived in the room he had rented from Dona Soco, in order to avoid seeing Gary every day like a zombie, and Dona Soco like a witch, but the cat kept meowing and had a hundred cars that followed Gibon from the time he got up until he went to bed, before, she ordered sabotage, but Gibon had passed all the tests, so she needed someone to notify her where he parked and what time he left when he got up, so she was informed of Gibon's moves, including who he moved with, she bribed all the friends who dared to approach Gibon, and the friends who were there before she arrived, and who were loyal to Gibon.

Anyway, Gibon tried to rent an apartment at 130 West 183rd Street in the Bronx, but because the crew followed him wherever he moved, she realized his purpose, and approached Peter the manager showing him an income of 7.000 dollars a month, 3.000 dollars more than Gibon had, and took advantage of that condition to seduce Peter and bribe him, making Peter rent the apartment to her, since she doubled Gibon's income, thus making Peter discriminate against Gibon in the apartment, besides that he had asked her about her origins, and Gibon had answered him that his origin was heaven and earth, and shamelessly Peter answered him that he was afraid that he would take the carriers that drove with plates from other states, Gibon answered him that he did not know anyone in that building where they had submitted the application and that he had nothing to do with reckless drivers who caused accidents and ran over innocent people, however everything obeyed the conspiratorial assembly of the occult sect and the organization of evil, who had decided to use the cat to do the dirty work against Gibon.

Four days later, Angelo, the super intendant who had insisted on renting the apartment to Gibon, informed him that the administrator had rented it to the cat.

In reality they sought to demoralize Gibon, but Gibon brought the strength to defeat them all, for he was the owner of a greater strength, which overcame all intentions, he was still awaiting the report of Robert Wolff, his lawyer, because he was convinced that even if the conspirators did what they did, or resorted to what they resorted to, having no power over him, they could not succeed in their plans against him.

What mattered to Gibon that the conspirators should not get away with it, and that he should be given all that he was born with, he did not care that public opinion should know the origin of that compensation, because for him, he who owed nothing owed nothing, would fear nothing.

Then when the time came, the time saviors who had seen what had happened to Gibon, and understood that the emissaries of the occult sect and the organization of evil were trying to change in free will what Gibon had assumed before he was born, intervened by strengthening Gibon's power, and inspiring them to part with what was not theirs, and give it to its rightful owner.

Some time had passed which led to Gibon's economic advancement, which allowed him to move into his own house, so Mrs. Soco and Gary, had increased the rent and due to the reduced amount of his retirement he had problems to complete the payment of the rent, and as Gary's income was barely enough to buy tennis shoes and clothes, they decided to imitate Nena, one who sold beans with candy at 182nd and St Nicholas, in Manhattan, and became head of a small business, they were put on a corner of the Bronx, to sell beans with candy and llaniqueque, a fried flour cake that was round like a disk.

In Bulley they had hired a girl named Ailin to help Frank and Ojitos to collect the carts, being an ideal help for them, and she used to make jokes to Gibon from time to time, but as there was never a hair in the soup, the pack had tried to insinuate that she was taking an interest in Gibon, so he was always looking for a way to avoid misunderstandings, so that they would not rehearse a montage of fallacies.

CHAPTER 43

PAIN AND VACCINATION

On December 11, 2021, the press had reported that the United States was in possession of the first doses of vaccine against the corona virus, COVID-19, and that over the weekend they would be distributed to the various states so that vaccination could begin immediately.

Many in the pack were reluctant to put it on, but Jochelo and Gibon had put it on and the pack saw that they didn't die and nothing happened to them, so Gibon, to reinforce the decision to put it on, gave a speech:

"Nobody dies a day before, nor a day after", "if you don't touch yourself even if you put on and if you touch yourself even if you take off."

Fear has always been the tool of destruction, because the mind in fear attracts the worst.

"Be positive and the light will define their paths and all the best will come to them as a blessing" He said, and from that day one by one went to different places and vaccinated, then when someone dared to provoke another inviting him to rehearse violence as a fist fight, the provoked answered him:

"I have already been vaccinated against rabies, so as not to let myself be provoked by the provocateurs" he said, and they chose to remain silent.

The planet had become a world where the romantics lived in disappointment because the inclement ones kept watching them, studying the way they would bring it down.

Many saw Gibon as an easy prey to hunt, so most of those who approached him did it with a second intention, to confuse, deceive and plunder him, and yet, he did not understand how it was possible that the world was invaded by hypocrites, ruthless, shameless and deceivers.

That was more than enough reason for him to have withdrawn confidence from the man, especially when he remembered the expression of the Galilean teacher Jesus of Nazareth who used to say "cursed is the one who believes in man".

Men had lost the concept of duty, before and after.

They had replaced love by ambition, and sanity had been eradicated from the human brain, by then their actions were robotic, programmed for deception, ethics at that time, had already been eradicated, it was easier to find rascals and louts, than sane men and goodwill.

Plutarco Rene Cariño had expanded his popularity among the pack, even over Donko's aspirations to replace him.

He had obtained a discount concession at the liquor store next door to Bulley's, and some of the pack would ask him to use it to their advantage, and they would even buy cases and send them to Santo Domingo, where they would sell it at double the cost, thus earning him two hundred percent.

Rene was always ready to enlist in everything that was raffle or orange blossom game, so it was easy to find him selling lottery of the republic, however, none of that clouded his solidarity, because if he had to share his food with someone, there he was ready to do it, if a tire was deflated, he appeared with a machine to help to put air, and so, always at the service, to win the appreciation of the beneficiaries.

Oh, I was going to miss it, the fate of Gary and Valentina, had closed the business for lack of liquidity to pay the rent, the savings had been exhausted which led to a separation, which is why the dwarf had returned to take refuge in the skirt of his mother, which to give him shelter, wrapped in the business of llaniqueques.

The Valentina went to the Dominican Republic, where she met a businessman, and they soon got married.

Instead, Arnulfo returned to Puerto Rico where he became a farmer, and the cat had been brought to justice for aggravated fraud, impostor, abuse of power and embezzlement, otherwise, the second coming, would define the cause.

Sometime later, when Gibon was going for Bulley, some of the members of the Pack said angrily: "Look at that one, he was carrying small purchases from here, and now that he has changed his life, maybe he doesn't even remember," they said, while another one in his murmurings answered him:

"If he didn't remember, he wouldn't even come here."

And Gibon, who knew by the movement of his lips what they were saying, thought: "who laughs last laughs best, even the cat humbled me, and in his mercy God lifted me up."

Galy Buchi was proud of his name because he understood that no other living being was the owner of such a name, he wrote it proudly on the waiting list and displayed it with the splendor of his honor on a post that held the list where each one of the pack could see behind whose turn it was.

On one occasion he was in favor of Gibon, but when they agreed to get Gibon out of his box, he was one of the first agitators.

The police had lost power, but crime was growing, not only in New York City.

Burdock pretended that from evil he had changed, but Gibon knew that a tree that was born affected, no earthly medicine would rebuild it until it returned to its original habitat, then the karmatic conditions had begun to manifest and someone came in wanting to work and trying to take some passengers, but as he always did, like a yard foreman, Burdock pushed him out and warned him:

"If you come back here, we're going to have trouble", and the guy was forced to answer him:

"Okay sheikh, when I come back this way, 'I'll come back as a thief in the night,'" she said, and left.

In fact, he and Rene had a brotherhood where they only allowed their relations and friends to ride one of Bulley's passengers, because if they were not from the flock, they would look for ways to create difficulties for him.

Burdock was a remnant of the generation of Sodom and Gomorrah, he was a soul of those who had rejected virgins for angels, so God got angry and a ship in space planted him and wiped him off the map at that time.

Now at that time he had returned to reincarnate without having managed to overcome the existential condition, because he had clung to the previous life to such a degree that the memory of that stormy past, had influenced the steps he had taken trying to move forward along the path of this new earthly existence, because his life in this new generation, had started from the chapter where he had been, and was so great the accumulated karma, which felt somewhat crystallized, so he tried to move forward by manifesting the agreement of changes assumed, so that everything was manifesting in a slow process.

A week later while Burdock was distracted, the spiteful individual who threatened to return as a "thief in the night" appeared, and with a bat on both knees struck him, and Burdock on foreign soil, falling to his knees with his arms outstretched, cried out to God.

The assailant fled the scene of the crime, everything was so fast that none of the dogs barked at him, only the howl of Burdock's ultra-grave was heard, and he was left sore on his knees.

A laywoman, who at the time of the incident passed by on the sidewalk in front, without knowing what had happened, marveled at seeing him on his knees and in a loud voice said:

"Hallelujah! Already the demons and the wicked are turning back to God!"

But the sound of the siren of the ambulance followed by the police made her aware of it.

Fredesvindo had called 911, which immediately assisted by

taking Burdock to the Montefiore emergency room.

Burdock had undergone emergency surgery, due to the absence of calcium that flooded his immune system was left in a wheelchair, and was so attached to the environment of Bulley, that although he could no longer drive, did not stop going, and his presence for some was a nuisance, because he had not left the habit even in a wheelchair to pollute the environment with his anal burps, so Petro when he saw him arrive the greeting he gave him was:

"The one who fart's here! How's the fart?"

Rene Cariño and he, who since they met were like partners, had developed a close friendship, Rene would take up a collection among the pack that Burdock would pick up every week, but some would protest and not give anything, and Rene would get angry with them.

Some of the pack considered him a low, shameless and vulgar being, and thought that what had happened to him was the regeneration of his Karma.

In any case, neither Guga nor her children knew about his double life, about his double personality of bird and dog, or rather, about his homosexual condition.

Anjo Jr., Rene Cariño's nephew, had gone to transport a passenger in New Jersey during the last snowfall of 2021, when he returned to Bulley, he found the traffic stopped, the vehicles were moving slowly, and he entered into a state of desperation, to the extent that as he lived in New Jersey he had decided to stay at home because of the slow traffic and when he tried to turn back, he felt cornered and turned wherever he could without realizing that he had taken a road of doom and was traveling a road of no return, the driver who was behind him tried to warn him, but he did not pay attention to him because his English was very limited and he did not understand. He drove like a sled sliding in the snow, until suddenly he found himself on a frozen lake that, when experiencing the weight of the van, cracked and sank. The driver, who from afar saw what looked like a winter shadow disappearing on the surface of the cracked ice, called the 911, and explained what happened so that in less than half an hour appeared on the scene, units of firefighters followed by the police, and although they made the best efforts, when they managed to pull it had already drowned, which brought great pain to the Pack, but especially to Anjo's father who was disconsolate that only said in his pain: "Alas, they took him away from me, such a young and hard-working boy."

And Rene Cariño for the first time in so long, he looked so sorry, he didn't look like himself.

On the other hand, Alonzo the boxer, had been pursued by a circumstantial cause, a kind of karmatic experience, which religions called sin, he was tempted by a neighbor who knew that he had been widowed and wanted to circumvent the vigilance of her husband, taking a spoonful of honey in her mouth, went and knocked on the door, and when Alonzo opened it she took him by the arm and took him out into the hallway and immediately led him to his apartment and without saying anything, she introduced the honey she had in her mouth in his and that was enough for him to forgot that his wife Crismar had only been death for six months. The widower got involved with the neighbor, but because of those circumstances of life, just when he was ready to have sex her, the husband reappeared, who had left the keys and the train card in his haste, he knocked, knocked and nothing was opened, until he thought of calling her on the phone, the call alerted the intention and Alonzo, the announcer, threw himself out of the second floor window, thinking that his condition of pugilist would help him to cushion the blow, but he had failed in his calculations, he had twisted his knees and had to undergo surgery, having been left with both legs twisted and on crutches, without being able to continue doing deliveries in Bulley.

CHAPTER 44

THE IMPOSTOR CAT

Gibon had gone quietly on vacation, and on his return to New York, he was taken into a room where the cat was waiting for him, and she came up to him and greeted him with a kiss on the cheek as she said:

"Welcome Gibon, how have you been?"

"Hi Cat, what are you doing here?"

"Obviously, I came to receive my husband, you are the key to my door, and I am the key to your key, God urges this union that obeys his purpose, and I am here for you," she said, while Gibon contemplated her in silence.

"Did you say my wife?," questioned Gibon, startled.

"Do not come to tell me that you do not know, because the Lord allowed me to enter under your blanket and introduce you between my body, and if I did it was for you to know that I am yours and you are mine, I am your beloved and you my beloved," she said, with a tender smile of love.

Gibon woke up startled and sweaty, and thought about how it was possible for the cat to chase him even in his sleep.

Just at that moment he received a call from Estrace that he

found surprising, since she hadn't communicated with him for several months, and she didn't give up to lead Gibon to the feline field, because in that call she invited him to accompany her to capture two cats that were walking on the escape stairs of the apartment of one of Xiomy, one of her friends who was a follower of feline protectionism, and Gibon, due to the time she was calling him, just replied:

"Let me think about it"

And he didn't take her call again, she was inviting him to be on the street at half past three in the morning and Gibon was retiring to rest at 8 o'clock at the latest.

However, he thought that they at that hour in the street hunting cat, could be mistaken for thieves and anyone who shoots could use as an alibi that they were stealing, so he thought how crazy and malicious the invitation was.

CHAPTER 45

ESTRACE AND KONKAT

Sometime after NASA had sent the exploratory capsule to Mars, in the last mission of the United States on Mars, already in the final stage of exploration, they had collected all the necessary evidence to find out if life existed on Mars, they were not wrong, but still, they were unaware that the beings that inhabited Mars, they were invisible to the human eye, because they had a body of light, they had seen everything that the crew did, and realized that the earthlings were interested in them, they chose to follow them, so they chose a planetary leader, assigning him a follow-up mission.

Before we get into the details, I must describe Konkat's place of origin: Mars, also called the red planet because of the rusty iron in its soil.

It was an apparently desert planet, because its inhabitants, as Konkat would explain, were invisible to the human eye, it had seasons and polar ice caps, climate, canyons and volcanoes.

But also, it was cold and had an extension similar to half of the earth.

When they were ready to return to earth, Konkat, who had chosen a man's body with the face of a cat, hypnotized the crew, entered the capsule as a stowaway, and when he arrived on earth, he woke the crew before disembarking and put in their minds what he wanted them to think and say.

He explained that they would never see the inhabitants of Mars because their body was of light, and invisible to the eye of man.

He told him that he assembled that body to be on earth, but if he wished he could leave it whenever he wished and return to Mars in the rays of the sun or in the light of the stars.

Washington was very impressed, no human could assassinate Konkat, so they offered him a job as an advisor on Middle Eastern affairs and space decisions, an offer that the very determined Martian gladly accepted.

I must add that Konkat in his condition of extraterrestrial, did not speak like humans, he listened and transmitted the answers by telepathy, he fed by absorption, different from how humans did, he did not use his mouth to speak or eat, since he absorbed the food through his cheeks.

Then he had to accompany an agent of the Department where he had been assigned in Washington to go to New York to visit a retired Jew who in the past had worked as director of the Department they were in at that time to consult with him about some decisions he had made in the past regarding the Middle East and that at that time, they needed to know if they would be suitable for other agreements.

When they arrived at David Erlich's house, that was the name of the Jew, they were informed that he was in the "Isabella Home", so they went from there to where he was.

Before this moment we had talked about Estrace, and her details, but I don't remember having told you that Estrace, in the previous life had been condemned to the stake by the Inquisition, returning in this life as a beatified in the service of the clergy, seen from the outside, she looked like an angel without wings, but inside her spirit, she had developed a fold of evilness, her ambition led her to the great deception, and although she had been used against Gibon, she had to give him back everything that was his and that she tried to retain, because of that feline spirit she brought, although she tried to join the brotherhood where Gibon interacted, he did not accept her, because when she should have informed him of what was happening, she kept silent, becoming an accomplice of the conspirators, wanting to use him for their benefit.

Her friend Tody, though she interacted, had no direct involvement and being less impulsive, never stretched beyond sass, and married a New York State corrections lieutenant.

But after the preamble, let's go back to Estrace's story, when we thought she would remain single, the unexpected and unusual happened, as we could not imagine what would happen next:

Occult Sect had gotten Estrace a job as a nurse's aide at Isabella Home, and coincidentally, she had been assigned to the care of the Jew David Erlich, and by the time Washington's entourage came in she had finished administering a serum and as she was about to leave she found herself face to face with Konkat in a platonic ceremony.

From the very moment he saw her, something strange happened, she looked into his eyes and her heart beat, she could discover that love was reborn, her heart accelerated and when she closed and opened her eyes, something strange happened.

Konkat had the body of a man and the face of a cat but she didn't notice it, she was in hypnosis trance, he asked her marriage, and Estrace very pleased the request accepted.

At the time of the wedding masked came, and because of the pandemic, the face to no one showed.

Estrace very pleased daily went on with her life, she always kissed the cats and when Konkat arrived, she began to kiss him more, her mother went to visit her who also had not seen him, and entering without warning her face came to look, and had a heart attack, a fright generated, and Konkat from the sofa, noticed once again and pausing his rest, to the surprised mother-in-law, he calmed her with a jump and she was hospitalized, her son-in-law appeared and before she remembered with hypnosis he erased her, and Estrace was very happy, and many years later she turned 99 and she was forced to leave the earth and the drama she was doing in life, ended there, then Konkat was called by the planetary council and they asked him to return, and a week later, after saying goodbye to his friends in Washington, he got rid of the body by putting it on the sofa and returned to Mars in the sun's rays, as his body did not decompose, they moved it to the alien museum, where it had been exhibited, according to the protocol.

Gibon arose in great glory, and all that had been withheld from him had been given to him. God inspired those who withheld Gibon's blessing to surrender it without further resistance.

Gibon emerged as the pillar of the new generation's orientation, even though by the time of the Lord's arrival, he had already completed one hundred and twenty-five years of having arrived on earth, and something extraordinary had happened to him, in spite of his age he remained healthy, young and strong, and he praised:

O Lord, what a glorification, whenever I open my mouth to speak, you make my heart beat and the grace of Your love is manifested, showing the splendor of Your greatness.

I don't want to be conjugated in the laziness that men incur in their sadness.

To me who bears grace in your splendor, who am the nature of your love. To me, who bring the greatness of the special profile of your beauty, manifested in your soul without sadness, to express itself without pain, in every tear that weeps for love.

Just as I found the manifest pearl of wanting, speculating in you, without much to think or say, today I relegated pain and suffering, to a life that has erased everything, to begin again, the grace and expression of its nature, and now I am love of the one who redeems, to be hope of your cause.

A few months later joy appeared in his life, Karen, his tender melody, whom he admired in the grace of his days, and a great change of life in harmony God gave him, bringing him out of spinsterhood, vindicating the cause of his honor, God granted him, grace and transformation, and it was an assignment of heroine and ideal companion, who was to break his loneliness.

Lucia as Gibon loved her, she was a lady of harmony, she was grand and preferred, she had a deferred grace, and she made herself a chair of her life.

Splendorous in everything, she was grand and so beautiful, that to the heart she seemed like a rose.

"Who knows the truth, refuses to rehearse,

what his heart prevents him from doing".

CHAPTER 46

THE WAITING CONSUMMATED

Time had passed since Gibon had left Bulley rich, and when many thought they would never see him again, the spirit led him there, some, upon seeing him arrive, felt joy and others, hoped to be blessed, Gibon distributed a hundred dollars at a time to those who were there, then they invoked a canticle of glory and thanksgiving.

How many unsolvable mistakes had been made against Gibon, and he wondered: How long would the criminal machinery continue to persecute and manipulate the innocent?

Would we still have to wait for the second coming to taste the sweet fruits of righteousness, or would we have to resort to the ancient laws of dracon?

All these questions were asked before Gibon was struck by the redemptive thunderbolt.

The time had passed from winter to spring melting pot, and when summer dawned, and something unusual had happened:

It was twelve o'clock, the pack was concentrated, a radiant sun was showing, suddenly the sun went down and the day got darker, something unexpected happened, slowly it started to get darker so that the day started to look like night, Burdock as usual was there in his wheelchair, waiting for the pack to bite, and in the middle of the darkness, a ray of radiant light appeared like a burning star, the pack was dumbfounded, everyone had become mute, a voice in the middle of the silence boomed:

"Gibon, the time of transformation has come, it is the hour of the Lord, lead the people that will join you to the destiny that I will assign to you, you are the tool of my redemption," he said.

All fell to their knees and prayed with intensity, the ray of light as a flash was reflected on the forehead of Gibon and he bent backwards, and when he was thrown forward, he saw that Burdock was still prostrate beside him without moving and not knowing what to do, he touched his knees while he said:

"God forgives those who repent, the Lord forgives you, get up and walk."

An energetic charge propelled Burdock out of the wheelchair and he jumped out of the wheelchair, and admiringly said:

"The Lord has lifted me out of the chair, He has removed my disability, He has made me walk, hallelujah."

He prostrated on his knees together with the others of the pack, and repentant preached the gospel to the pack and new creatures were, appeared ships, or rather flying saucers that emerged from below and others that came from above, the planet had been convulsed.

And Gibon said:

On the threshold of the portal I saw a reflection light up, all the grace expressed balanced my gaze, I walked where I went, where you told me to come, glorified in my soul, that's how you made me feel.

You are the glory and peace, you give me security, you are the divine grace that bestows happiness.

You are cause and you are essence, you are the lantern of goodness, you are the cause of existence, you are the abode of peace, you are light and you are virtue that inspires my heart, and wherever I go, I am a reflection of your love.

As the pack prayed some disintegrated and disappeared in plain sight, others were changed bodies, the darkness persisted.

On the fourth day, a bluish sun was appearing faintly until like a lantern intensified its rays, a new beginning redefined the planet, while a new species of men walked in front of the sun, looking with curiosity, the origin of the light, a voice echoed like an echo from a ray of the sun:

"Alba that is reborn in every dawn that is kept in the evening when the sun sets, raise your prayer and cry out for love."

And so, the serpentine curve of the ephemeral light, marked in its essence the spark of lightning, the rain announced its arrival.

The planet suffered a convulsion; the rays of the new sun made the seed of love germinate.

EPILOGUE

In times of chaos, the socially displaced were referred to the lines of the periphery, taking refuge in the mechanisms of survival, where whoever showed the strength to resist, prevailed over the majority.

The style of showing the crudeness, allowed to identify and distinguish the sophisticated from the vulgar, so the bite of the dogs shows you a daily picture of those beings that ignoring the levels of education required and assigned by society, had been dedicated to live as circumstances allowed and incurred in errors, typical of the experiences generated in a miscellaneous society.

Burdock's assiduous exaggeration in his interest to control the pack was a way to understand the levels of error that ignorance led to.

To the extent that even the way of breathing generated the conflicts of everyday life in Bulley, the family club where members came to acquire the food for their livelihoods, where those who made that food reach their homes, was that micro-entrepreneurial group, which often began to be beings that by interrelation altered the existential course of the daily life of each person involved.

They laughed, as did the members of the family cadres, to be angry and to forgive each other, to cry and to laugh.

Mariano Morillo B. PhD. The Chronicler of America, Author of this novel.

"The Bite of the Dogs" tries to give answers to questions that humanity rises about their daily lives, now presents the reality of how it survives and is tolerated in New York, a large line of immigration.

Where the pandemic led essential workers, ready to sacrifice to serve those who needed to stock up to meet the "stay at home" requirements, how in a fraction of days it changed the face of the planet, how grief and disillusionment gripped the generation.